The Black Stiletto

The Black Stiletto

The First Diary—1958

A Novel

Raymond Benson

Oceanview Publishing
Longboat Key, Florida

ISBN: 978-1-60809-020-4

Published in the United States of America by Oceanview Publishing, Longboat Key, Florida
www.oceanviewpub.com

10 9 8 7 6 5 4 3 2 1

PRINTED IN THE UNITED STATES OF AMERICA

For Randi

ACKNOWLEDGMENTS

The author wishes to thank the following individuals for their help: Michael Adkins, Tasha Alexander, Brian Babendererde, Michael A. Black, Michael Colby, Brad Hansen, Jeff Knox, Alisa Kober, Ganita Koonopakarn, Toby Markham, Christine McKay, James McMahon, Henry Perez, Heather La Bella, Justine Ruff, Pat and Bob, Frank, Susan, and everyone at Oceanview Publishing, and Peter Miller and the good folks at PMA Literary & Film Management, Inc.

Follow the Black Stiletto at www.theblackstiletto.net

AUTHOR'S NOTE

While every attempt has been made to ensure the accuracy of 1950s New York City and West Texas, the Second Avenue Gym, Shapes, and the East Side Diner are fictitious. Some liberties have been taken with architectural aspects of the Algonquin Hotel, the Plaza Hotel, and the New York Athletic Club Yacht Club, but for the most part the descriptions herein are extremely close to their actual layouts during the era depicted.

The Black
Stiletto

1
Martin
THE PRESENT

My mother was the masked vigilante known as the Black Stiletto.

I just found this out today, and I've been her son for forty-eight years. All my life I knew she had some secrets, but needless to say, this is a bit of a shock.

At first I thought it was joke. I mean, come on. My *mother*? A costumed crusader? Yeah, tell me another one. And the *Black Stiletto*, of all people? No one in a million years would believe it. I'm not sure I do, and here I am being presented with hard evidence.

The Black Stiletto. One of the most famous persons on the planet.

And she's slowly dying. In a nursing home.

Oh. My. God.

I really don't know how I'm supposed to react to this.

It was sure something I didn't expect when I was called to Uncle Thomas's office this fine May afternoon. He's not really my uncle; just a friend of the family. I suspect he was my mom's lover at some point when I was a kid, but they remained friendly and then later he acted as her estate attorney. You see, my mom—Judy Talbot—is seventy-two years old and she's got Alzheimer's. It's a terrible disease and it hit her hard and fast. It didn't creep up on her like it does with most victims. It was almost as if she was okay one day, and then a couple of years later she couldn't remember my name. Within five years of the onset of her illness, I had to put her into Woodlands North. An unpleasant but necessary thing to do; and I couldn't have done it without Uncle Thomas. The ironic thing is that she's somewhat okay physically. She was always in pretty good shape, even with all the drinking and depression. Then one day her mind shut down and she was no longer able to take care of herself. What bodily ailments she has now are simply due to atrophy from being held prisoner in a nursing home for the last two years. Yes, she's dying, and it's going to be slow and terrible. Her doctors don't know how long it will take. It could be years, it could be a few months. One never knows with Alzheimer's.

Uncle Thomas's office is in Arlington Heights, Illinois. That's a northwestern suburb of Chicago. I grew up there. I lived with my mom in a house near the downtown area, where we would catch a commuter train if we wanted to go into the big city.

Downtown Arlington Heights used to be a funky, quaint little place, certainly not much to talk about when I was a kid growing up in the sixties and seventies. Today they've built it up and made it more of a nightlife destination with movie theaters, trendy restaurants, nightclubs, and shops. But I don't live there anymore.

I live a little farther north in a suburb called Buffalo Grove. I'm a single dad. My daughter lives with her mother—my ex-wife—in Lincolnshire. All these places are close together. So it's not much of a schlep to see Uncle Thomas, or to visit my mom at Woodlands, which is in Riverwoods. And I do it. Visit my mom, that is. At least once a week. Aside from my daughter who sometimes visits her, I'm all she has—even though most of the time now she doesn't know who I am.

Janie, Uncle Thomas's secretary, welcomed me warmly when I walked into the office. We exchanged brief pleasantries and then she said I could go on in. I found him at his desk studying a pile of legal documents. Uncle Thomas is around my mother's age and still works eight hours a day, seven days a week. He looked up at me, smiled, and stood. We greeted each other, shook hands, and then he told me to have a seat. He walked around the desk and shut the door so we could have some privacy.

"So what's up?" I asked him. He had been fairly mysterious on the phone.

"Martin, I have some things I'm supposed to give you." He gestured to his desk and indicated a small metal strongbox, the kind used to hold files or valuables. Next to it was a nine by twelve envelope with my name and address typed on it.

"What is it?"

"It's from your mother." When I furrowed my brow, he continued. "She set this up a long time ago. Fifteen years ago, to be precise. In the event that she died or became incapacitated, I was supposed to see that you got these things. This letter and this strongbox."

"Where have they been all this time?" I asked.

"I've had them in safekeeping. In trust, so to speak."

"Do you know what's in them?"

"No, Martin, I don't. Your mother was very clear about the contents being private and confidential. I've debated with myself for a while when I should release them to you. I suppose it's time I stop the denial and admit your mother is indeed incapacitated. She will never recover from that horrible disease unless some kind of miracle cure is discovered, and the chances of that happening in her lifetime are unlikely. So, here you are. Sorry I've waited so long."

I wasn't upset with him. I understood his dilemma, but I was more concerned and curious about the stuff on the desk. What could she have possibly deemed so secretive?

"Well, let's see it." I held out my hand and he gave me the envelope first. It felt as if it contained a letter, certainly, and something metal and slightly heavy—a key to the strongbox perhaps?

I opened the envelope and sure enough, a small key dropped into my lap. I picked it up and put it aside for the time being. I took out the letter and read it.

I recognized the typeface as belonging to an old electric typewriter we once had in the house. She had hand-dated the letter and signed the bottom—"Judith May Talbot."

I had to read it three times before I could comprehend what she had written.

Uncle Thomas watched me eagerly. "You don't have to tell me what it says if you don't want to," he prompted. He was obviously dying to know.

For several moments I sat in the chair dumbfounded. I wanted to laugh. In fact, I did laugh, I think. I asked Uncle Thomas if it was a joke. He replied that it wasn't and then queried why I would ask that.

"Never mind," I answered.

I read the letter again. Shook my head.

It was a confession. In it, my mother admitted her name was really Judith May *Cooper* and that she was the Black Stiletto. She had kept this secret to herself since the sixties, when she retired her costume, changed her name, and tried to lead a normal life. She anticipated my skepticism and explained that the contents of the strongbox would lead me to the proof. She also granted me the rights to her life story. In short, she was leaving it up to me whether or not I reveal her secret to the world.

I folded the letter and stuffed it back into the envelope. Then I nodded at the strongbox. "Let's see that." Uncle Thomas handed it to me, and I used the little key to unlock it. I wasn't sure if I wanted him to see what was inside, and he sensed it.

"Maybe I should step outside?" he asked.

"Would you mind, Uncle Thomas?"

"Not at all, Martin. Just call me if you need me."

He left the room and shut the door. I opened the lid and found a folded piece of paper, three keys on a ring, and some other trinkets. I removed and unfolded the paper, revealing a floor plan of some kind. I studied it for a few seconds and then realized it was the floor plan of our basement. In the house where I grew up. Where no one has lived for the past two years. It's been on the market, but nobody was remotely interested in buying it. The real estate agent, Mrs. Reynolds, kept making the same old excuses—it's a bad market, it's the economy, the house needs fixing up, and so on.

So what were the keys for? Two of them were grey and appeared suitable for unlocking doors. The third was small and gold colored.

I looked at the floor plan again and then noticed a room that wasn't supposed to be there.

Hold on.

A wall separated the basement from that new space—a wall I never knew I could go through. The floor plan indicated there was a door in it. I'd never seen a door there. One or two of the keys must unlock it. And if that was true, what was the gold key for?

Even more puzzling were the other items, which I picked up and examined, one by one.

A heart-shaped locket on a chain, silver-plated, I think.

A Kennedy/Johnson campaign button, from 1960.

And a small canister containing a reel of 8-mm film.

I quickly put everything back into the strongbox, stood, and carried it to the outer office. Uncle Thomas was by the coffee machine and Janie was still at her desk.

"All done?" he asked.

"Yeah. Um, thanks."

"Is there anything I can do?"

"I don't know yet."

"You look a little pale. Is something wrong? What was in there, Martin? I assure you, as your mother's attorney, I—"

"I know. I appreciate it. I may consult you. I just need to process this. I'll call you later, okay?"

"Sure, Martin. Would you like a drink of water?"

I took him up on that.

The three-bedroom ranch house was a prewar affair on Chestnut that had seen better days. In 1970 I'm sure it was probably pretty nice. That was when my mom and I moved in. I was eight years old. Prior to that we had been all over. I was born in Los Angeles, but for the first few years of my life we were living on the road. I don't remember much of it, but I do have fleeting memories of traveling in a car, stopping in lots of hotels, living in apartments here and there, and finally coming to Illinois. I do recall we were in a small apartment in Arlington Heights before we moved into the house, and I distinctly recollect the day mom took me to see it. She picked me up at school—second grade—and said she had a surprise for me. We rode in her dumpy '64 Bonneville and there it was. A real house.

Unfortunately, Mom wasn't the best homemaker in the world. She didn't spend much time cleaning it or maintaining it properly. I didn't notice how much it had gone into decline until after I'd graduated from high school, gone away to college, and come back for a visit in the early eighties. By then, mom had started drinking more than usual. She seemed okay, though. She wasn't a drunk, at least not around me. There wasn't much I could do about it. But she still worked out and went on her runs and looked fit. Mom always had a punching bag hanging from the basement ceiling and, I swear, every day of her life she went down and beat on it for a half hour. She may have been an alcoholic and all that, but it didn't stop her from keeping her body toned.

As I visualized her slamming that punching bag over and over, day after day, I realized maybe this Black Stiletto stuff wasn't all horseshit.

At any rate, I drove straight to the house from Uncle Thomas's office. The FOR SALE sign was still in the front yard. It appeared that Mrs. Reynolds had replaced it recently. The last one was old and rusty, having been out there for a couple of years.

Yeah, the place was ugly. It needed a paint job in the nineties and here it was 2010. The real estate company took care of keeping the grass cut, but there were weeds everywhere. The shutters on the windows were broken. There were holes in the roof. Squatters wouldn't want to stay there. It was no wonder it hadn't sold. I really needed to get off my ass and hire someone to do some work.

I used my own key to get in the front door. The place smelled like mildew in that way old houses do. It was completely empty, for we'd moved out most of the furniture and Mom's stuff long ago. There was nothing in it but the soiled carpet and a chair or two.

Mrs. Reynolds kept some tools in the kitchen, so I grabbed a flashlight before going downstairs. The basement was dark, cold, and dank. I switched on the single bulb in the ceiling and found what appeared to be animal droppings on the concrete floor. Squirrels, probably; hopefully not rats. There were a few empty cardboard boxes lying around. Mom's punching bag was still hanging there in the middle of the room. I made my way to the wall in question and examined it. Looked to me like an ordinary wall made of, well, concrete. It was part of the foundation, directly under the stairs. There wasn't a door. I couldn't see anything except two blotches of caulk. One was eye level and the other a few feet below that. They seemed old and dry and completely flush with the concrete. I reached out to touch one and I felt some give. Using my fingertips, I pulled it away from the wall—it was actually a piece of *hinged plaster*! The caulked spots were really little covers built into the wall. And behind them were keyholes.

I quickly got the keys out of the strongbox and stuck one in the top lock. It turned easily. The second grey key worked, too, and as soon as the door unlocked, the frame seemed to pop out of the wall a quarter-inch, allowing me to pull it open with my fingertips.

I must have stopped breathing when I aimed the flashlight inside the small, closet-like space.

Hanging on the back wall were two costumes. Easily recognizable ones. Two sets of the most famous costume in the world, I dare say.

The Black Stiletto.

I stepped inside and touched them.

In both cases, the pants and jacket were made of thin black leather. One outfit was made of thicker material than the other, but was basically the same. Knee-high black boots stood on the floor beneath them. A knapsack lay beside the boots. The single mask was a half-hood with holes for the eyes , but to me it always resembled those kinky S&M things you see in sex shops. The Black Stiletto sure had that dominatrix thing going for her, and that was way before that kind of imagery was in popular media.

The legendary knife—the stiletto—was in its sheath and mounted on the wall next to the costume.

Amazing. Totally mind-boggling.

Sitting on shelves built into the side of the closet were stacks of newspapers, photographs, and comic books preserved inside plastic bags. Black Stiletto comic books—not a lot, but some of the very first ones. Worth quite a bit now, I suspect. She must have bought them when they first came out.

On another shelf was a holster with a gun inside. I picked it up and inspected it. I don't know much about guns, but I knew it was a semiautomatic of some kind. A Smith & Wesson, according to what was engraved on its side. Boxes of ammunition sat next to it on the shelf.

And then there were the little books. Diaries. A whole set of them. Each one was labeled with a year, starting with 1958.

Holy shit!

What had I just discovered? What had my dear mother left me?

Who the fuck *was* my mother?

I grabbed the first diary and went upstairs. I needed some air. This was all too much to swallow.

Outside, I sat on the wooden front porch and held the book in my hands. What was I going to learn from reading it? The truth about my father, perhaps? Mom had always told me his name was Richard Talbot and that he'd died early on in the Vietnam War. I never knew him. The really odd thing about it was there were no pictures of him in the house—ever. I don't even know what he looked like. When I asked my mom about it when I was teenager, she simply said she couldn't bear to look at his face after he'd died. She'd gotten rid of all his photos. I asked her about his family—my grandparents or any uncles, aunts, or cousins on his side—and she replied that there weren't any. The same with her own family. We were all alone.

I accepted all that as gospel.

I flipped through the diary, afraid to start reading.

My mom was the Black Stiletto.

I still couldn't wrap my brain around it. This was big. It was bigger than anything I could imagine. It was tantamount to finding out the truth behind JFK's assassination or the identity of the Green River Killer. The Black Stiletto was a *world-famous legend*, an international icon of feminist strength and power. And no one knew who she really was except the Stiletto herself. And now me.

Her existence had become the stuff of myths, just like that pin-up model Bettie Page, who had posed for underground nude photographs and films in the fifties and then dropped out of sight. In the eighties and nineties, pop culture had "rediscovered" Page and her images sprouted everywhere—even though the woman herself was nowhere to be found. The media exploited Page's likeness without her permission through movies, comics, and magazines—and then she finally made herself known. The elderly former model had been living quietly in seclusion, completely unaware of the attention she'd been getting until a friend pointed it out to her. Only in the last years of her life did Page see any profit from the use of her youthful image.

The same thing had happened to the Black Stiletto.

She was active in the very late Eisenhower years and some of the sixties, an underground heroine who made a name for herself as a vigilante. Although she was wanted by the law and would have been arrested had she been caught or her secret identity been revealed, the Black Stiletto was a competent and successful crime fighter. She battled common crooks, Communist infiltrators, the Mafia—and was responsible for their capture and, in some cases, their deaths. The Stiletto first operated in New York City, but when the police came too close to catching her, she moved to Los Angeles.

Where I was born.

And then she'd inexplicably disappeared and was never heard from again. No one came forward with knowledge of who she really was and most people thought she'd probably died. Why not? She was involved in dangerous, high-risk situations. It made sense that she'd been fatally injured or even arrested and sent to prison without the authorities knowing who they'd really locked up. For a while it was one of those big mysteries like "who shot

JFK?" *What happened to the Black Stiletto? Where is she? Is she alive or dead? WHO was she?*

A decade passed and people tended to forget about her until the mid-eighties, when a fledgling independent comic-book publisher began a fictional series about the costumed crusader. They proved to be extremely popular and sold all over the world. The History Channel did a documentary biopic in the early nineties that consisted mostly of speculation, as I remember. There was at least one biography published, but of course it contained nothing about the Stiletto's personal life. It was simply an account of everything that had been documented about her in the newspapers. Then came the toys and other merchandise—action figures, videogames, board games, Halloween costumes, you name it. A lot of manufacturers were making millions off the Black Stiletto and there was no one to defend her interests.

A feature film starring Angelina Jolie came out in the late nineties, before the actress had become a huge star. The picture was a hit but had very little to do with the real Black Stiletto. It was all fantasy with lots of gunplay, explosions, and unbelievable stunts. The real Black Stiletto was much more low-tech than what was portrayed in the movie. Still, it captured audiences' imaginations. There was talk of a television series, but it never came to pass.

Like most people, I, too, was fascinated by the Black Stiletto. If I'd been younger when the comics came out, I probably would have bought and read them.

Apparently, Mom was well aware of what was going on, seeing there was a little collection of ephemera in the closet. She never said a word. She could have capitalized on her past and made a fortune. But instead she lived quietly and in obscurity here in the Chicago suburbs until the onset of her illness.

I couldn't wait any longer. I opened the first diary and started to read.

2
Judy's Diary
1958

July 4, 1958

Dear diary, I thought maybe I should start writing all this stuff down. When I was a little girl I kept a diary. I wrote in it for about three years, I think. I don't know what happened to it. I guess it's still back in Odessa, sitting in a drawer in my old room. If my old room still exists.

I'm chronicling everything that's happened to me lately, just in case something bad happens. I'm not sure if I really want the truth to come out, but here it is. So much has occurred in the last six months. In a way, I'm more famous than the mayor of New York City! Well, not *me*, Judy Cooper. The Black Stiletto is. No one knows Judy Cooper is the Black Stiletto, and I hope to keep it that way.

Funny, I can hear Elvis singing his new song, "Hard Headed Woman," on someone's radio in the distance. He could be singing about me, ha ha. Whoever has that radio must be playing it awfully loud, 'cause right at this moment I'm sitting on top of the Second Avenue Gym building and watching the fireworks on the East River. Or it could be just 'cause my hearing is better than most people's. Sometimes it's hard for me to tell.

The gym is my home and has been for quite some time. Freddie Barnes runs the place. He's a trainer and former boxer.

He lives above the gym, and so do I. He's been letting me live in a room above the gym for a few years now, and I pay for it by working for him in all kinds of capacities. I started off being the janitor—cleaning and sweeping and washing the disgusting toilets in the men's locker room. Then he made me a cashier and assistant manager. Now I get to help with the training because I'm pretty good in the ring. Not many women are. Not many women do that kind of thing. It's fun. I like it. I hope to someday start my own self-defense program for girls. I don't want anyone growing up to be victims. No one should have to experience what happened to me when I was thirteen.

Right now I'm twenty years old. I'll be twenty-one on November 4. I've been in New York since I was fourteen. I guess you could say that's when my life really started, because before that I was in hell. Luckily, I managed to escape.

I suppose I should take up the first part of this diary with the past to bring it up to date. I'll spend the next few days writing and filling in the story and then, when I've reached July 4, 1958, I can just make entries on a daily or weekly basis—or whenever I feel like it.

So here goes, dear diary. This is my life, and I warn you—some of it ain't pretty.

Like I said, I was born on November 4, the year 1937, in Odessa, Texas. My parents named me Judith May Cooper. My father, George Cooper, was an oilman, a roughneck, which was the only kind of work he could get during the Depression. He worked on the oil rigs. I don't know how good he was at it. He'd moved to West Texas when they discovered oil there in 1926. My mother, Betty, cleaned houses. She was no better than the colored ladies who did the same thing. I actually think she brought more money home than my dad. It was a tough time. We were on the low end of middle class, or maybe the upper end of lower class. All I know is we lived in a shack on the edge of the town. There were still a lot of people who didn't have jobs at all.

I had two older brothers—John was five years ahead of me, and Frank, three years older than me. Growing up with two older brothers made me a tomboy from the get-go. All I wanted to do was play with them and do boy stuff—play ball, do sports, act out cowboys and Indians—you know, *boy stuff*. One of our favorite games was playing "Americans vs. Japanese," in which we'd take turns being the army, navy, or marines, and the other team was the Japs. I was particularly good at sneaking up on the Japanese "bunker" and surprising them. I think I always won when we played that game. So, yeah, I was really into doing stuff with the boys. Whenever I did play with girls I was bored silly. If I had dolls, I usually ended up breaking them or letting my brothers use them for target practice with their B-B guns. Sometimes I shot at them, too, ha ha. We didn't have any pets, although there was a stray cat that used to come around and I'd feed her. She didn't really like me, though. I'd try to pet her and she'd hiss and run away. I stopped feeding her and she didn't come around anymore.

I barely knew my dad. When the war started, he enlisted. It was 1942, right after Pearl Harbor, and he went out and joined the navy. I was still pretty young—I was four—so the last image I had of him was him waving goodbye to us as he caught a bus to take him into town. From there he went to boot camp and then was shipped off to the Pacific somewhere. He was dead just a few months later, one of the three hundred or so Americans killed in the battle of Midway. So, I never saw him again.

Things went downhill for us after that. Mom tried to make ends meet as best she could, but our family sank deeper into poverty. Looking back, I can see how bad it was, but at the time I was just a precocious little girl, always getting in trouble, rough housing with my brothers and their friends, and driving everyone crazy. By the time I started first grade at South Side Elementary, I could beat up most of the boys in the neighborhood if I wanted to. I was a tough little hellion.

Around the time I did start school, we lived near the corner of Whitaker and 5th Street. It wasn't a shantytown, but we weren't far from one. The Negroes lived just a few blocks south from us, across the tracks. I was too young to let it bother me. I walked to school with my brothers—John was in sixth grade and Frank was in fourth when I started first. It was a crappy school, that's for sure. Everyone who went there were oil field roughneck kids. No one with a whole lot of class, if you know what I mean. I didn't have many friends in school. I was a social outcast. Too much of a tomboy for the girls and too much of a bully for the boys, ha ha!

My best friends were my brothers, and it got to where they thought I was weird, too. Pretty funny when I think about it now. I loved my brothers, though. They usually stuck up for me when I got in trouble, which was a lot. Unfortunately, they didn't stick up for me when I needed them the most, and I'm not sure I'll ever be able to forgive them for that.

I guess people might say I was an angry child. I don't know what I was so angry about. I just liked to pick fights. There was a lot of aggression inside me, a temper that could be ignited on cue. There still is. I was born with it and I needed some kind of outlet. It drove my mom insane, or at least it drove her to drink. Well, it probably wasn't all *my* fault, but I know I was a handful for her. She did start drinking, though, after Dad died. She wasn't much fun to be around.

Despite all that, I was a good student. Learning just came naturally to me. I wasn't so hot at math, but I enjoyed science and history. I was particularly good at reading and writing, which is why I kept a diary for a while. I found that I liked reading books, so if I wasn't outside playing football with the boys, I was inside with the latest Hardy Boys or Nancy Drew adventure. I wasn't into comics, but my brothers were. Every now and then, I'd look at their Superman comics, but they just didn't do it for me. I thought they were silly. I like my adventure yarns to be a little more credible, set in the real world. Early on I had trouble with the *physical* act of reading, so my mom took me to a doctor to have my eyes examined. I remember she wasn't happy about paying the money for a pair of glasses, but I guess I needed them at the time. From then on, I saw perfectly—I just looked like an idiot. I hated wearing glasses and it only got me into more fights in the neighborhood when the other kids teased me.

Life pretty much remained the same until I turned twelve. When puberty kicked in, strange things started happening to me. I don't mean the *usual* strange things that happen to all girls— you know, starting periods and growing breasts and all that—but other stuff that wasn't quite normal. For one thing, I discovered I didn't need my glasses anymore. I could see without them. Twenty-twenty. In fact, my eyesight was better than perfect. I could read signs at distances most people couldn't. And I could decipher fine print without a magnifying glass. Another thing that changed was my hearing. Before I hit puberty, I could hear fine, but afterward *everything* was amplified. I could hear people whispering from across the room. It was *really* weird. I could under- stand conversations taking place in another room. I could hear them through the wall almost as if the people were in the same space as me. One day I went to the school nurse to ask her about it. She recommended I get my ears checked by a doctor, but I never did. I wasn't worried about it or anything. Actually, I thought it was great. I could eavesdrop on kids in the lunchroom, where it was usually pretty noisy, and I heard everything they said. I was able to play "he said, she said" better than anyone!

Something else changed that I didn't really notice until a little later. When something was going on behind me, I knew what it was. You know that expression, "eyes in the back of your head"? That's what it was like. No one could sneak up on me. I could simply *sense* when someone was in back of me. And if I was walking down the street, I could anticipate if somebody was around the corner up ahead. And sure enough, there was.

Another ability I developed, if you can call it that, was an acute intuition. Somehow, I just *knew* when my brothers were lying about something. And I'd catch them at it, too. I'd say, "Frank, you're lying. I can see it in your face." We'd argue for a minute but I'd point out the flaws in his argument, and eventually he'd admit he was indeed lying. By the same token, I could tell when someone was being honest. Just within a few minutes of talking to a stranger, I knew if he or she was a good or bad person. If someone had a good heart, I knew it. Or if they harbored hate or anger, I could tell that, too. I should have gone to Las Vegas and become a card gambler. I probably would've won a million dollars, ha ha!

At the time, I didn't know if something was wrong with me or not. I was afraid to talk about it or tell my mother. She'd just get upset at having to take me to the doctor again. And it wasn't like it was hurting me or anything. I realized it was special. I was different and I liked that. Now that I'm twenty and can look back objectively at twelve-year-old Judy, I understand that these heightened senses are unique to me. Nobody else I know of has them. These abilities certainly help me when I'm the Stiletto. I couldn't put on a costume and do all the climbing and jumping and fighting I do without this extra awareness. I tried reading about it in books on anatomy and psychology, but there was nothing I could find. I finally attributed it to the onset of puberty and the fact that I'm a female animal. Like a lion or tiger that protects her cubs. That sounds silly, I know, but think about it—all the senses an animal mother uses in the wild to protect her young— and herself—are these same things. Seeing, hearing, alertness, instinct.

I guess I'd make the perfect mother—ha ha! Well, maybe someday. That's certainly not on my horizon anytime soon.

Well, all this new stuff made me act even weirder, as you can imagine. My mother and brothers noticed I was different, but they just chalked it up to my becoming an adolescent. Nevertheless, I felt as if they all shunned me a little. I was an oddball. A freak. And so, life in the house became more and more uncomfortable and strange. Not only was I a social outcast at school, but I became one at home, too.

Anyway, once all this started happening and I realized I could control it, I started doing more sports at school—and I was *darned good*. I especially liked gymnastics. I was on the school team for a little while and outdid everyone. It was like the uneven parallel bars were a part of me. I practically floated on them. The coach was amazed and wanted me to compete in competitions. But I had a bad temper and would get mad if I wasn't the center of attention. I was a real bitch, if I do say so myself, and so I didn't last very long in a team configuration. So I practiced on my own, getting to where I could swing, handstand, dismount, and flip with the best of 'em. On a balance beam I was like a cat. I was agile, light, and could contort my body into a pretzel. So, yeah, I was athletic and I was good at it. There's no doubt that all this was an asset when I became the Black Stiletto.

Something occurred in the fall of 1950, while I was still twelve, that may have been instrumental in my deciding to become a costumed vigilante later. It was an event at which all of these new senses came together and drove home the notion that I was different and could use my "powers" to help people.

It was a weekend, so I wasn't in school. I liked to take walks by myself out in the oil fields. I'd take a bus out that way and then just go on a hike. I enjoyed watching the pumpjacks as they rocked back and forth. The derricks were majestic and looked like sentinels against the flat horizon. It was solitary and comforting. It was a refuge away from the awkwardness at home.

Anyway, I was walking along, lost in my thoughts, when I heard what sounded like a crying baby. My ears pricked up, I mean *literally*, I felt the muscles in the side of my face stretch. Out in the fields it would normally be difficult to tell where a sound was coming from. With the wind and sheer *flatness* of everything, noise tended to come from every direction. But not for me. I knew exactly where that baby was. The infant was over a hundred yards away, near one of the pumpjacks.

What was a baby doing in the oil fields? I wondered. Had one of the roughnecks brought his kid with him to work and left the child unattended? I was too young to fathom that someone might actually abandon an infant. It didn't cross my mind

Nevertheless, I set out running toward the sound. My eyes focused on a cropping of mesquite bushes and I knew that was where the kid was. My entire body felt more alive than it ever had—my skin was tingling all over. It was the excitement of discovery, the knowledge that I could pinpoint where the baby was hidden, and every nerve inside me directed me to rescue it. I couldn't help it. Again, it was that *mothering* thing that exists in wild animals. I had no choice but to find that baby.

Well, find it I did. It was easy. There was a basket placed under a small mesquite, and inside was a baby boy wrapped in a blanket. No note, no identifying marks. No bottle.

I stood and focused on one of the oil derricks, another hundred yards or so away. There were men working on it. I left the baby where he was and ran as hard as I could. When I reached the rig, I went to the first man I saw and told him what I'd found. At first he must have thought I was telling a story or something, but I finally convinced him to come with me and look. He and one of the other roughnecks followed me back to the mesquite tree. They were just as amazed as me.

Well, they called the police and it turned out the baby had indeed been abandoned, left out in the field to die. I couldn't imagine what kind of parents would do such a thing. It hit me like a sledgehammer—*there were evil people in this world.*

My mom wasn't too happy when she had to come down to the police station and pick me up. The policeman was nice and all that, but he brought me in so I could tell my story. And I did. I simply said I'd been walking alone in the field and heard the baby cry. It was the truth. The policeman said I was a "good girl" and that I'd done the right thing. I don't know what happened to the baby—I suppose he was sent to a foster home or whatever they did with abandoned infants back then.

But I knew I'd saved his life. And that felt good.

3
Judy's Diary
1958

When I was thirteen, in the spring of 1951, my mother remarried. Betty Cooper became Betty Bates when she hitched up with another oil field roughneck named Douglas Bates.

From the moment I met the guy, I knew he was trouble.

It was that weird intuition of mine. As soon as he walked in the door for their first date with that smarmy smile on his face and glint in his eye, I got the shivers. Looking back, I think he was more interested in *me* than in my mom. He couldn't wait to get his hands on a young teenaged girl, so he hastily married a woman he didn't care about so he could eventually trap his prey.

Douglas was ten years older than my mother. He'd been married before, gotten divorced, and gone through a succession of women before he met my mom at a bar. I don't know the circumstances of his earlier marriage, but I'll bet one of my toes that it was his wife who left him. Most likely for beating her up. Which is what he liked to do to my mother.

Oh, sure, at first he was friendly and helpful around the house. My brothers seemed to like him at the very beginning. They weren't around much, being in high school and all, and John was going to graduate that May. My mother doted on Douglas, simply because he was a man and he was paying attention to her. He didn't fool me one bit, though. I never trusted him. He was a liar and a sneak.

There was one weekend just after school was out for the summer when my mom was at work cleaning houses, and my brothers were outside somewhere. I was home alone in my room, reading a book. I thought I was by myself. Well, good old Douglas wasn't working that day, so he knocked on my door and wanted to come in. I didn't really want him to, but he was my stepfather, so I let him. At least he was clean—he must have bathed before knocking. Which also meant he was up to something.

He started sweet talking me, almost the way he did to my mom. Telling me how cute and pretty I was, and how I was "growin' up in front of his eyes." Yeah, right. He'd only known me for five months.

"Look what I got," he said. "A surprise!"

Then he had the audacity to pull out a flask of whiskey! He produced two plastic cups and poured a little in each, and then he *handed me one*! I was thirteen-years-old, for God's sake. I refused it.

"Come on, Judy," he pleaded. "You'll like it. It'll make you feel good."

Yeah, I'd seen what that stuff did to my mother.

"No, thanks."

"What's the matter? Too good for it? Little Miss Goody Two Shoes?"

"I'm trying to read. Please leave."

And then he said, "You know, Judy, you're growin' up and you're gonna start bein' interested in boys. And I don't mean playin' football with 'em. You're gonna want to know what to do."

I just looked at him like he was crazy. But he kept talking.

"I could help you, you know. I could teach you—things. Stuff your boyfriends will like. Don't you want that?"

"No. Get out of here."

"Now, Judy—"

And then I yelled at him. "*Get out of here! Leave me alone!*" I picked up a book and threw it at him. It hit him right in the face. Boy, did he get mad. His cheeks got all red and he moved forward like he was going to wallop me or something. But then we both heard the front door slam. Frank called out to see if anyone was home.

"Frankie!" I shouted.

Douglas backed off and stood in the doorway, trying to act nonchalant. Frank appeared and asked, "What are y'all doing?"

"Nothin'," Douglas answered. "I was just seein' if your sister wanted anything to eat."

"Well, I do," Frank said. He was oblivious to the situation.

Douglas just glared at me and then went away with Frank. I slammed my door shut. Unfortunately, I didn't have a lock on it.

From then on, Douglas just got mean. He yelled at my mom a lot and they were always fighting. Mom usually gave up pretty quickly, especially after he'd slap her. Once this happened while all three of us kids were present. We were shocked, and John stood up to the creep.

"Don't you hit my mom!" he threatened with as much menace as an eighteen year old could muster. John would have been a formidable opponent, but my stepfather was a big man. He probably had a lot more experience in serious fighting than John did.

Douglas just told him to shut up and then he left the house. My mom started crying and we tried to comfort her.

"You should leave him," I suggested.

She looked at me like I was mad. "How dare you!" she said. "How could I possibly do that? How would we live? Where would the money come from? We just got married. I can't go leaving a man I just married!"

I shrugged in response and glanced at my brothers. The looks we exchanged indicated they agreed with me. But they weren't about to come between my mom and our stepfather.

John was lucky. As soon as he graduated from high school, he left. He joined the military like my dad, only he enlisted in the army instead of the navy. Better to enlist than be drafted, he said. The Korean War was on and he actually wanted to go over there and serve. Mom didn't want him to go—none of us did, except for Douglas. The bastard was glad to get rid of the oldest kid. One less obstacle in the way of what he wanted—*me*. John went away to boot camp and, sure enough, was sent overseas to Korea. As I write this, I don't know what happened to him, whether or not he survived, or what. I was already gone by then.

If Douglas wasn't working in the oil fields or beating up Mom, he was out in a nearby vacant lot shooting one of his many firearms. He owned several guns—pistols and rifles—and he went out to target practice every few days. Sometimes he'd walk around the house with a handgun and pretend he was a cowboy gunslinger, doing quick draws from an old holster he had. He idolized John Wayne and other cowboys in the movies and thought of himself as an outlaw or something. Made me sick.

As time went on, Douglas made life hell for me and Frank. If my mom wasn't the object of Douglas's aggression, then it was Frank. My stepfather treated Frank like dirt. So, naturally, Frank stayed away from the house as much as possible. He was busy in high school, he had his friends, and he had a part-time job at a drugstore. So we hardly ever saw Frank.

Neither of my brothers was there to help me when I needed them.

It finally happened on Halloween night, 1951. I was in eighth grade at Odessa Junior High School. My birthday was the next week and I had dressed up as a witch to go to a costume party that some kids were throwing. There was a carnival and all, and that was the thing to do. I didn't really want to go, but I didn't care to stay at home either. Frank was out with his friends, so no one was at home except Mom and Douglas when I came in just after midnight.

Mom was asleep in their bedroom. In a drunken stupor, most likely. I noticed the nearly empty bottle of Jack Daniel's on the kitchen counter. Douglas was in the living room armchair doing nothing. We didn't have a television. No one we knew had a TV then. Douglas was drunk, too, but lucid enough to give me a lecherous grin when I walked in the door.

"Well, looky here," he said. "It's the Wicked Witch of the West."

I didn't answer him. I just wanted to go to my room, take off the stupid costume, and go to bed. I was tired and not in a very good mood.

"Got any candy for me, sweetheart?" he asked.

I shook my head and went to the refrigerator to see if there was anything to drink besides water. As I was looking, I sensed him standing behind me.

"Didn't you go trick or treatin'?"

"No," I answered, my back still to him. "I just went to a party. I'm too old to trick or treat."

"Oh, I don't think so. You're just the right age. In fact, your birthday is next week, ain't it?"

I ignored him. I shut the fridge and tried to move past him. He was blocking the way out of the kitchen.

"I'd like to go to my room, please," I said.

"Hold on, sweetie. We're gonna play a little trick or treat."

I wanted to say something to him I'd heard kids at school say. You know, the "F" word. But I didn't use that word in those days. I kept silent.

Then he reached out and caressed my cheek with the back of his gnarly hand.

I jerked back and hissed, "Don't touch me!"

After that there was fire in his eyes and he whispered, "Don't you dare talk like that to your father! You respect your elders, do you hear me?"

"You're not my father."

"I'm your stepfather. Same thing."

"No it ain't."

He got this sickly grin on his face and licked his lips. "My, my, ain't you the spirited one? You and I are gonna have some *fun*, sweetheart. I can see that, yes siree."

Douglas backed me up against the fridge and there was nowhere I could go. I could smell his rancid whiskey breath and, I swear, I could *hear* his heart beating furiously in his chest. It turned him on to be in such a dominating position over me.

He grabbed me by the throat and held it tightly—not hard enough to make a mark or choke me, just strong enough to keep me from moving. I was scared to death. I think I started crying, I'm not sure. For God's sake, I was still thirteen years old. I may have been a tough little street girl, but I was no match for a grown man who weighed two hundred and sixty pounds.

"You wanna go to your room? Let's *go* to your room!"

He then yanked me away from the fridge and, still holding me by the neck, marched me out of the kitchen, through the living room, and into the hall. I wanted to cry out for my mom, but the bedroom door was closed and I knew she was sleeping soundly. I could hear her snoring. I prayed for Frank to come home, but the chances of that happening were slim. It was hopeless.

When we got to my room, he threw me down on my bed and then shut the door. Douglas came at me and started tearing off my costume. He laughed and started chanting, "Trick or treat, trick or treat," as if this was *fun*—some game he thought we *both* enjoyed. I tried to kick and punch him, but it was no use. He held me down and ripped away my panties. Then he unbuckled his pants.

I couldn't stop him.

When he'd finished his business, he patted my face as if I'd done a household chore for him. "Thanks, sweetie. You done real good," he said. "That was definitely a treat, not a trick."

I don't remember if I was crying or what. I just know I was hurt. There was blood on my bed and I felt as if I'd been torn apart. I must have been in shock.

Douglas stood, pulled up his pants, and said, "Now don't you go tellin' anyone about this. It was your fault, you know. You teased me. You can't go around teasin' grown men or this is what'll happen. If your mother found out, it would kill her. You don't want to kill your mama, do you? She'd hate you for the rest of your life. You'd be in so much trouble. Maybe even get sent away to some juvenile home, y'know what I mean? A prison for bad girls. 'Cause that's what you are, sweetheart. A *bad girl*. Do you hear me?"

I didn't say anything.

"*Do we understand each other?*"

I nodded.

Then he left the room.

The rest of that night was a blur. I'm pretty sure I sat in the bathtub for a long time and then went to bed and cried myself to sleep.

Needless to say, my fourteenth birthday was the unhappiest of my life.

For the next several weeks, the hell of living at home was magnified tenfold. I couldn't stand to be there. I took long walks, stayed out late—for which I got in trouble with Mom—and spent more time at school than was necessary. Whenever I was home, Douglas would just leer at me, grin, and lick his lips. I knew it was a matter of time before he did it again.

Yes, he was planning it. I saw it in his face and eyes. That intuition again. The wild animal's instinct to protect itself.

I had to flee.

For three more horrendous months I endured existing under

the same roof with that evil man. At the end of January 1952, I decided I couldn't take it anymore.

I got hold of a bus schedule. I figured out how to get to the Odessa station in town and how much money it would cost to go somewhere far away. I packed a knapsack with some clothes and necessities. Then on a Sunday morning when my mom and Douglas were sleeping late, I crept into their bedroom. I could do that well. I called it "sneaky-weaking." Like a cat, I could open doors and go in and out of a room without making a sound.

So I sneaky-weaked into the room and grabbed Douglas's billfold, which was sitting on the nightstand by his side of the bed. He'd been paid the Friday before, and I knew his routine. He always cashed his check for the full amount, went for a drink at one of the roughneck bars, then came home with a wad in his wallet. On Monday he used it to pay bills, give some to my mother, and maybe put a little in the bank.

But this was Sunday.

I counted two hundred and fifty-two dollars in his wallet, so I took it and replaced the billfold. There was another hundred and twenty-five stashed in his nightstand drawer. I had managed to save a hundred dollars of my own money, so I thought I was rich. I had no idea how quickly that amount of cash would slip away out in the *real world*. But I didn't think about it, and I wouldn't have cared if I had.

I grabbed my knapsack and left the house. Caught the bus at the end of the block and rode it downtown. I didn't know where I wanted to go from there, so I studied the big board and the names of all the various cities. New York sounded the most exotic, so that's what I chose. I boarded the next bus to New York City and left behind my home, my brother, my mom, Texas, and that sick creep Douglas Bates.

As soon as I was in my seat, I vowed that one day I would get revenge on the bastard for what he did to me.

4
Roberto
The Present

My goddamned heart nearly stopped when I heard the guard shout, "Ranelli! Roberto Ranelli! Your ride's here!"

Holy Mother of God.

I've been waitin' for this day for fifty-two fuckin' years. Sittin' in this rathole all that time, gettin' old, just tryin' to survive. I knew they couldn't keep me in here until I died. I always thought I'd see the outside again.

They gave me some street clothes to put on. Some trousers that barely fit, a clean white shirt, and a dumpy sport jacket. I don't know where they got 'em. Probably some thrift shop in Ossining. Or maybe there's some kind of shitty charitable organization that provides civilian threads for parolees. Hell, I don't know. I don't care, either. I just wanted to get the fuck out of here.

The guard known as "Red," because of his flamin' red hair and freckles, approached my cell and gave the signal to the operator down the hall. No keys in this place, not anymore. Everything is automated. Run by computers. Amazin' inventions, those computers. When I first got sent up the river, there were no such things. They were science fiction. I'm glad I got to learn how to use one in the prison library. I witnessed the evolution of computers in that stinkin' library. I remember the first one they had was a stupid Apple IIc. We all thought it was a marvel. I think that was in nineteen eighty-four or somethin'. By 1990 we had real PCs that ran on DOS. Yeah, I learned what DOS was and how to manipulate it a little bit. Then Windows was the next big thing. Then things really started to explode. Computers got more sophisticated, faster, and smaller. Now we got these Macs in the prison library. Pretty nice machines. Hold on—*we* don't got 'em. *They* got 'em. I'm outta here. I'm fuckin' paroled. After fifty-two years. Unbelievable.

The bars slid open and I walked out. "Thanks, Red," I said.

"Sure thing, Ranelli. We're gonna miss you around here."

"Red, I was here before you were born."

"I know. You're like my goddamned uncle or somethin'."

"Take care of yourself, Red."

"You too, Ranelli. Just go on down to Roscoe, there, and he'll escort you to where you gotta go."

"Thanks."

As I walked down that hall of cells, guys I'd become friends with—and enemies, too—they all said goodbye and good luck. I waved and smiled at them. I didn't want to stop and talk. I didn't want to draw it out. Fuck 'em.

Roscoe was one of those stone-faced guys who'd been there forever. The place had some friendly guards, but most were cold-hearted assholes who didn't give a shit about you. Roscoe was one of those.

We went through a series of doors that opened and closed as a buzzer sounded. I passed Julio, another lifer who'd been in since the early seventies. He was paintin' a wall or something, some kind of work detail he was on.

"Hey, old-timer," he said. "You really leavin' us, huh?"

"Better take a good look at my ass when I walk out," I answered. "It's the last you'll see of it."

"Take care, Roberto."

"Thanks, Julio. You, too."

"Wish it was me, man."

"It will be someday. Don't give up."

"Right."

We went through another couple doors and finally entered the office where they gave you the official send-off. I'd already filled out all the paperwork, got it signed and approved and everything. There wasn't much more that needed done.

Some ancient guy—probably a lifer even older than me—worked the unit where they kept prisoners' personal belongings. Sing Sing had over two thousand inmates, so there was an awful lot of junk in there. I often wondered what they did with the crap that belonged to guys who died in prison. Did the guards use it for currency and play poker with it?

I signed the paper and they handed over a little plastic bag. Inside was my wallet I'd had in my pocket when I was arrested. Damn, it looked just like new. I opened it up and found my old driver's license, fifty years out of date. A business card from my bank with an account number scribbled on it. A few black-and-white pictures of my mother and father, and one of my brother Vittorio.

Vittorio. He would've looked just like me now if he'd lived.

There was also a comb, a wristwatch that didn't work anymore, a tiny notepad, a key ring, and a hundred and three dollars and sixty-two cents. That was the amount of money I had on me at that stupid New Year's Eve party. I stuffed the money into the billfold and stuck it in my pocket. The comb I shoved in my back trouser pocket. The wristwatch was useless, so I dropped it in the trashcan by the counter. I picked up the notepad and flipped through it. It had some names and addresses in it. At first I didn't remember why I'd had it. Then it came back to me. It was my little black book, so to speak. I was never good at rememberin' addresses and phone numbers, so I carried that little notepad around with me. The key ring—that was somethin' I needed. There were three keys on it. One opened my old apartment and another was for my long-gone Studebaker—those were garbage now—but the third key was important. I slipped the bad keys off the ring and tossed them in the trash. The good one I kept and put in my pocket.

"You need me to call you a cab?" the old man asked.

"I thought they said my ride was here."

The guy looked confused. "You had a ride comin' for ya?"

"No. I think it was just an expression."

"Oh. So you want me to call a cab?"

"No."

The geezer shrugged. His eyes looked me up and down. "How long you been in here?"

"In *here*? Sing Sing? Or how long has it been since I was arrested?"

"Whatever."

"I was arrested New Year's Eve—er, rather, early New Year's Day, nineteen fifty-eight."

The guy whistled. "How old are you, man?"

"Seventy-eight."

"No shit? You look pretty fit. I'd have said you were sixty-somethin'."

"Thanks. I guess."

"And they didn't parole you sooner? How many people did you kill, anyway?"

"I was convicted for one."

The guy nodded. He knew there were more. "You're lucky, man. Most lifers stay lifers. How'd you avoid the chair?"

I shrugged. "Had a good lawyer, I guess."

"Must have." He winked at me. He, too, knew I was connected at one time. The family had good attorneys with judges in their pockets. "You're a legend around here, Roberto."

"Better that than a fossil."

"Well, good luck to you."

"Thanks."

The doors opened.

I was free.

I walked out into the sunny streets of Ossining, past the shell that was old Sing Sing, the original prison that was declared some kind of historical buildin'. What a crock. A historical monument to pain and sufferin' and death. I heard they were gonna make it a museum. They closed it in the forties. Thank God it was before I got in. It was supposed to be really awful. The so-called modern facility was horrible enough. I'd seen a lot in Sing Sing. I knew guys who did the sit-down dance. They finally abolished execution by the chair, thank goodness. I was there for the riots of eighty-three, but I didn't participate. I knew better. I stayed the hell out of the way and made sure the guards saw I wasn't doing anything. That went a long way toward improvin' my conditions. I got offered more work/program assignments. My days of bein' the prison badass stopped after my first twenty years, so I became known as a "model prisoner." It took forever, but it got me paroled. Good behavior. And age. The heart murmur probably had somethin' to do with it, too. The prison doctor told me to have it checked out by a cardiologist when I got out.

Screw that. I had more important things to do with what time I had left on this stinkin' planet.

Like finding *her*.

The cab took me all the way down the FDR Drive to lower Manhattan. The driver was some Arab guy wearin' a turban. I didn't expect that. Luckily, he wasn't a talkative type, 'cause I didn't feel like chattin'. Man, things sure had changed. I hardly recognized the city. Well, parts of it were exactly the same. The skyline was different. More buildings. I wish I'd seen the Twin Towers. They were built and destroyed all durin' the time I was up the river. Do they still use that expression—"up the river"? It came about because you had to go up the Hudson to get to Sing Sing. There are probably a lot of expressions people don't use anymore and many more they do use that I don't know about. It's gonna be a learnin' curve. Will I reenter society smoothly? I had to attend some seminars in the joint that were supposed to help me "reassimilate." They didn't teach me a damn thing. Most of it was common sense. They told us about how technology had advanced, what we could expect when we tried to do somethin' as simple as makin' a phone call. Again, computers had changed the world. One of the first things I wanted to do when I got my dough was buy one of them laptops. I needed to get online. And I had to find some of my old friends—ones who were still alive, if any.

I told the driver to let me off at the corner of Wall Street and William. I paid him and then looked up at the buildin' I'd been dreamin' about for fifty-something years. Imagine my shock when I saw it. Forty-eight Wall Street was completely different. It was supposed to be the Bank of New York. It had changed. It wasn't a bank anymore.

What the hell had they done with my stuff?

I felt my heart skip a beat—that damned murmur thing again—but I took a deep breath and told myself to relax. They weren't gonna throw out anyone's money. The bank probably moved. So I went inside. The lobby was now some kind of museum of finance. I walked up to some guy that looked like he worked there.

"Yes, sir, can I help you?" he asked.

"Where's the bank that used to be here?"

He looked confused.

"The Bank of New York."

"Oh. You're in the wrong building. You want to go to One Wall Street."

"One Wall Street?"

"That's the Bank of New York. Actually it's now the Bank of New York Mellon."

"Mellon?"

"They merged. A few years ago."

"I see. Would they have all the stuff that used to be in this building?"

The guy shrugged. "I don't know. I guess so."

"Thanks."

I wondered if I should call my lawyer's office. They're the ones who've kept the trust money that paid the rent on my safety deposit box all these years. Wouldn't they have told me if my bank had changed? Maybe not. Fuckin' lawyers.

I left the place and started walkin' toward Broadway. It was a minor miracle I remembered where certain streets were and what direction they were in. Some things never leave you. Manhattan's in my blood. I lived here all my life.

And the women. My God, the women. They sure were different. I mean, they were still *women*, but sweet Jesus, were they amazin'. Short dresses. Long bare legs. Some had tattoos! Blondes, brunettes, redheads. All nationalities. Young, middle-aged, old. They were all fuckin' beautiful. I didn't see many women in the joint. I thought I'd have a heart attack right there on the street.

When I got to the corner and saw the really tall buildin', it came back to me. One Wall Street used to be the Irving Trust building. But now it wasn't. Now it was the Bank of New York Mellon. Interestin'. I just hoped to hell they had my stuff. I went inside—it looked like a bank lobby, so that was promisin'. There wasn't much of a line in front of the tellers, so I waited patiently. I admit I was nervous. This would be my first business exchange with someone on the outside—except for the Arab taxi driver, that is.

The teller was a young girl. She looked mighty pretty. I could barely speak to her.

"May I help you, sir?"

"Yeah, I, um, I used to have a safety deposit box back when the Bank of New York was at Forty-Eight Wall Street. What would have happened to it?"

I could see the question threw her for a loop. She blinked and asked, "When was the last time you accessed it?"

"Nineteen fifty-seven."

Then her eyes really bulged. "Oh, my. Have you been away somewhere?"

"Yeah. Prison."

She swallowed. "Just a second. Let me get the supervisor."

It took a few minutes, but she eventually came back with a squirrelly lookin' bald guy in a fancy business suit. I didn't think it was a coincidence that a security guard accompanied him and stood in back a few feet away.

"What seems to be the trouble, sir?" Squirrelly Man asked.

"No trouble. I just want to access my safety deposit box. But it's been fifty-two years since I've done so." I handed over my old driver's license, the key—which opened the old box, and the business card with my account number.

"What's this about prison?"

"Why does that matter?" I asked. My temper was risin' and I felt my heart start to pound again. "Yeah, I was in prison and I just got paroled. I came to get the stuff out of my safety deposit box. You still have it, right? It's supposed to be *safe*. That's the idea, ain't it?"

The fellow pursed his lips. "Let me look up your account." He punched the keys on the computer and then checked the information with my driver's license. "This license has expired."

"No kiddin'. I haven't had time to go get a new one."

Finally, the guy glanced at the security guard and nodded. Everything was okay. The guard walked away but hovered nearby, just in case. Then came the kicker. "I'm sorry, all the safety deposit boxes that were once at Forty-Eight Wall Street are now at the Chase Bank branch at Forty-Five Wall Street."

"What?"

He repeated what he said.

"You gotta be kiddin' me."

"Didn't you get a notice in the mail about the move?"

"No. I don't think so." I couldn't remember if I did or not. Besides, the lawyers would have got it. Maybe they didn't tell me.

"I'm sorry, sir. You'll have to go to the Chase branch."

Jesus H. Christ.

"Fine. Thanks for your trouble," I said to both him and the female teller. She smiled at me, which sent a lightnin' bolt down to my groin. I didn't think I'd still have feelin's there, but I did. Must've been the Italian in me. Nevertheless, I was too pissed off to respond in any way. I wanted to break somethin'.

But I took a deep breath and calmly walked out of the building. Went *back* to 45 Wall Street. I don't remember what it was in the fifties—in fact, I seem to recall the buildin' was under construction the last time I was across the street—but now it was a tall high-rise apartment buildin' complex with shops and stuff on the bottom. And a Chase Bank. So I went inside and did my song and dance yet *again* for a teller—this time a man; I'll call him Four Eyes because of the thick glasses he wore—and after a few minutes of exchangin' IDs and fillin' out papers, it seemed I'd finally hit pay dirt.

I followed Four Eyes through a door and down a corridor to another part of the buildin'. He talked me through the procedure, directed me into a vault containin' what appeared to be a zillion safety deposit boxes. The guy had a different key, which he stuck in one slot.

"Your key goes there," he said, pointin' to a different keyhole.

This was different from what it used to be. In the old days, it just took one key to open the door. Now it took two—mine and his. I guess it was a minor marvel that my key still worked.

"Do you need a private room, sir?" he asked.

"Yeah."

I carried my box to a series of booths with doors. The banker let me in one and showed me a button on the wall. "Press that when you want to return the box."

"Thanks."

He left me alone and shut the door. I sat at a small table and eagerly opened the box.

It was all there.

Unbelievable. I breathed a sigh of relief.

First I stuffed all the cash into my jacket pockets, and what didn't fit I crammed into my trouser pockets and even inside my underwear. By the time I was done, I was pretty well padded down. Forty-eight thousand dollars. Back in nineteen fifty-seven, that was a hell of a lot of money. A fortune. Today, probably not so much. Still, it was enough to get me back on my feet for the time being.

My beloved snubby Colt Detective Special and one box of thirty-eight special cartridges were there, so I loaded six into the cylinder, spun it once—it needed oilin', that's for sure—and snapped it in. The rest of the bullets I poured into one of the pockets with the money.

I stood and made sure I didn't look funny. Yeah, my pockets were bulgin', but I didn't think it would be too suspicious. I'd go straight to a hotel and regroup. Havin' my money and revolver made me feel like the king of the world. I hadn't felt this good since—well, way before New Year's Eve of nineteen fifty-seven, that's for damn sure.

I pressed the button to call Four Eyes.

Next on the agenda—the hotel, some decent food, and contact some of the boys if I could find them. And then I had to figure out how to locate the bitch. The Black Stiletto. I'd waited fifty-two years to avenge my brother's death. And by God, I was gonna get that woman. I wondered where she was. Was she alive? I hoped so. Was she still in New York? If she was still there, I'd find her. If not, I'd search every goddamned town in the country until I did.

At least I knew her real name. That'd help.

Judy Cooper.

5
Judy's Diary
1958

Dear diary, New York City wasn't what I expected. Actually, that's not true. Let's just say I naïvely thought it would be easier to leave home and start anew in another city. New York wasn't Odessa in any way, shape, or form. New York was like another planet, totally alien to anything I'd ever experienced. There were people everywhere, all kinds, of every race imaginable. Cars and buses and trucks and bicycles and lots and lots of people. And the buildings—they were huge and they were everywhere, towering over me like gods. It was overwhelming at first. I didn't have the first clue of what to do when I got off that bus at Port Authority.

I was fourteen, alone, with very little money. What the hell was I doing there?

Needless to say, I had to mature early and quickly. I remember going to a tourist information booth in the bus station and asking about a hotel. I stayed in some fleabag joint on 42nd Street for about a week as I explored the city, trying to conserve what little money I had. Eventually I found my way farther downtown and started kicking around East Greenwich Village. Somehow the Bohemian nature of the area appealed to me. I pleaded homelessness and got a temporary place to stay at the YWCA on Broadway and set about looking for a job. I'd been in New York about three weeks and the money was nearly gone. Then one day I saw a restaurant on the corner of Second Avenue and East 4th Street with a sign on the window that said HELP WANTED. It was called the East Side Diner and was one of those places that served breakfast, lunch, and dinner, opened early, and closed late. I thought, *what the hell.*

I went inside and the place was packed. It was eleven o'clock in the morning, so there were still customers eating breakfast and quite a few having lunch. There were two waitresses running back and forth like chickens with no heads. They constantly yelled orders to the short-order cook in the kitchen while dishing out sass to customers. "Where's my eggs over-easy?" "Cheeseburger, hold the mayo!" "Are you done, mister? Sorry, my legs ain't on the menu." That kind of stuff. They even had one of those new jukeboxes, which I later found out was very unusual for New York diners. I'd never seen or heard one before. I remember the song that was playing when I walked in—it was "Cry" by Johnnie Ray and the Four Lads.

One waitress, a pretty woman with blonde hair and a great figure, saw me standing by the door. She was probably twenty one years old or so.

"You comin' in, honey?" she asked.

"I want to apply for the job." I gestured to the sign in the window.

"Oh. Honey, we're really busy right now, as you can see. Can you come back after the rush? Say, two o'clock?"

"Sure."

"I'm Lucy. What's your name, honey?"

"Judy."

"Okay, Judy, see you later."

I felt excited. Maybe I'd get hired and start making some money. I immediately liked Lucy. She had a thick New York accent and it sounded funny to my ears. Funny in a good way. Lucy didn't seem to notice I was probably too young to work. I appeared older than I was. I suppose this is a good time to tell you, dear diary, what I look like. I was tall—still am—ridiculously tall for a fourteen-year-old. I'm not sure exactly how tall I was then, but now, at age twenty, I'm five-eleven. I was maybe an inch or two shorter when I was fourteen. So, yeah, I looked older. I had, and still have, dark hair—almost black—that comes down a little past my shoulders. My eyes are brown with flecks of green. My skin is pale—I used to get sunburned pretty easily. My legs are long, of course, and I'm fit. Since I did a lot of sports and all that gymnastics stuff, I was, and am still, well-toned. My boobs were growing fast at that time and were already something I noticed men stealing glances at. Today they're a nice full size that fit a 36C cup. Lots of men tell me I'm attractive. Some say I'm beautiful. That's nice, I guess. To tell you the truth, it makes me a little uncomfortable. The incident with Douglas put me off men for quite some time. That would change, though.

I killed time walking around the neighborhood. Two blocks south on Second Avenue was a gymnasium. It was called the Second Avenue Gym. Curious, I opened the door and looked inside. It was a pretty large space. There was a boxing ring in the middle of the room, and around the sides were all kinds of workout equipment like punching bags of all types and sizes, wall pulleys, rowing machines, and other stuff. A bunch of men were in there—a couple in the ring sparring and several others just exercising. White men, Negroes, Hispanics. I'd never seen colored men and white men working out in the same room before. That was surprising. For a few minutes I stood there and watched, fascinated by their sweaty, muscular bodies as they punched and jabbed at each other.

Anyway, I went back to the diner at two o'clock, and the place was much calmer. There were only a few customers in some of the booths. Lucy stood by the counter studying a stack of order tickets, trying to figure out something. She looked up and smiled.

"Hi, Judy. You came back, huh? The lunch rush didn't scare you away?"

"Nope."

She patted one of the swivel stools at the counter. "Have a seat."

"Are you the boss?" I asked.

"No, no. I'm the head waitress. The boss comes in at night, his name is Manny. He's a pretty nice guy, but he's strict and doesn't tolerate laziness or mistakes. That won't be a problem, will it, Judy?"

"No!"

"Good."

We spent the next half hour talking about the diner, my background, and how I'd run away from home. I was perfectly honest. At one point she frowned and whispered, "How old are you, honey?"

I looked down and told her the truth. Lucy took a deep breath and pursed her lips. "I think we'll just pretend you're sixteen, okay?"

"All right."

She handed me an application and a pencil and told me to subtract two years from my birth date when I filled it in. Lucy left me alone to fill in the pertinent information. For a residence, I put the YWCA.

Well, I was hired. I became a waitress at the East Side Diner and learned the ropes. I figured out when it was okay to flirt with customers so you could get a bigger tip, and I learned when to give them sass if they were getting out of line. I got to where I knew the menu by heart. Pretty soon, I was as good as any of the other ladies working there. And Lucy—Lucy Dempsey was her full name— became my best friend. She took me under her wing, so to speak. She lived alone in an apartment on St. Marks Place

and had a boyfriend named Sam, who came in the diner every
now and then. I didn't like Sam. He gave me the same kind of
bad feelings that Douglas had. Sam was cocky and full of himself. He bossed Lucy around and acted like she was his property.
I could tell she was embarrassed by his attitude but I also saw that
she really liked him, although I don't know why. One day, I think
it was in the summer, she confided in me. I had been in New York
six months and was still living at the Y, but the city was starting
to feel more like home than Odessa ever did. Anyway, Lucy and
I were off one Sunday and we went walking around the Village.
She told me that Sam could be very mean and hit her sometimes.
I told her she shouldn't put up with that at all. Lucy just shrugged
and said, "He's my man. I love him."

"He has no right to hit you," I said. "Don't you let him. If he
does, you tell me, I'll kick his butt."

She laughed. "You? Judy, how could you kick his butt?"

"I'm tougher than I look." And that gave me an idea. "Hey,
you know where I can go to learn to box?"

"What?"

"You know, box." I held up my fists and mimed punching.

"Why do you want to do that?"

"Self-defense. Wouldn't you want to be able to defend yourself
against Sam next time he hit you?"

"You mean like *fight* him?"

"Sure."

"Hell, no. He'd beat the crap out of me."

"But that's the point! You could maybe beat the crap out of
him!" I wasn't used to saying words like "crap"—but Lucy said
stuff like that all the time.

"Judy, you're nuts. Women don't learn how to box."

"Why not?"

"I don't know. They just don't."

"Do you know anything about that gym that's a couple of blocks south of the diner?"

"The Second Avenue Gym?"

"That's the one."

"Not really. I know the guy who runs it. He comes in the diner sometimes. You've seen him. His name is Freddie. Freddie Barnes. Middle-aged guy, late forties, I guess. Used to be a boxer himself. Has dark curly hair with spots of gray? Bushy eyebrows?"

"Oh, yeah!" I did remember the guy. He was always one of the nice customers who said hello every time he came in, and he left decent tips. "Do they let girls in there?"

"I don't know. I doubt it. A gym is where men go."

"Well, we'll have to see about that," I said.

It took me a couple of months to get up the nerve to go into the Second Avenue Gym. In the meantime, I worked at the diner, continued to live at the YWCA, and explored the city. New York was a fascinating place. Growing up in Odessa was like being in a vacuum. The whole world was at my feet in Manhattan. It was exciting and vibrant. I felt alive for the first time in my life.

They made me move out of the Y once they figured out I had a full-time job. I found a studio apartment on 8th Street near Sixth Avenue, but the rent was higher than I could afford. Noisy neighbors lived next to me, too, and I could hear them having sex at night. That drove me crazy. I knew it wouldn't be long before I moved again, but I tried to make it work for the time being.

It was September 1952 when I finally went into the Second Avenue Gym. I saw Freddie Barnes in the ring with a couple of young guys. Freddie was training them, playing referee for a practice fight or something. I took a position against the wall, stood there, and watched, trying to be inconspicuous. Nevertheless, all the men in the place stared at me. Now, in those days I wore just regular old boys' trousers, the blouses I'd wear at the diner, maybe a jacket or sweater if it was cold outside, and a baseball cap. Because of my height and build, I might have passed for a boy if it hadn't been for my long hair.

I was obviously a girl.

No one said anything to me, though. Maybe they figured I was someone's girlfriend. The men on the sidelines continued to jump rope, or work on the rowing machines, stand in front of the wall pulleys and use them to strengthen their arm muscles, slam into the heavy bags hanging from the ceiling, or punch the speed balls. The place was noisy and smelled like sweat. I liked it.

Finally the sparring was over. Freddie saw me and made a funny expression, as if to say, "What are you doing here?" After giving the two athletes some instructions, he climbed through the ropes and jumped to the floor.

"Hi," he said. "Judy, right?"

"Yeah. Hi, Freddie."

"Not workin' at the diner today?" Freddie had a thick Brooklyn accent.

"I'm working the dinner shift later."

"What can I do for you?"

"I want to learn how to box."

"You what?"

I repeated what I said. Freddie shook his head and replied, "Why?"

"So I can beat the devil out of anyone who bothers me."

Freddie didn't say anything for a few seconds, and then he laughed. I didn't appreciate that, and he must have sensed it. "I'm sorry, Judy, but girls don't learn how to box. How old are you, anyway?"

"Seventeen," I lied.

"No, you're not. I asked Lucy about you once. She told me

you're really not old enough to work at the diner, but she didn't tell Manny how old you really are. You're what, fifteen?"

I told him the truth. "I'll be fifteen in November. Look, Freddie. I think you could use my help around here." I made a sweeping gesture, taking in the entire gym. "This place could use some cleaning. And I know how to work a cash register. I could work behind the counter and sell all that soap and rent towels and stuff. And why can't girls learn how to box? Who says so? I'm a good athlete. I was on the gymnastics team at school for a while."

He still shook his head. "Judy, I can't let you work here. This is a place for men. Why, it's unheard of. Probably against the law, too."

"I don't think so, Freddie. I think it's just what people are used to believing about girls. We're not all the get married, stay-at-home, raise kids types."

"That may be true, Judy, but I can't. Sorry."

I was disappointed but I tried not to let it show. "Okay, Freddie. But I'll be back. You'll change your mind," I said confidently.

So I left. But I returned the very next day. Freddie was coaching a couple of different guys in the ring. He saw me but didn't smile or wave. I stayed and watched anyway. On my third visit to the gym, I stood watching a match and then spotted a mop and bucket over in a corner. I went over to it, grabbed the mop, and started on the area of the floor that wasn't being used. Freddie saw me but said nothing. I couldn't move to the section where all the men were working out, so I didn't try. Instead, I found a towel and started wiping down all the counters and a glass case that contained some trophies.

One of the young boxers, a teenager maybe eighteen or nineteen years old, said to me, "Hey, baby, I've got something you can clean." I ignored him and kept going. I'd seen the kid before at the gym; in fact, he was one of the trainees in the ring the first day I'd come in. He continued to harass me. "What's your name, sweetheart? Why are you doing that? You sure are pretty. Wanna go out with me? Let's go back and take a shower, what do you say?"

When he reached out, daring to touch me, I swung around and let him have it. I punched him right in the nose and he fell on the floor. Freddie stopped coaching the two fighters in the ring and looked up. The teenager I'd clobbered was mad as heck, and his nose was bleeding. But he sat there, his pride wounded. Suddenly, all the other men in the gym started laughing at him. Teasing him, you know, "Gee, Mack, you let a girl bust you one?" "What happened, Mack, you meet your match?"

Freddie came down and helped the kid named Mack onto his feet. His face was swelling up and there was a lot of blood. Freddie gave him some towels and ordered him to go wash up. Mack gave me the scariest glare as he walked past me—but it's funny, I didn't get that tingling sensation when I sensed someone meant to do me harm. You know, my animal intuition thing. I realized Mack wasn't dangerous. In fact, he was all bravado.

Freddie sidled up to me. "Judy, you broke his nose."

"I did? Gee, I'm sorry, Freddie."

"Why did you do that?"

"He was picking on me. Being fresh."

Freddie looked over at the mop and towels I'd been using. "What are you doing, Judy?"

"I told you. You could use some help. And I want to learn to box."

This time he chuckled. "I think you already know how."

And that's all it took. Freddie let me come in a couple of times a week to help clean the gymnasium. He showed me everything I was supposed to do and I did it better than he expected. Most of the cleaning was done at night, after hours. After a month of that, he let me start working the cash register and supervising the linens. He showed me how to maintain all the equipment, especially the punching bags. Freddie taught me the difference between the various kinds, like speed bags that are small and are the kinds you usually see boxers hitting in a constant rhythm; heavy bags, the large cylindrical kind suspended from the ceiling that you practice body punches on; and the double-end bag, which is round like a basketball and attached to the floor *and* ceiling.

And then, sometimes after closing, Freddie would give me a few lessons. They started gradually at first, but by the time I turned fifteen in November, we were making a regular thing out of it. He didn't pay me much to work there—we decided that the bulk of my salary would be in lessons.

I continued to work at the diner until Christmas. By then, Freddie and I had become good friends. He liked me—not in a sexual way, but more like a father-daughter thing, I'm sure of that. Freddie once told me he wished he'd gotten married, but hadn't. Maybe I was the substitute for the son he didn't have, ha ha. Anyway, he gave me a raise and I quit the job at the diner. Lucy and I remained good friends and I still went in there all the time to have meals and stuff.

Then, shortly after the New Year in 1953, I was complaining to Freddie about the apartment I was in and how the neighbors were nasty and noisy. He just said, "Come with me," so I followed him to the steel door that led to his quarters. I knew Freddie lived in an apartment above the gym, but I'd never been up there. Behind the door was a stairwell leading up two flights to compensate for the gym's high ceiling, and then to what would have been the building's third floor. Freddie led me to a door and opened it. It was a large, spacious room with a twin bed, a desk, a chest of drawers, and an adjoining bathroom.

"Want to live here?" he asked. "It's a spare bedroom I have no use for."

I squealed with delight and clapped my hands like a school-girl. Then I gave him a big hug.

And that's how, dear diary, I came to live above the Second Avenue Gym and become the assistant manager of the place.

The year 1953 was a blur. I was fifteen and I'd been gone from Texas for more than a year. Dear diary, I want to say something here. Seeing that I'm writing this in 1958, I've actually been away from home for five years. You might think I was awful to run away without telling anyone. I do think about my mom and brothers, and I often have dreams about them. Every now and then I feel a pang of guilt for leaving without telling my mom where I was going. She probably worried about me like the dickens. I'll bet she had the police looking for me. They've probably written me off for dead. Well, I can't give it too much thought. I hope my mom is okay and that maybe she's gotten away from Douglas. That creep is never far from my mind. The vow I made when I left Odessa still has meaning for me. I know I'll return someday and give him his comeuppance.

Sorry, I had to cry for a few seconds, dear diary.

Okay, back to 1953. I trained as a boxer. Freddie was great. He worked me hard after I told him not to treat me like a girl. He soon realized I was pretty tough and could take a lot of punishment as well as dish it out. He taught me about stances, different kinds of punches, defenses, and how to guard. My long legs were an asset for the "dance" in the ring. I eventually developed my own style of boxing, and Freddie said I was a classic "out-fighter."

That meant I could maintain a decent distance from my opponent and fight with faster, longer-range punches. Freddie told me that Gene Tunney, Billy Conn, and Willie Pep were out-fighters. Willie Pep was a popular professional boxer at that time. Anyway, when I say "my opponent"—ha ha—it was usually Freddie! There wasn't anyone else I could really spar with. He wouldn't let me spar with the boxers in the gym; in fact, he didn't let anyone know he was training me. Figured he wouldn't hear the end of it.

I did exercise during daytime hours when I wasn't working. I'd use the speed bag and got to where I was damned good. Sometimes I attracted an audience of guys who'd stand there and watch me keep it going for a half hour. They'd whistle and catcall at me; usually I ignored them but there was also a part of me that enjoyed the attention. I'd get on the rowing machine or use the wall pulleys, but most of the time I jumped rope. I was good at that, even with my long legs.

The men teased me and were sometimes downright abusive just because I was a female encroaching on their territory. But once they saw how *good* I was, they left me alone. Every now and then, one of the guys would spot me when I worked the heavy bag. When I exercised in front of the men, I'd wear men's long shorts, a polo shirt, and tennis shoes. I'd tie my hair back in a ponytail. When I was alone in the gym after hours, I wore a dance leotard and tights because they were easier to work out in. I couldn't parade around like that in front of the men, though; that'd been too much for them to handle, ha ha!

Every now and then some of the guys would make passes at me. They didn't know how old I really was. Several asked me out on dates, but I always said no. And then there was Mack, the teenager whose nose I'd broken. Ever since that day, he was as nice as he could be to me. He'd try to talk to me and on several occasions asked me to get coffee or something with him. Mack had improved as a boxer and was actually one of Freddie's promising trainees. I'd seen him win a few bouts in the ring.

On November 4, 1953, the day I turned sixteen, I finally accepted his offer to go out. We went to the East Side Diner for coffee. He even played a song on the jukebox for me, "I'm Walking Behind You" by Eddie Fisher. That was before the rock and roll stuff started, so I wasn't much of a music fan yet. Lucy was working that day and she winked at me, as if I'd made a conquest of some sort. I guess it was pretty obvious Mack was sweet on me. Funny that it had to take me breaking his nose for him to like me.

Well, we started dating. Mack and me. He was born and raised in Manhattan and was nineteen years old, as I suspected. I didn't tell him my real age. Mack wanted to be a boxer, naturally. As I said, he'd become pretty good in the ring since I busted his nose. To tell the truth, the broken nose made him more handsome. For the first time in my life, I started having feelings for the opposite sex. In a way, I was relieved—the experience with Douglas hadn't totally ruined me.

The first time I let him kiss me was on Thanksgiving Day. Freddie cooked a big dinner and I helped. Freddie was a pretty good cook, but I was even better. I guess some of my mom's ability rubbed off on me. Anyway, we invited a few of our closer friends from the gym—Mack among them—and Lucy and Sam.

It was a grand day and we all stuffed ourselves. While everyone was sitting around, completely satiated, Mack helped me clean up the kitchen. I was about to put away a pot or something, turned around, and there he was. He put his arms around me, leaned in, and kissed me. I still had the pot in my hands! Anyway, it was nice, so I put down the pot and put my arms around him. I'd never kissed like that—on the mouth and, you know, with the tongue—and I really enjoyed it. We spent the rest of the afternoon "making out."

I guess from then on we were sort of an item. A couple of times we double-dated with Lucy and Sam. I still didn't like Sam. He was a cad. He flirted with me behind Lucy's back. Once I asked him, "Isn't Lucy your girlfriend?" He answered, "Yeah, sure, but that doesn't mean I can't sample other items on the menu." I wanted to break *his* nose. I almost told Lucy what he was doing, but I figured it would just hurt her. She liked him too much, although I still didn't see why.

It was New Year's Eve, going into 1954, when I lost my virginity. Well, technically I lost it with Douglas, the bastard, but the first time I *wanted* to "do it" was after the party we had at the gym. Like at Thanksgiving, Freddie and I threw a small party, had a great dinner, lots of drinks—I was still legally too young to drink, but I did—and champagne. Okay, so I was pretty smashed when I took Mack up to my room. But I was perfectly aware of what I was doing. I wanted to. So did he—to state the obvious. What I remember of the event was nothing like the fireworks I expected. It was all right. I think I mostly just enjoyed the intimacy and the closeness more than the actual sex act.

And then the weirdest thing happened.

Mack didn't show up for a week. He didn't call or nothing. And would you believe—I didn't have his phone number, and the one Freddie had for Mack no longer worked. I couldn't call him. I didn't even know where he lived, only that it was somewhere uptown in the East Twenties. Was he hurt? Sick? What the heck was wrong? He'd certainly acted like he enjoyed what we did on New Year's Eve, so I couldn't imagine that he might not *like* me anymore. I had a good cry with Lucy and she told me not to worry—Mack would come around. Maybe he had to go out of town or something and couldn't get word to me.

Anyway, I didn't hear from Mack for two months. I was hurt and angry, but eventually I forgot about him. I went about my business, working at the gym, training, and trying to have fun. I didn't date anyone else.

And then in March, Mack showed up. He walked in as if he'd never been gone, started using the speed bag, and *ignored me*. I couldn't believe it. I overheard some of the guys asking him where he'd been, and Mack told them he'd moved and just "hadn't felt like coming." Well, everyone knew we'd been dating, so they all figured it was *my* fault or something. I was furious. The famous Judy Cooper temper reared its ugly head.

I went up to him and demanded to know why he hadn't called or come to see me. Mack just shrugged and said he didn't want to.

"Why not?" I asked. I was near tears, I was so mad. "I thought you liked me!"

He just looked at me with an expression of *disgust*—that's the only way I can describe it—and he said, "Not after that night."

Then he walked away.

I could've killed him.

Instead, I went over to where we kept the boxing gloves for people to rent. I put a pair on, went over to Jimmy, one of my friends at the gym, and asked him to tie them. Jimmy was a big Negro who didn't say much, but he asked, "What is it you-za gonna do, Judy?"

"You watch," I answered.

I climbed through the ropes and jumped into the ring. I stood in the middle and shouted to Mack, "Get up here, you louse!"

Mack just laughed.

"What's wrong, afraid a girl will beat you?" I taunted.

That got him. Some of the men were urging him to get up there and face me.

"What, are you *scared*?" I taunted.

By then, Freddie had walked into the room. "Judy! Get down!" he ordered.

"No, Freddie. This is between me and Mack," I said.

I guess he knew me well enough by then to know I was pretty stubborn. I wasn't getting out of the ring.

Finally, Mack couldn't take the ribbing the other guys were throwing at him. He put on some gloves and got in the ring with me. Freddie climbed in to referee.

"I want a real match," I told Mack. "No pulling back because

I'm a girl. I'm playing for keeps, so you'd better, too." Then I turned to Freddie. "I mean it. Treat this for real."

"Judy, are you sure about this?" he asked.

"Absolutely. I want to teach this *coward* a lesson."

That got Mack riled up. "Fine," he said. "I'm gonna beat your ass, *slut*."

I couldn't believe he called me that. I almost tore into him right then, but Freddie got between us. He pushed me to my corner and waited until Mack was in his. Then we started the match.

Round one.

I moved to the center of the ring and met Mack there. He swung at me hard and connected with the side of my head. I felt it, too, but it didn't stop me from delivering a powerful right hook—right on his nose! Mack stumbled back, but I kept moving forward. A jab, a cross, another jab, and a second cross. All four connected. I followed this barrage with an uppercut and then a slam into his stomach, which he didn't expect.

He moved back, an expression of total shock and surprise on his face. We pranced around the ring for another few seconds, and then I took the offensive. I moved in close and delivered a hard right hook and backed it up with a jab. Mack swung at me but I blocked the blow, ducked, and hit him with another uppercut. I followed this with two hard jabs and then a powerful cross.

Mack went down and didn't get up. It was over before round two.

Everyone in the room applauded and cheered for me. It felt great. Even Freddie gave me a huge grin and patted me on the back.

Mack never came back to the Second Avenue Gym.

Good riddance.

6
Judy's Diary
1958

I spent the rest of 1954 training, keeping fit, working in the gym, seeing Lucy when I could, and, for the first time in my life, having fun. Life was good. Freddie was a great "foster father" and I loved him. We became very close that year. I learned that he had been an up-and-coming boxer in the late thirties and early forties, but the mob had shut him out when he refused to play by their rules. He told me the Italian Mafia had such control over professional boxing that it was impossible to avoid them. I didn't know what the Mafia was until Freddie explained it to me. He said there were "families" that had a lot of money and basically ran most of the illegal activities in the city. Gambling houses, prostitution, drugs, protection rackets, bookmaking—that sort of stuff. And they had their hands all over boxing.

It was a good thing I was a girl and didn't have any aspirations to get involved with those guys. Little did I know, however, I would one day get in bed with them, so to speak.

For the most part, I ignored what was going on in the world. I was well aware of the Communists and how everyone was afraid of them. President Eisenhower made that speech about the dominos. People talked a lot about the atom bomb. I tried not to think about any of that. I was in my own little cocoon; my life took up a small section of a few city blocks of Manhattan. Every now and then Lucy and I would go see a movie. I saw my first Alfred

Hitchcock picture that year—*Rear Window*—and it scared the bejesus out of me! I liked listening to the new records on the East Side Diner's jukebox. I remember playing "Mr. Sandman" by the Chordettes over and over until Lucy wanted to scream, ha ha!

Anyway, I'm skipping ahead to the spring of 1955, when I was seventeen. In February of that year, Freddie allowed a martial arts tournament to be held at the Second Avenue Gym. I didn't know what martial arts were and neither did anyone else at the gym. When Freddie said a Japanese trainer had organized the event, everyone was suspicious. World War II had ended just ten years earlier, so anything Japanese was still not trusted. Freddie told me the man's name was Soichiro, but he had recently become an American citizen. He was originally from Japan and had family that had moved to America in the thirties. Supposedly they experienced a lot of hardships during the war years because Americans didn't like the Japanese—or the Germans and Italians, for that matter.

According to Freddie, in 1953 the Strategic Air Command invited Japanese martial arts instructors to visit American SAC bases for training programs. This opened communication between the U.S. and Japan, instigating a migration of many more instructors who set up shop in Asian neighborhoods around the country. Soichiro was one of these and he opened a small studio in Manhattan that practiced Asian fighting techniques. They had funny names like *judo* and *karate*. I had no idea what to expect. None of us had ever seen this stuff before.

On the day of the event, I helped Freddie with all the logistical and administration duties for the tournament. We rented a bunch of folding chairs and set them up, and I was in charge of collecting money and organizing the teams. Nearly everybody who participated in the tournament was Asian. Many couldn't speak English. Their ages ran from really little—six or seven years old—to middle-age. Soichiro himself was in his forties, *I think*.

It's hard to tell with Asians. They always look younger than they are. But I think he was probably the same age as Freddie.

Some of the gym's regular patrons came to watch the tournament, too. Jimmy was there with a small entourage of colored guys. I think everyone was curious about this martial arts business. Apparently it had existed in Asia for centuries, but we were just learning about it in the USA.

The tournament was a major revelation for me.

These guys got in the ring without boxing gloves or any other protection—they all wore white robes that looked like something you'd wear when you're having breakfast—and then they *threw each other around like they weighed nothing*! It was simply amazing. The stuff they called *judo* was like wrestling—that's the only way I can describe it—but they didn't really grapple much with each other; instead, the opponents would do a ceremonial bow to each other and then stand in a funny position, grab the other guy, and before you could blink, one was thrown over his opponent's back! Wham! I didn't understand how they did it, but they made it look easy. The other martial art, *karate*, seemed more brutal. In this one, opponents would hold their hands flat and spear-like—and they'd chop and jab with them, as well as kick with bare feet. The kicks were like circus acrobatics. Guys would jump really high, swirl around quickly, and *bam!*—a foot in the face. I'd never seen anything like it.

Well, after watching that all day, I was hooked. I wanted to learn it. I told Freddie that and he shrugged. "I don't know if they let girls, but you can ask Soichiro," he said.

"You don't mind, do you, Freddie?"

"I don't care, Judy. I just don't want you to get hurt. That looks like pretty dangerous stuff."

"I can handle it."

So I went over to Soichiro. They called him a "sensei," whatever that was. I guess it meant "trainer" in Japanese. I introduced myself and told him I wanted martial arts lessons. Soichiro had an expressionless face. He didn't smile. He didn't frown. It was just blankly serious. He looked at me as if I were an insignificant bug.

"You girl," he said.

"I am. Does that matter?"

Soichiro blinked a couple of times, but his expression didn't change. I could sense, though, that the wheels were turning inside his head. I also got a very nice feeling from him. My intuition confirmed he was a nice man.

"All right," he finally answered.

I wanted to hug him but instead I held out my hand to shake his. He didn't take it, though. Instead, he *bowed*. So I awkwardly did the same. He removed a business card from his pocket and handed it to me with both hands. It had the name and address on it. Studio Tokyo. In the West Village. That wasn't far.

"Great," I said.

"*Arigato*," he replied. I later learned that was Japanese for "thank you."

So, for the next year, dear diary, I took martial arts lessons from Soichiro at Studio Tokyo. I continued my training with Freddie, too. It cost me money for the sessions with Soichiro, but I went twice a week at first and then increased visits to three times a week. I started in a beginners' class and I was the only girl. Soichiro called it *kihon* and it was very basic. We learned fundamentals of *judo* and *karate*, and practiced extremely simple stuff. Lots of floor exercises and such. Mostly he taught us how important it was to be humble and polite to each other. That was why we bowed to our opponents before sparring.

After six months, Soichiro moved me into a more advanced *karate* class because I was better at that than at *judo*. I started learning what the sensei called *kata*, which consisted of very formal movements representing attack and defense postures.

Eventually I moved on to *kumite*, which was actual sparring with opponents. I had to practice at home, conditioning my hands and feet on blocks of wood and stone to toughen them up. It hurt like the dickens in the beginning, but I developed very hard calluses on the edges of my hands. Not very ladylike, but I didn't care. I wore one of those white robes, too, with white pants. They were similar to pajamas, I guess, and in fact the word for them, *karategi*, means "karate pajamas." In reality they are kind of a kimono and pants. Students advanced in rank denoted by the color of the belt worn with the *karategi*. I started with white, of course, which was the lowest rank. In six months I had gone through yellow and was working on green. It would take another year to get a blue. It was very hard work, but Soichiro told me privately that I was a better student than many of the males in his classes. I felt proud and pleased.

I remember one class very distinctly. It occurred in January 1956. I was eighteen years old.

For some odd reason, I was the only one who showed up for class. I found out later that Soichiro wanted to give me a private lesson, but at the time he pretended shock that no other student "bothered to show up for his honorable class." Anyway, Soichiro wanted me to learn some advanced self-defense moves, specifically because I was female. He told me, "In this world, men take advantage of women." Ha! I could've told *him* some stories about that. At any rate, he picked up a billy club and told me to think of him as an attacker on the street. How would I defend myself? I went through everything I'd been taught so far, but he always managed to break through my defenses and almost hit me, but he'd stop just before the club actually struck. It was very frustrating. Finally, Soichiro stopped the attack and told me to relax and breathe. He was *very* insistent on relaxing and breathing. I heard those two words a million times in his classes. Anyway, he asked me, "You know where one of most vulnerable spots is on man?"

Dumb me, I went, "Huh?"

"Kick him in private area."

"Excuse me?"

Soichiro stood in front of me with his legs wide apart. "Look how I stand. Easy to kick between legs. Just aim and kick. You disable opponent."

"But, that's against the rules, ain't it?" I asked, embarrassed and not a little shocked.

"No. On street you defend yourself best way you know how. In real situation, no rules. Now try."

"What?"

"Try kick me."

"Sensei, I can't do that. I don't want to hurt you."

"Do not fear. I will block. Come."

I prepared myself and he raised the club. He came at me. I eyed the apex where his legs met and lashed out with my long leg. Soichiro raised his right knee so quickly that I barely saw it. He slammed it into my calf, knocking my leg off target. It really hurt, but I got the idea.

"No one on street know that block," he said. "You not miss attacker on street."

Nodding, I rubbed my leg.

"Lesson over. See you next week." And he bowed.

By the fall of 1956, I was a blue belt. That was pretty high. I just needed to get through brown and advanced-brown, and then I'd get my black belt. That was the highest you could get—except there were also ten levels of black belt, ha ha.

One night after a lesson with Soichiro, I set out on the walk home to the gym from the West Village. I usually walked the distance between Second Avenue and Christopher Street, which was where Studio Tokyo was located. It was a nice hike. Anyway, it was dark but not very late, not even ten o'clock. I headed toward

Washington Square Park, my usual route. Just before I reached it, three hoodlums appeared out of nowhere and confronted me on the street. They wore black leather jackets and looked like characters from that Marlon Brando movie, *The Wild One*. Probably in their early twenties. White guys.

"Hey, baby, where you goin'?" one jeered.

I tried to ignore and push past them, but they surrounded me and wouldn't let me through.

"What's a pretty girl like you doin' out so late? It's dangerous on the streets. You might need us to protect you," another goaded.

"Get out of my way, please," I said. My nerves were setting off alarms, that animal instinct of mine was going nuts. Danger, danger! I felt my adrenaline soar through my body—I was ready for fight or flight, and I knew it was probably going to be fight.

"How 'bout a kiss?" the first guy taunted. He leaned closer to me—and I let him have it with a right hook, just like when I hit Mack on the nose that time. Well, it surprised the guy. He yelped and pulled back. The other two couldn't believe what I'd just done.

I assumed a fighting stance. Suddenly, though, I wasn't sure if I should go for traditional boxing or try some of the *karate* I'd learned. For some reason, I didn't feel as confident with the martial arts as I did with boxing. So I put up my dukes and prepared to jab and cross.

"Look, Stu," one said, "she thinks she's Jake LaMotta!"

The one I'd punched—Stu—spat and pointed. "Get her!"

They attacked.

Training and sparring in the gym or studio is practice. Sure, you can get hurt, but you're not going to *die*. In a real-life situation like the one I found myself in, anything can happen. I was fighting for my life—and suddenly everything I'd learned went out the window. I couldn't think straight. I just punched and kicked and fought like a banshee. I knew my blows connected, but some of theirs did, too. The pain was terrible. For a few seconds I had no confidence.

And then some of Soichiro's words came back into my head. I assumed a traditional stance and applied the techniques I'd been taught. *Relax. Breathe.* The boxing jabs became knifehand chops. Instead of girly kicks, I performed perfect *karate* front kicks—*mae geri*. A roundhouse kick—*mawashi geri*—actually knocked one opponent to the ground. And a side kick—*yoko geri*—caused one guy to double over and vomit! That left Stu, the leader.

He produced a switchblade out of thin air.

"You're gonna die, bitch!" he hissed.

The sight of the weapon surprised me so much that I froze. He jumped forward, his arm swinging. I felt the blade strike my shoulder and slice through the front of my shirt, just over my right breast. It penetrated the skin—deeply. I cried out in pain and leaped backward. He kept coming, though, wildly swinging the knife in unpredictable directions. This was where my boxing training came in handy—I danced around him, barely avoiding being cut again. But then he backed me against the wall of a building. He stood a few feet in front of me, legs apart, the knife pointed at my belly.

I saw my opening and unleashed a vicious front kick to his groin.

Stu's eyes went wide as he bellowed in agony. The blade dropped to the ground. He fell to his knees and then rolled over into a fetal position.

All three guys were down.

I ran.

When I got to the gym, Freddie took one look at me and almost started crying. "Judy! What happened?"

There was a big mirror near the punching bags, and I saw the damage. My nose was bleeding and my upper lip was busted. There was a big red welt on my left cheek. Worst of all, though, my shirt was drenched in blood.

Freddie helped me take it off. There was a six or seven-inch cut that went from my right shoulder down to the top of my breast. It was deep, too.

"Judy, we gotta get you to the hospital. That has to be stitched."

"No," I said. "I've seen you stitch up some of the guys here. You do it."

"Judy, I can't do something like this."

I didn't want to go to the emergency room. I don't know why, but I was afraid of hospitals. Besides, I didn't want to go through having to talk to the police.

"Yes, you can, Freddie. Just do it. I'm gonna wash my face. You get the stuff."

"It'll leave a bad scar if I do it."

I didn't care. "Now, Freddie!"

And so Freddie stitched me up. It hurt like hell—I guess I can say that word now, I'm a big girl. I drank a quarter bottle of Jack Daniel's while he was doing it. By the time he was done, I felt great. It sure was ugly, though. I tried not to think about that as I put on a robe to cover myself.

I still have that scar today. I'm still self-conscious about it and try to hide it—no bare shoulder dresses for me.

Freddie made some scrambled eggs and bacon for me. It hit the spot. I was pretty looped and exhausted from the adrenaline rush, but I gave Freddie a hug and thanked him.

Before retiring to my room, the idea came to me. It wasn't a foolish notion wrought out of liquor, either. I meant it when I said, "Freddie, next I want to learn how to fight with a knife."

7
Martin

The Present

I shut the diary at that point and sat there on the front stoop of the house.

Dumbfounded.

My mom? Boxing? Taking *karate?*

Holy shit.

I glanced at my watch. The afternoon was gone. The last several hours had vanished. I was due back at the accounting firm where I worked in Deerfield long ago. My cell phone had rung two or three times while I was glued to the pages of my mother's confessional, but I ignored it. I pulled it off my belt and checked the caller IDs. Yep, the office called twice and my daughter once. I listened to my voice mail messages—nothing urgent, the boss was just wondering where the hell I was. Gina had gymnastics practice that afternoon and wondered if I could pick her up at school later. Her car was in the shop and Carol—my ex—was busy.

Gymnastics.

Geez, did this stuff run in the family? I wasn't athletic in any way. I was more of a pencil pusher, all my life.

Come to think of it, Gina was very athletic and had been since she was a toddler. I remember my mom watching Gina closely with a smirk on her face. Was she secretly proud? Had she seen herself in her granddaughter? Now Gina was a senior in high school, having participated in every sport imaginable while she was growing up. She was also into the drama and acting thing, which was a little weird, so go figure.

I called the office back and let them know I wouldn't be back in today. Then I called Gina and left a message on her cell to say I'd pick her up at seven, as requested. Then I pondered what my next course of action should be. My brain was fried and I felt emotionally drained. I couldn't think straight.

Nevertheless, I had the presence of mind to decide I shouldn't leave any of Mom's stuff in that secret room. I had to get it out of there and store it somewhere safe.

Hell, it had been safe where it was! I just didn't want to leave it in a house that might someday be sold.

I went back inside and down to the basement. Among the empty cardboard boxes that were still there, I found one that would work as a container. First, I lined the bottom of the box with the remaining diaries, the comics, newspapers, and the gun. I then carefully removed the costumes, mask, knapsack, and knife from the wall and placed them on top of the other stuff. The boots went on top. The lid closed, just barely. I locked the secret door with my keys, picked up the box, and carried it upstairs. There was some packing tape in the kitchen—I used that to seal the carton. The diary I was currently reading—1958—I stuck in my pocket.

Making sure the house was locked and secure, I drove away and then realized I had no idea where I was going to put the stuff. I didn't really want to take it home. I'm not sure why. It felt, I don't know, somehow kind of sleazy. I still couldn't get around the knowledge that my mother was famous—or rather, infamous.

As I drove along Euclid Avenue toward Route 53, I passed the bank that was once my mother's. We had closed all her accounts when she moved into the nursing home, but I knew they had safety deposit boxes there. On an impulse, I turned into the driveway and parked.

They knew me at the bank. It didn't take long to rent a large box. The carton fit neatly inside the bigger container and was then locked safely in the vault. I put the key on the same ring with the other two that had come in mom's surprise package.

As I left the bank's parking lot, I felt the diary practically burning a hole in my jacket pocket. There was something I needed to do before heading back home.

I had to see Mom.

Turning the car around, I got back on Arlington Heights Road and headed north, through Buffalo Grove, and then turned east toward Riverwoods. Woodlands North was located on Deerfield Road, just east of Milwaukee Avenue.

As I drove, something else hit me.

Richard Talbot. My father. Had Richard Talbot even existed?

I signed in, walked down the long hall to the Alzheimer's Unit, punched in the code for the door—it was no secret, it was posted in plain sight—and went inside. Strode through the common room and into another corridor toward the dining room. Mom's room was on the right.

She was all alone, sitting in one of the chairs by her bed, just staring at the portable television. It wasn't on. Her roommate wasn't there.

"Hi, Mom!" I said as cheerfully as I could.

She looked up at me and wrinkled her brow. The raven-colored hair she once had was now grey and white, but it appeared as if it had recently been shampooed and styled. Her eyes were still a piercing brown with green specks, just as she'd described in the diary. Unfortunately, they looked at me blankly.

"It's me, Martin. Your son."

Her head moved back to the television. I'm not sure if she comprehended what I said or not.

"It's not happy," she said.

"What?"

She didn't repeat it.

"What's not happy, Mom?" I sat in the only other chair and faced her. "How are you today?"

The woman who was once Judy Cooper merely sighed loudly.

"Your hair looks nice. Did you go to the salon today?"

She nodded, but it could very well have been yesterday.

"How come you're in here all alone?" I asked. "Don't you want to go out to the common area where all your friends are? It's almost time for dinner, I think."

"Is it?"

"Yeah. Are you hungry?"

"It's not happy."

"What's not happy, Mom? Are you not happy? This is a real nice place. Everyone here is very sweet to you."

She nodded and smiled at me. Maybe she did recognize me.

I decided to go for it. I pulled out the diary and held it in my hands. Her eyes went to it, but she didn't react.

"Do you know what this is?" I asked her. I held up the diary and showed it to her.

Her face remained expressionless.

"Mom, what did you do in New York and Los Angeles before I was born?"

She sighed again and shifted her long body in the chair. My mother had remained tall, but now she was terribly thin.

They were risky questions. I'm not sure I even had the right to ask her. I didn't want to upset her, but I had to know if any of it still meant something to her. "Do you remember?"

"New York?" she asked.

"Yeah. You lived in New York at one time. Remember?" Remarkably, she nodded. "Did you ever put on a costume?"

There was a flicker of *something* in her eyes. Her brow creased. "Mom?"

"He was late."

"What? What did you say? Who was late?"

"Fiorello was late."

"Fiorello?" *Who the fuck was Fiorello?* "Who's Fiorello, Mom?"

"I was worried. That's why."

"Why, what? Mom? Who's Fiorello?"

Geez. Was he a boyfriend? A lover? *Oh my God,* could he have been my *father?* Was Fiorello "Richard Talbot"?

"Mom, tell me who Fiorello is. Was he someone you knew?"

She nodded and tears came to her eyes.

"Can you tell me anything about him?"

Mom tried to say something but was unable to do so.

"Mom, Fiorello wasn't my dad, was he?"

And then, with surprising coherence, she looked at me and answered, "No, Fiorello was murdered long before you were born. I loved him." She then turned her head back to the blank television set and stopped speaking. The conversation, such as it was, was over.

I guess I needed to read more of the diary.

8
Judy's Diary
1958

Dear diary, I fell in love for the first time shortly after my nineteenth birthday.

With a gangster.

Ever since the attack on the street, I'd been hounding Freddie to find me someone who could teach me how to wield a knife. I don't know why, but I was fascinated by the weapon. Sleek, flat steel with a sharp edge, shiny, silent, beautiful. Maybe it was because I'd been cut by one. I have no idea. All I know is I started looking in shop windows at displays of knives. I'd go inside and ask to see them—combat knives, hunting knives, stilettos, folding knives, sliding blades, Bowie knives, switchblades, and even Swiss Army knives. I loved the feel of the handles in my hand. It just felt right. Mind you, my intention was not to kill anyone. I wanted to learn how to use a knife simply because I found it—sexy. There, I said it. There was something about the *concept* of a knife, that it could pierce flesh so easily and draw blood. That sounds icky, I know, and it wasn't really anything I looked forward to actually doing. I honestly hoped I'd never have to use one in self-defense. I just wanted to know how.

It was around Thanksgiving when Freddie finally relented. We were sitting in the common living room upstairs above the gym. He had recently bought a television and we liked to watch *I Love Lucy* and *The Honeymooners* together. They made us laugh.

One of the first things we saw on the new set was the *Ed Sullivan Show* when Elvis Presley was on. I went crazy. I loved Elvis and still do. I can't get enough of him. Freddie couldn't stand him, but I bought a little portable record player and, when I could, I bought some of Elvis's records and played them in my room. I guess I liked that new rock and roll music. I wore out my copy of Bill Haley's "Rock Around the Clock."

Anyway, I'd been bugging Freddie some more about knife fighting, and he said, "Back when I was boxing, I knew some of the mob. There was this young guy, an Italian, naturally, who was real good with a knife. I didn't know him very well, but he was one of the few fellas in that bunch of weasels who was nice to me. He was friendly. I mean, he was probably a killer. He was in the Mafia and he was an expert with blades. It doesn't take a genius to figure that one out."

"When can I meet him?" I asked.

"I don't know, Judy. He's dangerous. That whole group is dangerous. It's best to stay away from 'em."

"I'm not afraid. When can I meet him?"

Freddie agonized over this for days. I kept pestering him until he finally set it up. We'd meet his "friend" at a restaurant shortly before Christmas.

When the evening finally arrived, I did my best to look good. By then, I'd saved some money and started actually buying nice women's clothing. Lucy and I had gone out a few times to some nightclubs like Jack Dempsey's and the Copacabana. It was fun to see how men reacted when I dolled myself up. Lucy had given me some makeup tips, which was something I'd never learned prior to that. She told me to buy Maybelline mascara and taught me how to apply it, so I guess I looked pretty good.

Anyway, Freddie and I splurged and took a cab down to Fulton Street for the appointment. The restaurant was a really old fancy place called Gage & Tollner's, an establishment that had been around since before 1900. They still had gas lamps. It was dreamy.

When I first saw Fiorello, I swear my heart skipped a beat. That was his name—Fiorello Bonacini. He was in his twenties—later I'd find out he was twenty-seven. Fiorello had wavy black hair that reminded me of Elvis Presley, amazing blue eyes that penetrated my own—like *knives*—and the kindest smile. When Freddie introduced me to him, I immediately expected that crazy animal intuition of mine to kick in and send off alarms—but it didn't. In fact, my instincts told me Fiorello was an honest, benevolent human being. Yes, I sensed there was danger behind those blue eyes, but I found it exciting. Absolutely, I understood the man was a killer—I could feel it. He had taken lives. There was no question about it. But he had such charisma, an indefinable magnetism that rendered me speechless.

He was already at a table; he stood when he saw us.

"*Buona sera,* Freddie," he said. "It is good to see you again."

"You, too, Fiorello. May I present Miss Cooper? Judy, this is Mister Bonacini."

I offered my hand. He took it and actually leaned over to kiss it. "A pleasure. Please call me Fiorello."

"Thank you. You can call me Judy."

"Please sit." He actually pulled my chair out for me. No man had ever done that before.

Well, for most of the dinner—which was exquisite—the men talked. I sat there like a dummy, smiling like a fool. Whenever Fiorello addressed me, I answered in monosyllabic sentences. But he continued to grin at me and there was a twinkle in his eye that made me melt.

It was over dessert when he finally got down to business. "So, Judy," he said, leaning closer to keep his voice down, "Freddie tells me you are an excellent boxer and that you have been learning Japanese fighting techniques?"

"That's right. It's called *karate*."

"I have heard of it." He shook his head. "Very foreign. I prefer the ways of the old country. More traditional, I suppose. Old-fashioned. But it has always worked for me and my people. The boxing I understand. But why in the world would a beautiful girl like you want to learn how to fight? You should be learning how to cook instead."

I was too enthralled to be insulted. "I do know how to cook."

Freddie added, "She's a pretty good one, too."

"Then why aren't you married and having babies?" Fiorello asked. "You would be a prize on the arm of a very lucky man."

I felt my face flush. "Thank you, but no, that's not what I want out of life right now."

"What *do* you want?"

Put to me like that, I didn't know how to answer. I shrugged. "All I know is I don't want that. Not yet, anyway."

"So you want to learn how to use a knife."

"Yes."

"Why?"

I thought before replying. "I feel it's a calling. All of it. The boxing, the martial arts, and now knives. I was born to know this stuff."

"But women do not fight."

I held up a hand. "Ah, Mister Bonacini, there you're wrong. I was attacked just two months ago, right on the streets of Manhattan, by three thugs who wanted to do bad things to me. One of them had a knife and he cut me badly. Freddie here had to sew a few dozen stitches into my skin. It's healed, but I'll have the ugly scar for the rest of my life."

Freddie interrupted. "What Judy didn't say was that she clobbered the three hoods anyway. Knocked 'em flat."

"Really?" Fiorello raised his eyebrows. "I'm impressed."

He sat back in his chair but continued to gaze at me. I felt an odd sensation I'd never experienced before. It was like electricity, and it went down my spine and straight to—well, between my legs. This man was the most handsome, sexiest thing I'd ever laid eyes on.

"All right," he said. "We will have a trial session, for lack of a better word. If that works out, we will continue. We'll discuss terms then."

So he was actually going to charge me money. Stupid me. I thought perhaps he'd be so taken with me that he'd provide lessons for free, ha ha!

He wrote down his address and phone number on a card he pulled from his pocket. We agreed on a day the following week, between Christmas and New Year's. I'd come to his place in Little Italy—he said it was big enough to "work" in—and we shook on it.

Fiorello picked up the tab.

In the taxi on the way back to the gym, Freddie said to me, "Be careful, Judy. I saw what happened back there. Watch your feelings. Don't lose control."

Too late for that. I already had.

It was snowing outside when I arrived at Fiorello's apartment. I loved New York in the winter. In Texas it rarely snowed, certainly not like it did in Manhattan. I stopped at the Ferrara Bakery and picked up some pastries to bring as a gift. Fiorello expressed delight at the thought, but took the dainty box aside and told me the treats would have to wait until after the lesson. Once again, I almost swooned when I saw him. He was dressed casually in dark trousers and a pullover sweater—and he wore cologne that drove me wild. I had no idea what it was, so I asked him.

"Colonia," he replied. "By Acqua di Parma. Fine Italian eau de cologne. You like?"

I exaggerated a sniff and went, "Mmm, I do."

He took my coat and led me into his spacious living room. The place wasn't huge, but it was certainly bigger than my bedroom. He had already pushed the furniture against the walls to make an open space on the floor.

We spent a few minutes with small talk. He asked me where I was from and I told him. He also wanted to know how old I was.

"Nineteen."

"Ah, a grown woman, and yet still a young girl." His eyes glistened.

He told me he was from Palermo, a city in Sicily. I didn't know Sicily was part of Italy until I looked on a map later. Fiorello had been in America since he was a little boy. His parents lived in Brooklyn. He didn't mention his *other* family.

Then we got down to business. Fiorello produced an array of blades. They were of varying sizes and weights. He started with what he called a "trench knife," a weapon used for close-quarters combat.

"This is a U.S. Marine KA-BAR. The blade is seven inches long. Try it."

I picked it up. I liked the feel of it.

He showed me various ways one could hold a knife, depending on whether it was for offensive or defensive purposes. Fiorello mostly used a forward grip, with the edge facing out. There were also several variations. For example, a "hammer grip" was when you make a fist around the handle. If you placed your thumb on top of the handle, it was a "saber grip." Fiorello preferred a modification of that by positioning his thumb on the flat of the blade.

Next, I learned several exercises on how to thrust and slash, keeping the knife firmly in my hand. Fiorello brought out a store mannequin—where he got it I don't know—and had me practice on it. It was a male and it had no clothes, which was a little weird. Nevertheless, I dutifully punctured it.

The second knife I tried was a stiletto. It *really* felt natural in my hand. As if it was a part of me. I loved its thinness and length, like a tiny sword. It was just the right weight for me, too. Even Fiorello commented I seemed to have a knack for that particular knife.

After an hour, we stopped to rest and eat the pastries. He made coffee and then he pulled the sofa and a table back to their original positions on the floor.

"You are a natural with the blade," he said. "I can see why you wanted to learn."

"Thank you."

We talked about New York and its wonders. He said he never grew tired of the city. The only thing he liked more were visits to Sicily, which weren't often enough.

It was probably a tactless thing to do, but I came right out and asked him. "Are you in the Mafia?"

The question surprised him, but he laughed.

"Dear Judy, if I were, I wouldn't tell you. And people in the Mafia don't call it that. It's just—a family."

"You are, aren't you?"

He just smiled. The blue eyes glowed with warmth.

"Do you have plans for New Year's Eve?" he asked.

"No. Not yet. Freddie and I usually throw a party at the gym. Why?"

"Come with me to a different party. I would like you to be my guest."

"Really? What kind of party? Where?"

"Black tie, formal, but not too formal," were the only clues he gave me. Even though I didn't own an evening gown, I accepted. I'd have to call Lucy and go shopping. New Year's Eve was only three days away.

The lesson was over, so I made an excuse to leave, even though I really didn't want to. He went along with it, though, got my coat, and helped me put it on. At the door I asked him, "You mentioned something about payment. How much are these lessons going to cost me?"

He waved his hand, dismissing the thought. "I find you very attractive," he said. "Perhaps you would honor me by accompanying me to dinners, to Broadway plays, to nightclubs for dancing, and to more parties."

My God, he was asking me to be his girlfriend! And I barely knew him.

"I think I could manage that," I answered.

He kissed me on the cheek. "I will call the gym and let you know about New Year's."

"All right. Bye!"

"*Ciao.*"

I think I floated all the way home.

Lucy took me shopping for the big date. She advised me not to get an evening gown and instead buy a really nice party dress. I ended up buying a cute one made of black velvet. It had gold metallic embroidery; the full and swishy skirt was made of sheer chiffon. I picked out a crinoline slip to wear underneath. Lucy insisted I buy some black stiletto heels. She said they'd accentuate my calf muscles and make my legs look great. The dress came down to mid-calf, so there wasn't that much leg to see, unless I twirled around and caused the dress to spread like a parachute. Lucy told me to do that as often as I could, ha ha! The heels were very awkward for me at first. But after I strutted back and forth across the shop floor a few times, I got the hang of it. The shoes were Di Orsini Black Satin Originals, very classy and elegant. And sexy.

I never thought of myself as sexy before.

When Fiorello picked me up, there was a limousine parked on the street. I'd never ridden in one. I felt like a princess. Fiorello

wore a tuxedo and looked astonishingly gorgeous. Freddie didn't
see me off—he didn't want to come off as a "dad" or anything like
that. He just wished me Happy New Year earlier at dinnertime
and retired early. The annual gym party was cancelled. I think he
wasn't feeling very well.

The party was at the Algonquin Hotel on 44th Street, which
had a lot of history in the arts and such. Supposedly stars such as
the Marx Brothers liked to congregate there a couple of decades
before. When you first walk into the lobby, there's the front desk
to your right, as well as a phone booth and an egress that leads
to a short hallway perpendicular to the front desk. I knew the
ladies' room and a staircase to the second floor were in that hallway, for Lucy and I had been to the hotel for lunch a couple of
times. Normally there was a cocktail seating area to your left, but
since that space was being used for the party, a partition had
been set up to separate it from the rest of the lobby and front desk.
An old grandfather clock stood at the head of the partition. Just
ahead, past reception and the elevators, was the entrance to the
Rose Room, where the bar was located. This was also the spot of
the famous "round table." The hotel also had two restaurants, the
Oak Room and the Chinese Room, but they were closed. The
party took up all of the Rose Room and the partitioned cocktail
section of the lobby. A makeshift dance floor was between the
two, and the band was set up at the street side of the cocktail
lounge.

As soon as we walked in, I felt everyone's eyes as they gawked.
They all knew Fiorello and greeted him like one of the family, ha
ha, which I guess he was. He introduced me as "the lovely Miss
Cooper," to anyone we spoke to. I was so flustered and over-
whelmed that it was difficult to engage in intelligent conversations. Besides, I mostly just wanted to hang on Fiorello's arm and
allow him to lead me around. It was nice not having to think for

myself for a change. I had always been independent and solitary, so having a man like Fiorello in charge was a welcome novelty.

Everything was all decked out in New Year's decorations and the place was full of Italians. There was a Guido and a Rafael and a Tito and a Carmine and a Federico and a Vito amongst the men; the women were called Theresa and Francesca and Giulietta and Aurora and Mariangela. I thought I stuck out like a sore thumb with my southern ways and Texas accent, but everyone was really nice. Fiorello obviously commanded respect. He was a big shot in this crowd. It was very exciting.

The food was out of this world. All kinds of pasta dishes, salads, veal chops, incredible desserts that rivaled Ferrara's, and wine, wine, wine. And the best champagne I've ever had. Fiorello called it Dom Perignon, "a French concoction," he said with displeasure; but he admitted it was very good.

There was a dance band situated in what was normally the lobby's cocktail lounge. They mostly played songs from the forties, but there were a few from recent years. Fiorello and I danced—something else that was fairly new to me. Lucy and I had danced a little at the Copacabana, but nothing as intense as this was. Fiorello was a terrific dancer—his lead was all I needed to follow along and not make a fool of myself. I was hoping the band would maybe play some rock and roll music, but they didn't. They did, however, play Elvis's song, "Love Me Tender," and Fiorello held me *really* close when we danced to that. I was in heaven.

At one point, a man around Fiorello's age came up to us and the two men greeted each other like long lost brothers. The guy was heavy, with the largest nose I'd ever seen on a person. He had the sweetest eyes, though. My intuition liked him immediately.

Fiorello introduced us. "Judy, this is my fellow *paesano,* my *compare,* Tony the Tank. Tony, this is the lovely Miss Cooper."

Tony the Tank bowed, took my hand, and kissed it. "A pleasure, madam, a pleasure. Any friend of Fiorello's is a friend of mine."

"*Grazie*," I said. Fiorello had taught me the Italian word for "thank you." "Please call me Judy."

Tony immediately attempted a Cary Grant imitation that failed miserably. "Judee, Judee, Judee, how lovely you are this evening! Happy New Year to you."

After he moved away, Fiorello said, "Tony is my best friend in the whole world. We grew up together."

"Why do you call him Tony the Tank?"

Fiorello patted his tummy. "Isn't it obvious? Tony doesn't mind. We all have our little nicknames."

"Oh? And what's yours?"

"Sometimes they call me Flash."

"Flash?"

"*Sì.*"

"Why?"

"I don't know. Maybe because I'm flashy?" He winked at me and I laughed. It was truly a novel experience having a man around who made me laugh.

At that moment, I felt something change in the room. Everyone seemed to direct their attention to one end, where a large man had just entered with a small entourage. He was in his sixties, I guessed, also heavily built, with grey hair and a dour expression. He had his arm looped through the arm of an elderly woman who, in contrast to her escort, was beaming with delight. Obviously the man's wife. Behind them were two men who were the same person—well, they were identical twins. Their faces were oh-so-serious, as if they were angry at being there.

"That is the don," Fiorello whispered.

"The don?"

"Don Giorgio DeLuca. The boss. He is the head of the family. A very important man. The reason why we are here tonight. He is our host."

"Is that his wife?"

"*Si*. We call her Mrs. DeLuca."

"And who are the other two guys? Are they twins?"

"Can't tell them apart, can you? I understand even Don DeLuca has trouble identifying them. They are his bodyguards, a couple of the family's enforcers."

"They look scary."

"They *are* scary. Very tough men."

"Have they killed people?"

Fiorello just raised his eyebrows, put a finger to his lips, and shook his head.

"What are their names?"

"Vittorio and Roberto Ranelli."

Needless to say, the New Year's Eve party was one of the best evenings of my life. I had so much fun. Got pretty drunk, too. Nevertheless, I met Don DeLuca and his wife at some point. He was very gracious. He, too, kissed my hand. I could feel the power oozing off of him, but my animal instincts didn't like him one bit. I started getting those weird tingles as soon as his eyes fell on me. He was definitely a very dangerous and cruel man. From the wife I detected a palpable amount of fear and resignation. She was probably extremely unhappy with the marriage, despite their wealth and status in the Italian community. When I met the don, the two creepy twins looked me up and down. I *really* got the bad feelings about them. I didn't even want to say hello to them. Fiorello didn't introduce me, thank goodness. At any rate, I knew for a fact those two were killers.

In the limousine on the way back from the party—at two o'clock on the morning—Fiorello asked me if I'd like to come to his apartment.

I accepted.

And, dear diary, I won't go into any details about *that*, ha ha!

To make a long story short, we became an item. For the next two months, we were together *all the time*. Well, not really. I still did my lessons with Soichiro three times a week and trained with Freddie the other two days. My job as assistant manager of the Second Avenue Gym was still in full force. So, there was all that. But when I wasn't exercising, training, working, or sleeping, I was with Fiorello. I had a real boyfriend for the first time. And I loved it. And I loved him. He loved me, too, I could tell, although he never said it in so many words. He was kind to me, though. He showered me with gifts, clothes, and jewelry, took me to dinner, went dancing with me, and we had sex—lots of sex. I had qualms about it, believe me. It wasn't something I jumped into without thinking about it. We took precautions. I didn't want to get pregnant. Even so, there was a part of me that thought I was being a very bad girl. But then I watched all the other girlfriends at the parties and places where Fiorello took me—and they were having sex with their men, too. I could sense it. This sounds crude, but my heightened sense of *smell* affirmed it. People were very sexually repressed on the outside, but in private a lot more went on than you'd think. They just didn't talk about it. There was the Kinsey Report thing that came out recently, and all the women read it and still talked about *that*. Lucy said it was her Bible. Fiorello had copies of a fairly new magazine called *Playboy* that actually had photos of naked women in it. I was shocked at first, but as I looked at some of the issues, I understood it took a very healthy approach to the idea of sex between unmarried people. It was really society—and religion—that made people feel guilty about doing that stuff outside of marriage. The truth was they were doing it anyway. I didn't know that then, but I do now.

In March of 1957, I moved out of the gym and started living with Fiorello. Now *that* was sinful, I suppose. And yet, it felt like the right thing to do. We sometimes talked about getting married but ultimately laughed about it. Neither of us really wanted that, although Fiorello did mention he'd like to have several children "someday." Freddie wasn't happy that I moved out. Like I said, he thought of me as a foster daughter, and he wasn't comfortable with me associating with Fiorello's "crowd." It's a wonder they accepted me—I wasn't Italian, I was a hillbilly Texan with a funny accent, and I was *very* naïve about what those people did.

Over the next several months, though, I learned. Fiorello never talked about what he did for the family. Eventually I found out he was considered a "soldier" and an "earner." As a soldier he was a member of a team and he did whatever he was told. If he had to rough someone up, he did. His expertise with a knife *was* legendary. Opposite numbers were afraid of him. Fiorello wasn't an enforcer in the same way the Ranelli twins were, but I have no doubt he'd been called to commit murder at some point. Probably several times. As an earner, he was the boss of two or three bookies on the Lower East Side. He collected money from them once a week, delivered a good chunk of it to Don DeLuca, and got to keep the rest for himself. Fiorello told me he was on his way to being made a *capo*, which was a ranking member of the family. He was going to be "made," probably when he turned thirty. Fiorello said it was unusual for someone so young to become a "made man."

Okay, I knew these people were doing illegal things. But you know something? Somehow they made it all seem to be a necessary evil. As an ethnic minority, these Italians felt they never got a fair shake from established authority in the United States. Their methods and customs came over from Sicily. It was in their blood, it was just the way they did things. And usually their "victims" were other criminals—members of a rival family or drug dealers or what have you. They never targeted what I thought of as "innocent" everyday people. I'm not saying what they were doing was right, but it didn't bother me as much as it might others. Well, that was *then*.

Of course, my love for Fiorello probably blinded me to the truth about the Mafia. I was hoodwinked by the glamour and attention.

Living with Fiorello opened my eyes to a whole new way of thinking about men. Even though I'd grown up with two brothers—and a pervert for a stepfather—I didn't really pay much attention. Fiorello was a funny guy. He was a great cook, he sang opera with records he'd play on the phonograph, and he liked comic books. Fiorello was a huge fan of Batman and Superman— that kind of stuff. Those comics were all over the place. I looked at them every now and then, just as I'd done back in Texas, but I couldn't understand what he saw in them. I preferred mysteries and crime novels, especially Mickey Spillane. And I read *Ladies Home Journal*. I know, I'm weird.

One thing I can say for my romance with Fiorello is that my wardrobe improved. He bought me a lot of new clothes, and I was no longer the tomboy dressed in men's baggy trousers and polo shirts. I wore dresses, high heels, and stockings. The black stilettos I'd bought with Lucy became a staple. I loved them. My ability at applying makeup had improved and Fiorello often said I could be a "cover girl." That pleased me.

It was a wonderful life. While it lasted.

Everything changed, though. It always does, doesn't it?

It was just after my birthday, 1957, and I was twenty years old. We'd known each other for nearly a year. Fiorello had promised he'd be home by eight o'clock in the evening so we could go to Sardi's for dinner—one of our favorite spots. He was late. I didn't worry about it at first, it happened sometimes. But by ten o'clock, eleven o'clock, I started getting nervous. It wasn't like Fiorello. He would have called me if was going to be very late.

At midnight, I decided to go to bed. I was uneasy—my instincts were going haywire—but I had a drink of whiskey to settle me down. I bathed, dressed in my nightgown, and went into the kitchen to get a last glass of water before retiring.

The phone rang.

It was Tony. He sounded very upset.

"What is it? What's wrong?" I asked. My heart was beating furiously because I knew. I *sensed* it.

Fiorello had been murdered.

9
Martin
The Present

After seeing my mom, I went to the office but couldn't do any work. So I picked up the damned diary and started reading where I left off. Then my boss, Brad, called and wanted to see me. So I put down the book and went to his office. Brad is one of those managers who never praises his employees but doesn't hesitate to find faults. I've worked for him a long time, and I never so much as got a "Good job, Martin," from him. Well, it turned out he just wanted to chew me out for taking off work so long that day. I explained I had some comp time, but he didn't give a shit. Said I was behind in some audit reports, which I was. I promised to get them done. On the way back to my office, I saw George, a fellow auditor, at the water fountain.

"The axe is gonna fall soon," he said.

"What do you mean?"

"Layoffs. Ten to twenty percent of the staff are gonna get pink slips."

"No. I don't believe it."

"It's what I hear." George was always a fatalist.

"Well, they can't touch me," I said. "I have seniority."

He raised his eyebrows and walked away. Screw him. I went into my office, shut the door, and picked up the diary. And then my cell phone rang. It was Gina.

"Dad?"

"Yes, honey?"

"What's for dinner tonight?"

Dinner?

Damn, I'd forgotten she was staying with me over the weekend. Carol and I had joint custody and it was my turn. The whole arrangement was kinda pointless now, seeing that Gina was seventeen, had her own car, and could basically do whatever she wanted. I almost told her to stay home if she preferred, but I didn't.

"You want to go out?" I asked her.

"Maybe. Can we go to Big Bowl?"

That was the popular Asian place. "Sure."

"Awesome. After that I have rehearsal."

"Rehearsal? On a Friday night?" She was in some play. I didn't know how she managed to do sports and drama at the same time, but she did.

"Well, it's not a rehearsal at school. I'm getting together with Nick and Jon to go over lines. We need to work on 'em."

"Nick and Jon?"

"They're in the play with me."

"I see." Hey, I was still her dad. I took an interest in who she hung out with. "When's your car gonna be ready?"

"Maybe Monday. I hate not having it. It's been over a week."

"That's what happens when you have an accident, sweetheart. Body shop work takes time. You need to—"

"—be more careful, yeah, I know, dad. Geez, it wasn't my fault. We've had this conversation, what, three dozen times?"

She was right. I probably dwelled on crap like that way too much. It's all part of being an accountant, I think. I'm always thinking about the numbers. Money. Insurance. Dollars. Taxes. Bills.

I decided to change the subject. "Heard from any of the colleges yet?"

"Um, can we talk about that at dinner?"

"Sure. So you've heard?"

"From a couple."

"Which ones?"

"Dad!"

"Gina, tell me. I want to know."

"Well, Illinois State said yes and DePaul said yes."

"Terrific!" They were schools with good business programs.

"But they're not my first choices."

Yeah, lately she'd been going on about studying theatre. Can you imagine that? Who makes a living in theatre? I told her she was nuts and I wouldn't pay for it if that's what she wanted to do. It's been a little bone of contention between us.

Becoming an accountant was a no-brainer for me. Sure, it's not a glamorous job, but it's what I can do. And I've made a living. My firm, Bailey and Catlow, specializes in corporate taxes. I'm one of the senior auditors. I have exciting and wonderful opportunities of spending days, sometimes weeks, in some high-rise in Chicago going over some company's records. Sometimes I go over and over and over them. And then I do it again. Whatever it takes. It's thrilling, I gotta tell you.

"Honey, you have to think about where you're gonna get the best training for a career. We've talked about this."

"I know, I know. Look, I gotta go. See you at seven?"

"I'll be there."

I looked at my watch. There was a little time before I had to get to the school, so I kept reading the diary.

10
Judy's Diary
1958

I was devastated. I simply couldn't believe it.

Tony didn't have any more information at that point, so he hung up after saying he was sorry. I think he was crying. It wasn't long before I was as well.

After a sleepless night, drowning in tears and whiskey, I passed out and didn't open my eyes until noon. I missed Soichiro's class, so I called him and told him what had happened. He knew I'd been seeing Fiorello, although the two men had never met. Then I called Freddie, who was busy in the gym. He said all the right things, asked if I was okay, and inquired if I would like to come "home." I told him, thanks, but I wanted to stay in Fiorello's apartment, if I could. I had no idea if I'd be able to take over the lease or not.

As a matter of fact, a week later the landlord dropped by, looking for the month's rent. He was an old Italian guy who had respect for Fiorello, but the man wasn't connected. He expressed concern and shock at the news, but then he made it clear that the rent would still have to be paid. He gave me until the end of the month to pay it, but by then, of course, December's rent would be due the following week. The landlord was nice about it, but he intimated that if I couldn't pay the two months' rent, I'd have to leave. Fiorello and I weren't married. I was tempted to tell him I knew "people" that could convince him to let me stay, but I didn't have the heart. After all, the landlord was in the right.

Anyway, on the morning after Fiorello's murder I was determined to find out what had happened. I phoned Tony, who didn't answer. I tried a couple more of Fiorello's friends in his crew. They didn't have any details—only that there had been a shooting at one of the bookmaker's establishments on the Lower East Side. Fiorello wasn't the only one dead; the bookie had also been killed. Someone hit them, most likely a rival family looking to take over the bookmaking business in that area.

It wasn't a very satisfactory answer. Not for me, anyway.

I put on my coat and went out. I knew where Don DeLuca lived—it was in Long Island, a town called Glen Cove. I'd been there twice with Fiorello—once for a dinner party in the spring and again on the Fourth of July. On both occasions he was friendly and treated me like I might have been Fiorello's wife. That's one thing I noticed about all the mobsters—they respected everyone's wives. So I thought, naïvely, that Don DeLuca would tell me the truth about what happened to one of his men, providing he knew himself.

I took the Long Island Railroad from Penn Station and arrived in Glen Cove around one o'clock. I hailed a taxi and asked the driver to take me to the Don's address. Even the driver seemed to know who lived there; he looked at me with suspicion, as if I was a gun moll or something.

The don's house was like a small fortress, a huge two-storey mansion on expansive grounds. There was a guy at the gate who motioned for me to roll down the cab window. He didn't know me.

"I'm here to see Don DeLuca. Tell him it's Judy Cooper, Fiorello Bonacini's girlfriend."

The guy made a face and went to the guardhouse by the gate.

He made a phone call, spoke for a minute, made funny gestures with his hands, and then hung up. The gate opened.

The cab drove inside and pulled into the circular drive in the courtyard adjoining the front of the house. Several cars were parked in a row on one side of the drive—all belonging to the don's men. There were always troops of them at the home. I'm sure Mrs. DeLuca loved that.

A fellow I knew named Carmine met me at the door.

"Judy, I'm so sorry," he said. "We just found out this morning."

"What happened, Carmine? Do you know?"

"No, I don't. Why did you come here, Judy? It's not, well, it's not appropriate."

"I don't care. I'd like to talk to Don DeLuca."

Carmine made a face. "He'll see you, but I gotta say, this is out of the ordinary. If you was *married* to Fiorello, it might be different."

"What's that supposed to mean?"

He didn't answer. We went into the large foyer, where a couple of other goons stood at attention. One of them had a gun in plain sight, holstered on his belt. Sheesh.

For the first time, I felt uneasy in the place. My other two visits were with Fiorello and we had attended social affairs. I had previously ignored any negative sensations I may have felt from the house, but this time I sensed a strong, unpleasant ambiance. There was an invisible ugliness in the home that chilled me to the bone.

Carmine led me into the don's study, where the big man sat behind a desk. It might have been the office of a great lawyer, for the space was surrounded by bookshelves full of leather-bound tomes. A large picture window looked out into the spacious backyard.

Don DeLuca stood as I came in. He held out his hands and took mine. "Miss Cooper, I am sorry about Fiorello. It breaks our hearts," he said.

The man was lying. I sensed it. The old instinct kicking in.

"Thank you, Don DeLuca." I actually curtsied to him. "And thank you for seeing me."

"Please sit down. May I offer you something to drink? It's a little early in the day for me to indulge in something strong, but I have fruit juice, coffee, tea."

"No, thank you." I took the seat in front of the desk, and he reclaimed his chair behind it. "Don DeLuca, I just—I want to know what happened to Fiorello. No one seems to know."

"I'm afraid we don't either," he answered. Again—*a bold-faced lie.* I saw right through him.

"Please, Don DeLuca, I know more than you think about Fiorello and what he did for . . . for you and the family. I understood the risks involved. But I loved him. I have a right to know."

The Mafia boss considered my words and sighed heavily. "Miss Cooper—Judy, that's it, isn't it?"

"Yes."

"Judy, you and Fiorello were not married. We of the Catholic faith have strong feelings about that. Of course there are many men who have affairs, even married men who keep a *comare*, but it is rare for one of our own to openly live with a woman and not be married."

So much for treating me like one of the wives. His attitude toward me was palpably changed. I was taken aback by his words and must have had a blank expression on my face, for he added, "Please understand I didn't mean that as a condemnation, only an observation. I loved Fiorello like a son. I was hoping he would marry you."

"Are you saying you'd be more forthcoming with me if I was Fiorello's wife?"

Don DeLuca looked away and stared out the window as if he hadn't heard me. I got it, though. These men weren't forthcoming about their business even to the women in their lives.

After an awkward silence, the don spoke again. "Fiorello was reckless, my dear. He made some mistakes. Our opposite numbers in New Jersey got to him. We will take care of it. This is men's business. I am sorry."

I realized that was all I was going to get from him.

It was a complete fabrication. He knew who killed Fiorello, and it wasn't an "opposite number."

I nodded and thanked him for his time, and then got up to leave. He stood, took my hands again, and said, "I hope we'll see you again sometime."

"Give Mrs. DeLuca my regards."

"I will, dear."

On cue, the study door opened. This time, one of the Ranelli twins escorted me out. Once again, my nerves reacted negatively.

As we walked toward the front door, he spoke with a perceptible sneer, "I already called you a cab. Did you find out what you wanted to know?"

"No." I looked at him and studied his face. "Which one are you?"

"I'm Roberto."

"Roberto, do you know what happened to Fiorello?"

The thug shrugged his shoulders and made a tsk-tsk sound. Again, that was an indication that they all knew the real story but they were intentionally hiding it from me. Fiorello was one of their own—why were they so unconcerned?

Were they somehow responsible?

Roberto Ranelli waited with me at the door without saying a word. He just stared at me, the same way Douglas had. With lust. Ill intentions. I desperately wanted to get away from him, but there was nowhere to go. Finally, the taxi arrived and pulled into the courtyard circle. It was a relief to get away from the darkness and evil that permeated that house.

As the cab went through the gate, I looked back. Roberto hadn't moved. He stood in the doorway, watching me with menace in his eyes.

I spent the evening crying again as I sat in Fiorello's apartment—*our* apartment—all too aware of the overwhelming emptiness.

I was convinced Don DeLuca was hiding something. They all were. I had honed my ability to read faces and body language. Fiorello was not killed by enemies of the family. I hated to consider it, but what *felt* correct was my lover had been murdered by his own people. The question was *why*?

I tried calling Tony again, but there was still no answer. Where was he? Did all this have something to do with him?

Eventually anger overtook the pain. I had no proof, but I was certain Don DeLuca was responsible for Fiorello's death. I vowed to find out the truth, and then I was going to do something about it. If I didn't, who would?

As I drank another glass of whiskey, my eyes fell on a stack of Fiorello's comic books. The latest Batman was on top. I picked it up and thumbed through it. In my foggy state of my mind, I read a bit and couldn't help but laugh a little. The premise was silly—some millionaire dressed up in a costume, had a secret identity, and went out to fight crime. Who would really do such a thing?

I suppose that was the germ of the idea that would change my life.

11
Judy's Diary
1958

July 5, 1958

I woke up late today because I stayed up all night writing! Anyway, here I am again, continuing where I left off back in 1957 at the point when I decided to become the Black Stiletto.

I never called it a costume, dear diary. I considered it a "disguise."

The first thing I did was draw some sketches on paper. I wasn't much of an artist, and I definitely didn't know how to sew—but I learned quickly. Stabbed myself in the finger with a needle several times in the process, too. I went out and bought material, which was the most difficult part. What should it be made of? I wanted it to be black for no particular reason other than I liked the way Batman could blend in with the night. I ended up buying some expensive, thin black leather. I spent a month in a trial-and-error process until I came up with a design I liked. All the time I was working on it I played the latest Elvis Presley records over and over on my phonograph—"All Shook Up," "(Let Me Be) Your Teddy Bear," and "Jailhouse Rock."

While this was going on, I did my duty at the gym, still attended my martial arts classes—I was a brown belt by then, working on my black—and managed to find time to train and exercise. And I did everything I could to find out what really happened to

Fiorello. Tony the Tank was missing in action. No one knew where he was. I began to fear something bad had happened to him, too. All of Fiorello's other friends observed the *omerta*, the Mafia's code of silence.

It was a difficult time, for I was very depressed. To top it off, Fiorello's landlord ended up evicting me. I offered to pay the rent for November and December in installments, which was all I could afford. The man was sympathetic but insisted on sticking to his guns. There was nothing I could do. I packed my things, threw in a lot of Fiorello's stuff that nobody would ever want—including his comics—and then, with head hung low, I went back to Freddie and asked for my old room. He was happy to have me, even though it was a tough thing for me personally. It was all about pride, I guess. It was a step backward, but in the long run it turned out to be good. Freddie was "family"—*real* family, not Fiorello's family, if you know what I mean. And to tell the truth, living at the gym made the commute to work and to martial arts lessons much more convenient. I got over the pain of leaving Little Italy pretty quickly.

Moving on from losing Fiorello wasn't so easy.

Freddie gently lectured me about associating with people like Fiorello. He said they were "evil" deep down, even when they were nice and loving on the outside. "Nothing good would have come out of the relationship," Freddie told me. This hurt to hear, but I knew he was probably correct. Nevertheless, I loved Fiorello. I never saw his bad side.

Being upset those few weeks in November and December also made me think back to Texas and what happened with Douglas. I was happier than I'd ever been when I was with Fiorello, so I was able to push the stepfather incident out of my mind. It came back full force. I really hated Douglas and other nameless men like him in the world. My anger resurfaced, and I probably wasn't very pleasant to be around. Once, I was with Lucy and Sam at the diner, and Sam said something stupid and insulting to Lucy. I called him a "creep" to his face and stormed out. It didn't bother him at all, I'm sure, but I think it hurt Lucy's feelings. She never said anything about it, though, and I never apologized. I meant what I said.

I also remember a distinctly vivid dream I had about my mother. She was crying and in pain. I desperately wanted to tell her I was alive and doing just fine, but of course she couldn't hear anything I said. You know how weird dreams can be. And then I started crying and woke up feeling bad. For a day or two I considered sending a postcard to Odessa, just to let her know I was all right.

But I never did.

Tony the Tank reappeared two days after Christmas. Why is it that significant events always happen to me around the holidays? I'll never know. Anyway, he called me from a pay phone in California, of all places. The phone in the gym rang around the time I was collecting all the towels that the men just leave lying around. Wash day. Anyway, I heard the ring and my sixth sense, or whatever you want to call it, told me it was something important. I ran across the gym floor and grabbed the phone. I was really pleased to hear Tony's voice.

"Judy, is that you?"

"You bet it is. Where the heck've you been, Tony?"

"Long story. I'm in Los Angeles right now."

"L.A.? What for?"

"Longer story. How you doin'?'

I sighed. "I'm okay."

"You don't sound okay. I hear it in your voice."

"I miss him, Tony."

"So do I, sweetheart."

I suddenly got the feeling Tony was in trouble. Why else would he be in California? "What's going on, Tony? You can trust me."

"I know I can. I have to smooth over some stuff with the don, that's all. In the meantime I have to steer clear of New York."

"Is it anything to do with Fiorello?"

"In a way. Yeah."

"What happened, Tony? Why was Fiorello killed?"

"Judy . . ."

"Please tell me, Tony. It's been driving me crazy. I gotta know."

I heard some shuffling on his end. Then he said, "Judy, Fiorello tried to cheat the boss. I hate to say that, but it's true. He was skimmin' off the top. Keepin' more money for himself than he shoulda. The boss found out. They clipped him. Him and his bookie, who was in on the deal."

"Oh, my God."

"I'm sorry, Judy."

"Were you involved in it, too, Tony?"

"Not really, but the thing is—I *knew* about it and didn't report it. And now the boss knows that. It's not an offense bad enough for them to clip me, but they can make life difficult. I have to make amends. Do the don some great favor or service that proves I'm still loyal. I'm out here tryin' to arrange that as we speak."

"I see." I wished I could see Tony's face. It would help me determine if he was telling the truth or not, but I sensed he was. "How did Fiorello die?"

"Typical execution, Judy. A couple of plugs in the back of the head. I'm sorry."

Tears came to my eyes again.

"Don DeLuca gave the order?"

"Sure he did."

"Who killed him?"

"You mean who pulled the trigger?"

"Yeah."

"Had to have been the twins. They usually work together, so I imagine they were both there. As to which one of 'em actually did the deed, I have no idea. Probably Roberto did one guy and Vittorio did the other. I heard they're both wanted by the cops for a couple of other jobs. I doubt they'll be showin' their faces in public."

My bile rose. From then on I felt nothing but disgust for Fiorello's so-called family.

"I'll kill 'em, Tony."

"Don't be dumb, Judy. Best to try and forget about it, darlin'. Just remember Fiorello for the kind heart he had. He cared about you a lot, you know."

"Yeah, I know. Thanks."

"I gotta go. You take care now, Judy, y'hear?"

"Sure. You, too, Tony."

"*Ciao.*"

Then I got an idea. "Hey, Tony."

"Yeah?"

"Is the don having another New Year's Eve party like he did last year?"

"Yeah. It's an annual event at the Algonquin. It's always a nice party. Unfortunately, I won't be there this year."

"Okay. Thanks. *Ciao*, Tony."

"Goodbye, sweetheart."

We hung up and I turned to face the empty gym.

New Year's Eve. The don's party.

I decided they'd have an uninvited guest.

On December 31, 1957, I finished making my disguise. I was amazed at how good it looked. It was tight, sleek, and, in my opinion, sexy. The thin black leather worked well. It was heavy enough to keep me warm during cold weather, but pliable enough to move in with my better-than-average agility. The fit was skin tight and almost resembled a rubber diving suit except it was sleeker and, well, *prettier*, if I do say so myself. The mask covered my head down to the bottom of my nose. I'd made holes for the eyes and I punctured tiny outlets on the sides so that I could hear—but my ears were still covered. My hair had to be folded in a bun before putting it on.

I had recently purchased some light-weight, knee-high black boots to wear over the pants. They had a bit of a heel on them, but this didn't prevent me from running, climbing, or kicking. At first I thought the boots would hamper my movements, but they were so streamlined they were practically part of my legs.

The knife training with Fiorello had been a constant throughout our romance. At our last lesson, he'd told me I was better with a blade than anyone he knew—besides him, of course. He didn't lie about things like that, either. Fiorello was, in many ways, a stricter teacher than either Freddie or Soichiro. I'd learned a lot and was very proficient with the weapon. As to which type of knife I wanted to use, I'd chosen the stiletto very early on. As I mentioned before, it just felt right in my hands. Fiorello bought a U.S. Marine Raider Stiletto for me. I liked it a lot. It was a fairly recent design from the Second World War. It was hilt heavy, so it fit snugly in my hand. The double-edged, sharp-tipped blade was around seven and a half inches long and had an oval crossguard. The slender, symmetrical grip was bottle shaped. I figured the knife weighed almost a pound and a half. Easy to throw, too. There were times when I actually beat Fiorello in our games of target practice.

I strapped the stiletto's sheath on the outside of my right thigh. This position allowed for rapid-fire access to the hilt. For months I'd practiced a quick-draw maneuver, over and over, until I could unsheathe the knife, raise my arm, and throw the weapon at a target—in one second. Nine times out of ten, the stiletto hit the intended object. Made me think of that bastard Douglas and all the times he pretended to be a gunslinger, quick drawing his pistol in the house. I sure wanted to meet *him* outside the saloon on Main Street, ha ha!

Fiorello taught me another trick I employed, and that was to carry a second, concealed knife. He owned a homemade six-inch flat blade "wrist dagger" he said was once used by an OSS operative he knew. That's a U.S. spy agency that was active during World War II. I took the dagger and sewed the sheath onto the inside liner of my left boot. If I had to, I could reach over and pull out the blade.

Taking a cue from some of the superheroes in Fiorello's comic books, I fashioned a belt to wear and carry other items I thought would be useful—a thirty-foot-long coil of rope, a small flashlight, and Fiorello's lockpicks. Yes, Fiorello owned some lockpicks he used on a few occasions, mainly to get through locked doors. Sometimes they worked on safes, or so he said. I didn't press him on that, but he showed me how to open doors with them. I figured they'd come in handy.

I put on the disguise and looked at myself in the mirror.

Not bad. A little scary looking. Which was good.

I looked at the time. Nine o'clock. The party at the Algonquin had already begun.

As I prepared to leave through my room's fire escape window, I noticed Fiorello's comics on my bed. I thought it would be funny to come up with a name, the kind those superheroes had. It would be an inside joke between Fiorello, wherever he was, and me. The name came to me with little effort.

The Black Stiletto was born.

12
Roberto
THE PRESENT

I found this shitty furnished studio apartment in Brooklyn, on the east side of Prospect Park. It's the basement of a brownstone, and it seems the entire neighborhood is black. I'm the only white guy on the whole block. Big deal. There weren't many white guys in Sing Sing, either. I probably could've afforded something better, but I don't know how long my money will last. Just in the short time I've been out of jail, I spent 20 percent of my small fortune. I have to watch it from now on.

It's been tough settlin' in, I gotta admit. The world has changed so much. I opened a checkin' account at a bank and was given a plastic card—a credit card—that I'm supposed to use to withdraw money. Never heard of that. I mean, I'd heard of debit cards, but I never had one. Think I'll stick to cash transactions. It's how I always operated.

I hadn't begun trackin' down the old crew. That's next on the agenda. I wonder who's in charge of our *thing* now. That's what we'd say, it was this *thing* of ours. I know the family ain't what it was. The crew I belonged to don't even exist anymore. Wiped out by the feds durin' the sixties. So organized crime mutated into something else. I know it still exists, just not in the way I was used to. I just gotta learn the new ropes. I may be an old man, but I'm still handy with a gun. And I have a brain that still works. I could be useful to somebody, somewhere. I know it.

The sorry excuse for a desk in my apartment was so small I could barely get my legs under it, and I'm not a big guy. It musta been made for a child. In fact, the more I think about it, everything in the room appeared to be leftovers from some dumb kid's room.

I thumbed through my black book, recognizin' some names and not havin' a clue about others. I hadn't splurged to get a phone in my room, but I might have to. Or get one of those cell phone contraptions. I went lookin' for a pay phone on the street yesterday and couldn't find a damn one. Actually I found one near the subway entrance by the park, but it was outta order. Looked like it hadn't worked for ten years. Yeah, I'll probably get one of them cell phones. That's what everybody uses now. I'd look like a dumbass without one.

The weather was warm outside, so I left the apartment and went for a walk. It was nice walkin' on the street after being cooped up in Sing Sing. It was supposed to be good for my heart murmur, but sometimes too much exercise made me dizzy. I couldn't stop gawkin' at the women. I couldn't help it. I thought about findin' a hooker or somethin' and spend some of that money. It's been too long. I may be old but the plumbin' still works. Thank God for that. The last time I got laid was during the day on New Year's Eve, nineteen fifty-seven. Gloria. Nice dame. Italian. We mighta had something if it hadn't been for the party. The don's New Year's Eve party. That's when I got pinched.

And it was all because of the fuckin' Black Stiletto.

Almost had her, though. I was so close. She was lucky, that's all I can say. There's no way, under any other circumstances, that she coulda beat me in a fight. She was good, but I was better. I know it.

And I'm gonna make her pay for what happened to me. I hope to God she's still alive and kickin' somewhere. I don't care about anything else. I don't mind if it's the last thing I do before I die. I'll go to my grave in peace.

Somebody must've tipped off the Black Stiletto that Don DeLuca had given the order to clip Fiorello. And that same somebody probably let her know the don gave the job to Vittorio and me.

I always found it hard to believe the cops never found out who the Black Stiletto really was. To me it was obvious. Who else woulda had such insider knowledge of the family? Who else was takin' lessons on how to box? Who else lived with Fiorello Bonacini, the best knife man in the crew?

Judy Cooper.

I still remember the first time she stuck her nose in our business. It was at the New Year's Eve party a year earlier, the one that rang in nineteen fifty-seven. She was Fiorello's date, before they'd become a real item. Damn fine lookin' woman. After that, she was always with the guy. He shared everything with her, I know. That time she came to the don's house in Glen Cove, the day after we whacked Fiorello, she was all up in arms. Wanted to know who was responsible. Any other dame woulda shut up and let the men handle it. She was up to somethin'. That's one thing that gave her away to me. And then there were the eyes. Brown, with some little green specks. I saw those eyes close up, face-to-face. I'd recognize 'em anywhere. And I swear I saw those same eyes behind the Black Stiletto's mask.

Searches on my new laptop computer didn't yield any results. All the Judy Coopers that came up in the search engines weren't the woman I was looking for.

I guess I have to shadow her old haunts. The trouble was hardly anything that was in Manhattan durin' the late nineteen fifties still existed.

I asked myself who else mighta known? Did Fiorello? Probably not. The Black Stiletto's first appearance was that New Year's

Eve party, just as nineteen fifty-eight had reared its ugly head. But who were Fiorello's friends? I know he was close to Carmine and Guido. And Tony.

Yeah. Tony the Tank.

Fiorello and Tony were like brothers, they were so close.

Findin' Tony would have to be a high priority. He might know somethin'.

Yes, sir. The day was lookin' brighter.

13
Judy's Diary
1958

It felt very strange moving through the city in my disguise. I had to stick to the shadows. I couldn't just get on a subway train or a city bus. I found that sometimes it was easier to travel by rooftop if I was going east or west on a single block. Most of the buildings downtown were so close together that I could jump between them. I tried it for the first time that night. It was easier than I would've thought. In fact, it was exciting. As I leaped from structure to structure, I felt my blood pumping through my veins, the adrenaline giving me a spark and an edge. I was alive.

A couple of times when I was on the street, I was spotted by pedestrians. Couldn't be helped. They pointed and said, "Look!" "Who is that?" "*What* is that?" I ignored them and kept going. I imagine they thought I was on my way to a costume party. I didn't really care about them. I just didn't want to be seen by the police. They might've tried to stop me, I don't know. At that point, I'm not sure what they would've done. All the bad stuff with the cops happened later.

Anyway, I tried to keep out of the lights as I approached the Algonquin Hotel, which was on 44th between Fifth and Sixth Avenues. The time was around eleven thirty as I stood across the street in a dark spot to survey the place. I could hear the band in the Rose Room. The front of the building was crowded, the street was busy with traffic, and the lights under the awning were bright—I certainly couldn't go in that way! But to the right of the main entrance I could see an opening to a narrow, internal alleyway that ran parallel along the side of the building. A steel door to the alley opened and a guy wearing a white apron came out with bags of trash. He placed them at the curb and then went back into the little alley and closed the door.

I hadn't thought the plan through. How was I going to get inside?

The answer was simple. I simply took off my mask and removed the knife from my leg. Became one of the pedestrians, albeit with some very strange clothes on. That's when I got the idea to add a small knapsack to the disguise—something I could wear on my back to carry stuff in. I made a mental note to work on that when it came time for improvements. Anyway, I walked across the street in plain sight—yeah, I probably looked odd. But it was New Year's Eve in New York City. Several pedestrians did double takes as I walked past in that slinky black outfit—but they were looking at my body, not my face. I then stuck close to the buildings and approached the alley door just as the doorman at the front entrance went inside for something.

I was in luck. The man in the apron hadn't closed the door securely—it was ajar. I quickly slipped inside and moved against the side of the building, lurking in the gloom. There, I replaced my mask and knife. So far, so good.

The alley stretched along the hotel to a door midway down. I quietly advanced and carefully opened it, detected that no one was inside, and went in.

I was in a narrow, carpeted hallway. From my recollection of being there a year earlier, the corridor was perpendicular to the lobby, south of the front desk. The ladies' room was there in the hall.

To the right, through a swinging door, was the kitchen. I looked through the porthole window—it was a beehive of activity. Cooks were busy at the stoves and waiters and busboys were all over the place. This was the kitchen's back entrance. To get to the Rose Room and the party, waiters and busboys had to go through double swinging doors on the opposite side, or into the service elevator to deliver room service. I figured I was safe from discovery unless a busboy took out another bag of trash.

I turned and crept along the hall, past the ladies' room and across the bottom of the staircase leading to the second floor, toward the opening to the main lobby. A grouping of planters with tall, artificial greens sat in an alcove there, so I hid behind them to look and listen—I had a full view of the hotel lobby. I could see the partition that had been set up to divide the lobby for the party, as well as the entrance to the Rose Room, where most of the guests had congregated.

The party was in full swing. The band, set up on the other side of the partition, was loud, and the place was noisy with sixty or seventy people laughing and talking and drinking.

I suddenly thought—it wasn't going to work. I couldn't just barge in there in this getup. I was beginning to think I'd gone mad. What the heck was I doing?

Then I saw one of the twins come out of the Rose Room. I didn't know which one he was—Vittorio or Roberto—I guess even though they were wanted by the cops for murder, they weren't afraid of going to the New Year's Eve party. Anyway, the twin stopped at the phone booth next to the elevators, but someone was in it. He started walking toward me—there was another phone booth in the lobby just past the egress where I was hiding, but the twin stopped and cursed to himself. Apparently that booth was occupied as well, although I couldn't see it.

He turned to the receptionist at the front desk and asked, "Is there another damn phone down here?"

"Yes, sir, in the corridor by the ladies' room. Just go through that archway."

That meant right where I was. There was indeed a phone booth built flush into the wall next to the ladies' toom, the kind with one of those hinged shutter-like doors with windows in it. The Ranelli twin headed toward me, moved *right past the planters without seeing me*, turned the corner, and walked to the phone booth. He opened the door and went inside. Throwing caution to the wind, I stepped out from behind the planters and slithered down the hallway, my back to the wall. I could see the booth. The Ranelli twin's back was to me; he had just picked up the receiver and placed coins in the phone. I moved to the other side and then, still keeping my back to the wall, I stealthily moved toward the booth. I pretended I was a marine commando sneaking up on Japanese bunkers, just like I'd done with my brothers when we were kids. Worked every time.

I stood to the left of the booth door and could hear the twin's muffled voice. Images of Fiorello flashed through my mind—his warm smile, the feel of his kisses, his hand upon mine—and I saw red. My anger surfaced and I wanted to tear the Ranelli twin to pieces. But then I heard Soichiro's voice in my head, commanding me to relax and breathe. *Relax and breathe*. "Anger never wins," was one of his axioms. So I replayed that maxim over and over as I stood there, exposed. The odds of being caught were tremendous.

Yet, I slowly unsheathed my stiletto.

I told myself the man in the phone booth was a murderer. An evil person. Worse than—worse than—*Douglas*.

I pushed the hinged doors in on the killer, but his body blocked them from opening much. He turned and looked at me, and his eyes grew wide.

"What the—?" he muttered.

My stiletto flashed through the slender opening, cutting his hand. He yelped, dropped the receiver, and immediately went for the gun inside his tuxedo jacket. The knife struck again, almost as if it had a mind of its own. The pistol fell to the floor. The twin yelled something, but the noise from the party drowned it out.

With both hands wounded and powerless to retrieve his weapon, the killer attempted to push the doors closed and keep me out. All it took was a single forward *karate* kick, and the heel of my right boot shattered the glass in the door. The twin tried to bend over within the confines of the small space and get the gun. I reached through the broken window, grabbed a tuft of his oily, black hair, and pulled back his head. The eyes bulged at me in terror.

"This is for Fiorello," I said as I used my hand to chop the front of his throat, crushing his Adam's apple.

I immediately let go of him. He thrashed around inside the booth, unable to breathe. Knowing he wouldn't survive, I quickly ducked into the ladies' room. Thank God it was empty. I went into a stall, shut the door, and sat on the toilet seat.

My hands were shaking.

I had just killed a man.

I couldn't believe it.

I told myself he deserved to die. He'd helped to kill my lover, if he hadn't done it himself.

Then I realized I should do something about the body. If he was found, the rest of my plans would be shot. I quickly got hold of myself and exited the stall. Opening the washroom door, I peered back and forth into the corridor, and then returned to the phone booth.

The twin's body lay crumpled over the seat. I managed to get the door open and pulled him out by the shoulders. He wasn't a very heavy man, but dragging the dead weight—ha ha, *dead weight*, that's funny—was harder than I expected. I did it, though.

Got him into the ladies' and into the stall where I was before. I propped him on the toilet, shut and locked the door, and then crawled out from under. I took stock of my appearance in the mirror, making sure there was no blood on me. Unfortunately, there were some splotches on the tile floor leading from the washroom door to the stall. I quickly grabbed some paper towels and wiped them up.

Then I heard footsteps in the corridor outside.

"Vittorio! Where the hell are you?"

It was the twin's brother. So I knew my victim's name—I'd killed Vittorio. Roberto was just outside.

Was there blood in the corridor as well? Would he see it? Was there a trail leading from the phone booth to the ladies' room? Would I be discovered before I could finish my mission?

I held my breath and listened at the door.

Nothing.

Then I heard footsteps run back toward the lobby.

I waited a few seconds to make sure the coast was clear. I cracked the door open and looked out. The hallway was empty. There was no blood on the carpet, none that I could see. The phone booth, however, was a mess. Broken glass, the phone hanging off the hook, and blood smeared on the inside wall. Roberto must've seen it.

I figured I'd best avoid trouble by going up to the second floor, so I quickly ascended the staircase—and passed a bellboy. He looked at me with wide eyes and mouth open; I held a finger to my lips, winked at him, and kept going. Once on the second floor, I scurried into what was the elevator lobby. It was in the center; two corridors of hotel rooms branched away from me in opposite directions. Just then, the UP light dinged on the passenger elevator, indicating it had just arrived and its doors were about to open. I quickly chose one of the hallways, darted into it, and prayed that whoever was getting off would go in the other direction and not toward me. Flattening my back against the wall, I held my breath and willed myself to be invisible. I heard the doors open.

"Thank you," someone said to the lift operator. "This way, Don DeLuca."

My heart skipped a beat.

I didn't sense anyone moving my way, so I dared to take a peek.

The big man himself, Don DeLuca, and his wife were being escorted down the opposite hall by three bodyguards. Roberto Ranelli wasn't one of them. I watched as one guy unlocked a door at the end and let the couple inside. I hugged the wall again as two of the goons made the return journey back to the elevators. They'd left one man to guard the door.

Apparently the alarm had been sounded. The don wasn't safe, so they'd stashed him in one of the rooms.

A clock, sitting on a credenza in the elevator lobby, suddenly chimed twelve, scaring the wooly-bullies out of me. I heard shouts of "Happy New Year!" resound throughout the building. Fireworks in the distance outside. The strains of "Auld Lang Syne" coming from what seemed to be a hundred different sources. My hearing was so acute that it was all one big cacophonous torrent.

Nineteen fifty-eight.

I heard the elevator DING once again and the two gangsters stepped into the car.

"Down, please," one said. The door closed.

I then carefully peered into the lobby. It was empty. The thug at the end of the other corridor paced back and forth in front of his boss's door, not moving more than two feet in either direction. He wasn't looking at me.

This was my chance.

I took a deep breath, exhaled, pictured in my mind's eye *exactly* what I was going to do, and then stepped out from the wall.

The mobster noticed my movement out of the corner of his eye, so he turned.

I set off running toward him. Fast. Through the elevator lobby and into the other corridor.

His eyes widened.

Faster, ready to leap.

His hand went for the pistol inside his jacket.

Closer. Closer.

The man opened his mouth, ready to shout a warning.

I leaped, turning my body in midair so that my right leg bent at the knee toward my chest and the left one jutted straight out. Propelling my body like a weapon. My heel slammed into his face with such force that his head bounced off the don's door and left an impression in the paint.

Just as I used to do in gymnastics when I was in school, I landed gracefully on both feet. I even held the pose for a beat, as if it was the most natural thing in the world to do.

"What do you want?" the don called from inside. He thought someone had knocked.

I used my foot to push the unconscious goon out of the way. Then, using the lowest vocal register I could muster, I said, "We brought you and Mrs. DeLuca some champagne, sir."

Sounds behind the door. The big man was coming closer. The latch slid back.

As soon as the door opened, I kicked it in and barged inside.

Mrs. DeLuca, standing in the suite's living room, screamed.

Don DeLuca stood there, shocked and amazed by the sight of me. I used my foot to kick the door shut behind me. I drew the stiletto and pointed it at the boss.

"Who are you? What do you want?" he stammered.

I didn't answer him. Snapping the knife toward his wife, I growled, "Go in the bedroom. Shut the door." Scared to death, she did as she was told.

Then I swung the blade back to the don. I whispered, "You had Fiorello Bonacini killed, didn't you!"

The boss wasn't so powerful anymore. He was trying desperately to keep his cool, but I could sense he was frightened out of his wits.

"I . . . I . . ."

"What? I can't hear you."

Then he suddenly went for a gun that was holstered at the small of his back. I let loose with a roundhouse kick—*mawashi geri* in Japanese—and knocked the weapon out of his hand. The man stumbled backward and fell over a chair. His head struck the edge of the coffee table *hard*—I heard a horrible *snap!*—and then his heavy body landed on the carpet with a thud.

I leaped like an insect from where I was standing and landed on top of him, straddling his big round paunch.

His face turned red. The eyes exhibited pain, not fear. My instincts told me that something else was happening.

The don's eyes rolled up under his eyelids.

I got off of him.

He seemed to be having trouble breathing, but he wasn't moving. "Help . . . me . . . !" he managed to say.

Oh, Christ, I thought.

I certainly couldn't kill him then. My sense of honor, drilled into me by Soichiro, came into play. I sheathed the knife, went to the phone on the desk, picked it up, and dialed the front desk. When the receptionist answered, I said, "Call an ambulance for Mr. DeLuca." I told him the room number. He asked who was calling. "This is the Black Stiletto," I replied, and hung up.

Then the suite door opened. Alas, I hadn't bothered to lock it when I'd shut it.

Roberto Ranelli stood there, his mouth agape. For a moment, I swear—time stood still. We were frozen, unable to move.

Then he reached for his gun.

I performed a *yoki geri*—a side kick—and cracked the gun out of his hand before he could grasp it firmly. He lunged for me. I deftly avoided his blow and was about go into full defensive mode—when I saw through the open door half a dozen men running toward the room from the elevator lobby.

I pushed Ranelli out of the way and burst into the bedroom. Mrs. DeLuca sat on the bed, her face white as a sheet. Thinking quickly, I shut the door behind me and locked it. I then went straight for the window, tore down the drapes with one hand, and used my boot to kick through the glass. The woman screamed again.

"Get away from the door, Mrs. DeLuca," I said. "They're about to start shooting."

As I kicked away more of the windowpane, the woman nodded in comprehension. She jumped up, ran to the bathroom, and locked herself in.

As expected, a barrage of bullets perforated the bedroom door, just as I ducked outside through the window to the fire escape. I merely had to grab the ladder and pull it down, as it was on rollers attached to the rails. But that led to the street. There would be people, cars, and probably more gangsters with guns. Metal flights of stairs led upward toward the building's third-floor landing and beyond, all the way to the roof, twelve stories higher.

I chose to go that way.

14
Martin
The Present

I had to stop reading and pick up Gina at Stevenson High School in Lincolnshire. By seven o'clock, the usual traffic jams in the parking lots and access roads surrounding the school had dissipated. I can remember days when I *hated* taking or picking up Gina during the normal start or let-out times.

Gina came out the back by the gymnasium section of the building, wearing a shockingly short skirt that revealed her long bare legs. I guess she inherited those from her grandmother. My daughter also must have gotten her good looks from her mother. She certainly didn't from me. I'm not a bad-looking guy, but Carol was damned gorgeous. Gina is too, and as she gets into her twenties, I'm sure she'll be a stunner. She has dark hair—almost black—just like my mom did. Brown eyes. Pretty face. No wonder I get a little concerned about the boys she sees.

Why didn't I inherit some of mom's physical genes? I'm not tall. In fact, you might say I'm short for my weight, which makes me a little pudgy. Mind you, I'm not *fat*. Just, well, let's say I could stand to lose a few pounds. Unlike my mom and my daughter, I hate to exercise and was never into sports. I was always the nerd who excelled in math and science, made good grades, and never dated cheerleaders.

Gina got in the car and said, "I took a shower and changed already."

I just shrugged. "Whatever. You ready to go eat now?"

"Yeah, Jon's picking me up at eight thirty." As I pulled out of the school parking lot, she asked, "Can I have your car tonight, Dad?" It was a BMW E90.

"What?"

"I'm kidding. Scared you, though, didn't I?"

There was the usual twenty-minute wait when we got to Big Bowl. Gina spent most of that time on her cell phone, either talking or texting, leaving me to stand and stare at the waitresses. A couple of 'em were cute. Eventually we got seated, placed our order, and had father-daughter face time.

"So how's your mother?" I asked to be politically correct.

"She's okay. I think she has a boyfriend." Like me, Carol hadn't remarried.

"Oh? Who?"

"Some guy named Ross."

"What does Ross do?"

"I don't know. He's a lawyer, I think. Mom says he's rich."

I'm not sure why that irked me, but it did. I wasn't *rich*, but I did okay. Well, sort of okay; George's doomsday prediction of layoffs at Bailey and Catlow was a little disconcerting. The recession had taken its toll on the firm, just like with everyone else.

"We gonna go see Grandma tomorrow?" she asked.

Usually if Gina visited me on a weekend, we'd go to Woodlands on Saturday to see her grandmother.

"Sure, that'd be a good idea. She'd be happy to see you."

"She doesn't even know who I am."

"She knows she loves you, though."

Actually, Gina seemed to communicate better with my mom than I could. They often had somewhat coherent conversations, whereas with me it was usually a series of non sequiturs.

"Didn't she live in New York when she was young?" Gina asked.

"Yep. Why?"

"Just wondering."

We finally got around to talking about college. I asked Gina again about the schools she applied for and whether or not she'd decided to go into business or education. For a couple of years I'd been pushing her to go in one of those directions. With her athletic skills, she'd make a great girls' coach at a high school somewhere. And, like me, she was very organized. I could see her as VP or even a president of a company.

"Okay, Dad," she said, "listen. I don't want to have a fight."

"Fight? Who's fighting?"

"You will be when you hear what I'm gonna say."

"What."

"Dad, I don't *want* to go into business or education. That's not who I am. I've tried to tell you this a million times."

Great, I thought, *here we go again*.

"Geez, honey, I thought we'd settled this. We met with your counselor and all that. I thought we were agreed."

"Dad, I never agreed. You just thought I agreed 'cause you don't listen to me. You never hear what I say. Mom says the same thing."

Terrific. It figured Carol would take her side.

"Well, Gina, are you sure you can get an athletics scholarship? What will you do with the degree? Either you go and be a professional athlete—and the last time I looked, there weren't a lot of women making big bucks on balance beams—or you teach."

"Dad."

"What?"

"I want to study theatre."

I thought I was going to spit out my pad Thai. "No you don't."

"Dad! Listen to me. I'm a good actress. It's what I really love. I mean, I love gymnastics, too, but that's more of an exercise thing.

Something I do because it feels good. I don't want to make a living doing it."

"You can't make a living as an actress."

"Plenty of people do."

"Gina, an extremely small percentage of actors actually makes money. They all can't be Julia Roberts."

She made one of her *dad-you-are-so-not-with-it* faces.

"Sweetheart, I want you to study something practical. It's a tough world out there. You need a skill you can make a real living doing."

"What, like being a boring *accountant*?" She said it as if it was the lowest career move possible.

"It's put food on your table and clothes on your back, young lady."

She didn't apologize.

You know, it hurt to hear what she said. My daughter thinks I'm boring. I suppose I could say this was the kind of thing all fathers experience with teenage girls—and boys—and I should just shrug it off. But I couldn't. It really bothered me.

We spent the rest of the dinner in an awkward silence. When we were done, we went to my house. She went up to her room and then primped in the bathroom for five minutes—and then *Jon* came and picked her up. He seemed nice enough when Gina introduced me to him. At least he didn't seem gay or anything, like some of those drama types.

I figured she'd come in late and I wouldn't see her until morning. Still stinging a bit from Gina's denigration, I fixed myself a cocktail and sat down to read more of my mom's diary.

15
Judy's Diary
1958

When I climbed over the roof edge and landed on my feet, I looked below. Someone was chasing me up the stairs. A single guy. It was difficult to see his face—only the top of his head was visible and he was moving fast. I turned and quickly surveyed the landscape.

Rooftops. Of various heights.

Maybe going up wasn't such a good idea after all.

I had to do something, so I sprinted across the roof to the back. Lucky for me, there was one of those bunkhouse type structures with a metal door presumably leading to a stairwell that descended back into the hotel. I grabbed the doorknob.

Locked.

Thinking quickly, I pulled the lockpicks out of the pouch on my belt, fumbled with them for another second, and then poked one into the keyhole.

Gunfire!

A bullet ricocheted off the metal door a few inches from my head. I stole a quick glance back. The man chasing me had reached the roof and had fired from the edge.

It was Roberto Ranelli.

The lockpick didn't work. I had to try a different one.

The enforcer fired a second shot. This time the round struck the roof near my right foot, spewing a cloud of cement chips and debris.

He ran toward me. The next shot wouldn't miss.

Thank God the second lockpick did the trick and the door opened. I spun inside and slammed the door shut, locking it behind me. The stairs descended to the thirteenth floor, the highest in the building. I set off, taking the steps two at a time; but when I reached the next landing I heard two more muffled gunshots above me. Roberto had shot out the lock in the door. I kept going to the twelfth floor, then the eleventh. At one point he leaned over the rail and fired a shot at me down the center of the stairwell. The bullet didn't hit me—I don't know where it went—but the noise was monstrously loud and echoed all the way down to the bottom.

Nothing I could do but keep running. If I had to fight my way out the front door of the hotel, I would.

It was a good thing I had spent the last few years training with Freddie, otherwise I would have run out of breath long before. I had a feeling it wasn't so easy for the man chasing me—I could hear him panting heavily, even from the distance between us.

The stairwell finally came to an end on the second floor. I'd have to expose myself by going out to the elevator lobby and taking the open staircase down to the ground. Unfortunately, the lobby outside the door was full of people—mostly mobsters. My handiwork in the ladies' room and in the DeLuca's suite had obviously been discovered. The sound of running footsteps above me grew closer. He'd be on me in a few seconds. There was no other option. I burst out of the stairwell and flew down the staircase toward the back exit near the kitchen.

Someone shouted, "Hey! Look there!"

I was out the door in a flash and in the alleyway that ran parallel to the building. I reached the outer door, opened it, and erupted onto 44th Street. The front of the hotel was mobbed, no pun intended. An ambulance stood at the curb, along with two police cars. I didn't linger. I bolted across the street, barely dodging oncoming traffic. Horns blared, attracting attention my way. Once on the other side of the street, I ran west toward Sixth Avenue, zigzagging through pedestrians and New Years Eve revelers. As soon as I got to the corner, I heard a single pair of running footsteps behind me.

Ranelli had continued the chase alone.

I darted back across 44th Street, heading south along Sixth. More people. Shouts of alarm as I rushed past. I took a chance and attempted to cross Sixth Avenue. A taxicab screeched to a halt and slammed into my left side, knocking me to the ground. If the driver hadn't braked, I'd be dead. Still, the impact stunned me and I don't know how long I laid there before I was able to pull myself up. I heard the driver say, "Lady? Are you all right?"

The pursuing footsteps reached the avenue.

I leaped to my feet, running as hard as I could.

A gunshot. Screams.

My left leg hurt badly. I was going to have a heck of a bruise there the next day, if I lived to see it. But I made it to the west side of Sixth Avenue and continued running south. I fell when I reached the corner of 42nd Street and Sixth. I don't know what I tripped on, but I did. Maybe it was a wet spot on the pavement, or maybe it was an empty champagne bottle—I have no idea. At any rate, I went flying and did a belly flop on the sidewalk. It hurt so much I wanted to cry out, but I didn't.

Roberto Ranelli reached the corner just as I stood. He pointed his pistol at me—onlookers gasped and at least two women screamed at the sight.

I was dead. I knew it.

The killer pulled the trigger.

Click.

The gun was empty. He'd fired six shots and hadn't stopped to reload.

I faced Roberto and assumed a defensive position—legs apart, arms raised, hands flat and stiff.

"I will kill you for this," he spat as he holstered his gun. "Whoever you are. You and your entire family!" And then he attacked.

A fist flew at my face. I deftly blocked it by chopping it away with a knife-hand blow to his forearm. He grunted and tried again, but missed. I saw an opening best suited for a boxing cross, so I let him have it. My fist connected with his jaw and his head jerked back. He recovered quickly and moved closer. I wanted to strike again, but I froze. I'm not sure what happened to me, but I *forgot* everything I was trained to do. I was a brown belt in *karate*, for Christ's sake, and I couldn't remember the first thing of how to defend myself.

Before I could react at all, he clobbered me with a powerful right hook that connected with my left cheekbone. I swear I saw stars as lightning bolts of pain shot through my skull. His other fist slammed into my mouth, once, twice, and then he got me with another right hook. Reflexively, I brought up my leg and attempted a front kick—but he was too quick for me. He *caught* my leg, as if he'd been expecting my maneuver, and held it tightly. I hit him hard on the chest with a *shotei uchi*—a palm heel strike—but he used my instability to his advantage and toppled me. I fell hard and tried to roll away before he could kick me in the side, but I wasn't fast enough. The toe of his shoe crashed into my right ribs, sending intense explosions of agony up my spine and into my brain. And then he kicked me again as I rotated, catching the blow this time in my stomach. It seriously knocked the wind out of me, but I had the presence of mind to lash out from my balled position at his stationary leg with a side kick. He yelped in pain and also dropped to the ground. I hoped I'd broken his tibia.

I crawled onto my hands and knees, desperately attempting to catch my breath. My lungs wouldn't work. I simply gasped in pain and struggled to relax the spasm in my diaphragm.

Breathe, Soichiro would say. *Breathe.*

Yeah, right.

Roberto's face was distorted in a grimace as he held his lower leg, writhing on the ground. Perhaps I *did* break it.

Then, precious oxygen finally filled my lungs. Sounded like a wheezing motor when I finally inhaled. The blinding stars in my vision slowly dissipated, so I got to my feet and shook my head.

Pedestrians stared at me. I heard police sirens. I had to get out of there. But there was something I had to do.

I drew the stiletto from its sheath and approached Roberto. I kicked his arm, causing him to let go of his leg. With one hand, I grabbed him by the neck and slammed his back onto the sidewalk. I held him there and touched the tip of the blade to his cheek. He opened his eyes and stared at me—looking past the mask and into my own eyes. He squinted and then his pupils flared.

Did he recognize me?

"This is for Fiorello," I said. I raised the stiletto, ready to plunge it into his chest—when a police car screeched around the corner, its lights blazing. The crowd around us immediately dispersed, making room for the cruiser to drive on the sidewalk and stop just a few feet from where Roberto and I lay in a frozen tableau.

Then a *second* patrol car roared around the corner and pulled up behind the first.

Policemen jumped out of the cars, took cover behind open doors, drew their guns, and aimed at me.

"Freeze!" one shouted.

I hesitated. My acute hearing picked something out of the street noise that didn't belong. A low rumbling. A train. Below me, underground. Out of the corner of my eye, I saw the 42nd Street and Sixth Avenue subway entrance about ten yards away.

Slowly, I lowered my hands and sheathed the stiletto, and stood. I don't think the police had seen the knife, otherwise they would've ordered me to drop it.

"Put your hands up!"

I showed them my empty palms and raised my arms, elbows bent, my hands at shoulder level.

And then I bolted.

"Halt!"

One of the cops fired his gun and missed, but whoever was in charge shouted, "Hold your fire!"

I dashed into the subway entrance and practically flew down the steps. As I ran, the pain in my ribs increased—I wagered at least one was broken. Reaching the station below, I leaped over the turnstile, and felt a sudden wave of nausea as I ran down the platform. Fighting the dizziness, I continued running, prepared to jump onto the tracks if I had to—but the train I'd heard was just pulling in. Several policemen followed me down and gave chase. The train stopped and the doors opened. I pushed through the crowd getting off and boarded several cars ahead of the cops. Had they gotten on? I didn't know.

The doors closed and the train pulled away from the station. I wasn't sure which platform I'd been on. Was I going uptown or downtown? I didn't care, I just had to move forward and be ready to jump out at the next stop. As it was late on New Year's Eve, the train was full of people. They looked at me as if I were an alien creature from one of those dumb science-fiction movies that were so popular. I ignored the stares and moved forward in the car until I came to the door at the front. I pulled it open and stepped out, between the train cars, and opened the next one. Before I went farther toward the front of the train, I suddenly realized I'd be too far from the subway exit on the platform when I got off. The turnstiles were usually situated in the middle. So I stayed put.

I never saw the cops. The train slowed and eventually stopped. Thirty-Fourth Street. I was on a downtown train, thank God. I joined a throng of passengers as they poured out of the car. Sure, there were comments: "What the—?" and "Who are you, lady?" and "Get a load of this!" and "What are you supposed to be?" But I pushed through them, made it to the turnstiles, exited like a normal paying customer, and hobbled up the steps.

I was at Macy's and Herald Square.

The rest of the trip home was a blur. I was in pain and scared out of my mind. I really don't remember how I did it. It was on foot the whole way, I can tell you that much. But I managed to avoid people, stick to the shadows, and stay as invisible as possible.

So much for the Black Stiletto's first "adventure."

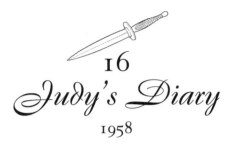

16
Judy's Diary
1958

The next morning was difficult, to say the least. I was sore all over and my head hurt. Roberto Ranelli had really slammed me with a few good ones. I had a large discoloration on my left cheek and my eye above it was bloodshot. My lips were puffy and cut. My entire right side and stomach was bruised from Roberto's kicks and my left leg was stiff and marked from being hit by the taxi. I walked with a limp, but nothing was broken.

When I came into the kitchen, Freddie was sitting at our little dining table, the *New York Daily News* in hand. Coffee and breakfast. He glanced up and his mouth dropped.

"Jesus, Judy!" He stood.

"I'm all right," I said, gesturing him back down. "Just let me get some coffee."

"You sit, I'll get it." He kept his eyes on me as I sat at the table and slid the newspaper over in front of me. Poured some coffee and set the cup on the table. "Eggs?"

"Sure. Thanks."

The headline read: MAFIA HEAD DEAD. In smaller lettering was a subheading: POLICE SEARCH FOR MYSTERY FEMALE ASSASSIN. I winced and then read the story.

Don DeLuca had died in the ambulance on the way to the hospital. His neck was broken. His wife was quoted as saying that a "woman dressed entirely in black" had threatened them in their

Algonquin Hotel suite. Mrs. DeLuca was convinced the "mystery assassin" killed her husband, but I knew that wasn't true. The man fell and hit his head on the coffee table; he broke his neck in the process. I may have been indirectly responsible, but I didn't *kill* him. The story went on to say the hotel receptionist testified someone calling herself "the Black Stiletto" had phoned for an ambulance from the DeLuca suite.

To further complicate things, a second homicide had occurred elsewhere in the hotel. The body of Vittorio Ranelli was found in the ladies' room on the first floor of the hotel. Cause of death was not revealed, nor was the mystery woman from the DeLuca suite implicated. Several arrests had been made, including that of Roberto Ranelli, Vittorio's twin brother and alleged Mafia hit man. Like Tony had said, both Ranellis were wanted for questioning in several murder cases. The surviving Ranelli had been treated at Bellevue Hospital for a head injury and a broken leg, and then released into police custody. Most of the other arrests involved possession of illegal weapons and using them in a public place.

New York's Mayor Robert Wagner was quoted as saying that Giorgio DeLuca was a known criminal, the head of a powerful Italian organized crime operation, and that he "got what he deserved." DeLuca had been arrested numerous times over the years on a variety of charges, mostly racketeering, but the police never had sufficient evidence to bring the don to trial. The mayor went on to say, "Whoever this mystery woman is—this 'Black Stiletto,' or whatever she calls herself—what she did was wrong in the eyes of the law. But in reality she did the city a favor."

Nevertheless, Police Commissioner Stephen Kennedy reiterated the woman was wanted for questioning and asked that anyone with information pertaining to the assassin's identity should come forward. He added that the police were pleased Roberto Ranelli was apprehended "at last."

The U.S. Attorney for the Southern District of New York, Paul Williams, declared there was enough evidence against Ranelli on one case to bring him to trial for murder and that the mobster "would be going away for a long time."

It was all scary stuff, but I felt avenged. The don had died—not by my hand—but I suppose one could argue it was because of me. Vittorio received his comeuppance. And it appeared Roberto would spend the rest of his life in prison. That was good enough for me.

Freddie slapped the plate of eggs on the table and retook his seat.

"So," he said.

"So what?"

"It was you, wasn't it?"

I got a sinking feeling in my stomach. I was hoping he wouldn't figure it out, but I guess it was kind of obvious, considering what I looked like.

"Freddie—"

He held up his hands. "I'm not tellin' anyone. Don't worry."

"Look, I—"

"You don't have to explain anything, Judy. I think I understand why you did it. I don't *approve*, but I understand. I strongly suggest, though, that you never do it again. You could have been hurt pretty bad. Or worse. Hell, they coulda arrested you. You'd be tried for murder, even if the victim was a Mafia hit man."

We sat in silence for a few minutes as I tried to eat. He was right, of course. But what Freddie *didn't* understand was how the whole experience had made me feel. Donning that disguise—the costume—empowered me. It gave me some sort of entitlement I didn't have as normal, everyday Judy Cooper. It provided me with a purpose for all the lessons and training—the boxing, the *karate*, the knife wielding. I really didn't think I could give it up. Not yet, anyway.

"Judy, promise me you won't do it again."

I sighed and shook my head. "Oh, Freddie. I don't think I can. I've always wondered what I was going to be and do when I grew up. I think I just found out what that is."

17
Martin

THE PRESENT

Gina and I went to the nursing home on Saturday to visit Mom as planned. I've read much of that first diary, was about halfway through it. Pretty incredible stuff. I suppose it's all true—why wouldn't it be? Unless my mom lived in a fantasy world and made it all up, which I don't think is possible.

It's been driving me crazy that there was so much about my mom I didn't know before. This whole business has put me in a funky mood, and I woke up this morning angry. *Why didn't I know?* One thing really puzzles me—how come Mom never told me about her brothers? My *uncles*. I wonder if they're still alive. Did they know about their sister? From what I've read so far, it appeared my mom left Texas behind and never looked back. I don't know if I should try and look them up. Wouldn't know where to start.

At Woodlands, I signed us in and checked Mom's mail. When she moved out of the old house, I had all mail forwarded to the nursing home. She normally didn't get much, but today there was a letter. From New York. There was a handwritten Queens address on the envelope. I opened it and saw it was dated a couple of days earlier and was signed "Tony."

Tony.

Tony the Tank?

"What's that?" Gina asked.

"Just mail for your grandma."

"And you're reading it?"

I looked at her like she was bonkers. "Well, *she* can't read it."

"Oh. Yeah."

I was still a little upset with my daughter. Anyway, I read the letter, which was short and to the point. Tony said it'd been a long time since he'd written, for which he apologized. He also gently chastised my mom for not writing him, too. He hoped her address hadn't changed; if it had, he trusted the post office to forward it. Tony spent a few sentences saying his health "had improved," whatever that meant, but that he was old and cranky. He still lived alone and was able to take care of himself, which he considered a blessing.

Then he wrote something that sent a chill down my back. He said, "The main reason I'm writing is to let you know Robert Ranelli was paroled. He's out of jail. I don't know where he is or what he's doing, but he's alive and he's free."

Damn.

Surely it couldn't be a big deal. How could Roberto Ranelli have any idea where my mom lived now? And he's older than she is—probably pushing eighty. Over fifty years had passed. He'd be in no shape to come looking for her.

Or could he?

Nah.

Tony closed by wishing her well and admonishing her to write. I folded the letter, put it back in the envelope, and stuck it in my pocket.

Had she been in touch with Tony all these years? I never found any evidence of it when I'd gone through all her stuff in the house. All her correspondence, personal papers, and such were kept in a desk drawer in her bedroom or in a filing cabinet in what we called the "guest bedroom." I don't remember ever having guests. It was the catchall room for stuff that didn't go anywhere else.

I had her address book at my house. I'd have to remember to go through it and take a closer look at what was in it. Maybe Tony's address and phone number was there and I never knew it. I could call him. Maybe. Tell him about my mom's condition.

Wait a minute!

If Tony was warning Mom that Roberto Ranelli was out of prison, then Tony must know Mom was the Black Stiletto!

That would be at least two people who knew her secret—Tony and Freddie Barnes, the manager of the gym where she lived and worked. Were there more?

I put all these thoughts aside. Gina and I went to the Alzheimer's unit to see Mom. The nurse on duty stopped me to say Mom's roommate had died. She'd eventually get another one, but for the moment Mom would be alone in her room. I didn't know if this was a good thing or a bad thing. When we got there, mom was just sitting on her bed, staring across the way at the other empty bed. She was dressed in a nightgown.

"Hi, Mom!" I said as cheerfully as I could.

"Hi, Grandma!" Gina said, mimicking my enthusiasm.

Well, Mom's eyes went straight to Gina and they lit up. A big smile spread across her face and she held out her arms. My daughter dutifully went to her and gave her a hug.

"How are you, Grandma? You doing okay?"

"Oh, I don't know," my mom answered. "I guess so."

I took one of the chairs in the room; Gina sat on the bed with Mom. "Well, you're looking pretty," she told her.

"I am?"

"Sure."

I was amazed. It wasn't entirely clear my mom knew who Gina was—or me either—but you could see that the old gal was aware she had a connection with my daughter. And they had a decent conversation. Much better than I'm ever able to do.

"Ask her about New York," I ventured.

"Hey, Grandma, isn't it true you used to live in New York?"

Mom's brow furrowed. "New York?"

"Yeah. New York City?"

Then mom smiled and nodded. "That's right, I live in New York."

Gina laughed. "No, Grandma, not now. You live *here* now. But when you were younger you lived in New York. Remember?"

"Of course."

I wasn't so sure she did remember or was just saying that. But then she said—

"I live at the gym."

Gina laughed again. "The gym? You live at the gym? I didn't know you could live in a gym, Grandma."

I'm sure my jaw dropped.

"You're joking, right, Grandma? You didn't live in a gym."

"I did," she answered.

Gina looked at me. I just shrugged.

"Well, Grandma, who knows, maybe *I'll* live in New York, too. I don't know if I'll live in a gym, though."

Wait a second. "New York?" I asked.

Gina waved at me to shut up and continued talking to her grandmother. "You know I graduate from high school soon. I'll be going away to college in the fall."

"That's nice," Mom answered.

"But I'll come and visit you as often as I can."

"I'd like that."

Gina got up and went to Mom's dresser, where we keep a portable CD player and a few CDs. Mom doesn't operate it herself, but sometimes the staff will put on music. Gina picked out a CD of Elvis Presley's greatest hits—I'd bought it for Mom a while back because I knew she liked him.

"Feel like dancing a little?" Gina asked her.

"Gina, I don't think she's up to dancing," I said.

"Sure she is." Gina put on the CD and skipped to the track "Blue Suede Shoes." The King started belting out the song. Gina held out her arms—*and my mom took her hands and stood.*

And I sat there fascinated as Gina and my mother moved around the center of the room together. Gina did most of the real dancing while holding my mom's hands, but Mom managed to sway back and forth on her feet. Her huge smile indicated she was obviously very happy.

Astonishing.

18
Judy's Diary
1958

Time passed and I healed, dear diary. I trained harder at the gym, continued my work with Soichiro, and tried my best to forget about what I had done on New Year's Eve. The thing is—I had no regrets about it. Had a few nightmares and woke up with the shakes a few times, but that eventually passed. I kept telling myself Don DeLuca and the Ranelli twins got what they deserved, and that helped. The newspapers were full of speculation and innuendo about me—well, about *her*—and most of it was insulting and ridiculous. One paper suggested the Black Stiletto was really a man. Another claimed the mayor and the police force actually knew the Stiletto's identity and it was their underhanded way of striking at organized crime. Witnesses appeared on the radio, on local television newscasts, and in print, describing the Stiletto's appearance and the "superhuman" feats she was able to do. One claimed I'd bent steel with my bare hands and "flown" like Superman. Oddly enough, not one person snapped a photo of me that night. Several artist depictions were published, though, and none of them was remotely correct.

By the end of January, the urge to don the disguise again was overwhelming. My prophetic statement to Freddie became a reality. I *was* the Black Stiletto, and she needed to make an appearance again. My injuries no longer hurt and I was able to run, jump, and kick even better than before.

I picked a lousy night to go out. It was snowing, the streets and sidewalks were wet and slippery, and it was cold. The leather suit kept me warm, but my hands and fingers nearly froze. I decided to incorporate gloves the next time. I did fashion a black knapsack to wear on my back. Inside it I carried a few more miscellaneous tools—additional rope, a screwdriver and small hammer, a first-aid kit, and street clothes. If I suddenly needed to become a normal pedestrian, I could strip off the mask and don a trench coat over my disguise. I didn't know what I'd do for warmer weather, but I'd think of something.

Anyway, it was around ten o'clock at night. I was close to Washington Square Park, near NYU, darting from shadow to shadow. It was a game I played with myself—I tried to get from one part of town to another without being seen by a soul, even though dozens and dozens of people were on the streets. I was successful most of the time. If someone did happen to see me, I'd skedaddle so fast that he or she was left unsure of what they'd seen.

My second altercation with "bad guys" came when I saw a young couple leave the Waverly movie theater on Sixth Avenue and head along 4th Street toward the park. They were about my age, probably college students, obviously in love. The boy had his arm around the girl and they were giggling and cuddling, enjoying the snowfall and the intimacy of walking together. I followed them for a bit simply because they were attractive and made me feel warm inside. Not many people were out—it was a bad-weather weeknight—and the stretch of 4th Street was deserted.

As the couple approached the intersection of Thompson and 4th, three hooligans emerged from the park and stood in front of them. I sensed fear from the couple; the newcomers weren't known to them. My acute hearing picked up harsh words from one of the thugs. The boy started to fumble with something in his pocket and then pulled out his wallet. It was a robbery, right there on the street.

My heartbeat increased and I felt an adrenaline rush. It was what I'd secretly hoped would happen. Okay, I was looking for trouble. I wanted to test myself again and see if I was ready to tackle another challenge. This incident fell right into my lap, so to speak.

I was on the opposite side of 4th, lurking in the shadows. I ran across the road and stood some ten feet away from the group.

"Don't give him your wallet," I said.

Everyone looked at me. I saw terror in the girl's eyes. The three muggers jerked their heads toward me and practically snarled.

"What the hell?" one said.

"Who are you?" another asked.

"Who do you think I am?" I took a couple of steps forward.

"I don't know, but you're a freak, whatever you are." the first guy said.

"Turn around and go home," I ordered. "Let these people pass."

"Screw you, lady."

Then I saw the knife. One of them had a switchblade.

"You really don't want to use that, do you?" I asked.

"Sure I do. Come closer and I'll show you."

I tried to laugh, you know, be cool. The truth was that I was just as scared as I'd been the first time I was the Stiletto.

Nevertheless, I stepped closer.

"Come on." I gave him a little beckoning motion with my hands.

He came at me awkwardly, untrained and unsure of himself. I easily disarmed him, knocked the knife out of his hand, twisted his arm behind his back, and pushed it up over his shoulder blades.

The creep cried out in pain.

I didn't break his arm, though.

"Tell your friends to beat it," I said.

He resisted, so I put a little more pressure on his arm. He yelped and then said, through his teeth, "Beat it, guys."

But the other two weren't having it. They looked at each other, nodded, and then rushed me. I released Clown Number One and pushed him hard at the other two. They collided like bowling pins. Before Clown Number Two could throw a punch at me, I performed a front kick to his solar plexus. He doubled over, staggered away, and left the path clear for me to take care of his friends. Clown Number Three was on top of me by that time. He tried his best to hit me, but I dodged him easily, gave him two hard straight lefts, and then a right hook to the face. Out like a light. Clown Number One ran away.

The couple backed away from me.

"It's okay," I said, holding up my hands. "Are you two all right?"

They nodded, speechless.

"Do you have far to go? You want me to walk you home?"

"N-n-no, that's okay," the boy said. "Thanks."

"Yeah, thanks," the girl added.

"You're welcome." And, believe it or not, there was this awkward moment where none of us knew what to say next. Finally, I went, "See you around. Bye." and started to leave.

"Wait!" the boy said.

"Yeah?"

"Are you that lady? The Black, um...?"

"Stiletto?"

"Yeah?"

"Could be." I winked and then ran.

I thought it was a pretty classy exit.

I sat in the East Side Diner the next day with the newspaper. There was another story about me. Apparently the couple had called the cops when they got home. Somehow the *Daily News* found out and went over to interview the kids. The couple was enthusiastic in their praise of my "heroics," but the paper spun it in a way that led readers to believe I might have set the whole thing up as a publicity stunt. You know, *hired* the muggers, just so I could save the couple and get some press. Sheesh.

Once again, there was an artist's sketch, using the couple's description of my disguise. It was the most accurate yet. Alas, none of the thugs came forward to provide additional information, ha ha.

"I think she's great," Lucy said, setting down a cup of coffee for me.

"What?"

"I said I think she's great." She nodded at the article. "The Black Stiletto."

"Oh. Yeah."

"I wonder who she is."

I shrugged. "I don't believe she really exists."

"No? Why not?"

"It's kind of silly, isn't it? Some woman dressing up like a costumed hero? Who would do that?"

"I don't know. But enough people have seen her. She's got to be real."

"People claim to see flying saucers, too, Lucy. That don't mean they're real."

"I know."

The new Elvis Presley song, "Don't," started playing on the jukebox. I'd only heard it a couple of times, and I squealed, "Oh, you got the new record!"

"Yeah, the guy came in this morning and put new ones in it. You heard he got drafted, right?"

"Who, Elvis?"

"Uh-huh."

"Yeah, I heard that before Christmas."

"Would you believe they're letting him finish his new movie before he goes?"

"Really?"

Lucy rolled her eyes. "How many other people would the U.S. Army do that for?"

"I don't know. I'm happy for Elvis. I think he's dreamy."

"If you say so." She walked away to tend to more customers.

I tapped my hand to the music and reread the article about me.

The Black Stiletto made numerous but inconsequential appearances in February and March. Nothing happened. I couldn't find a crime to save my life. I went up and down the Bowery and even into parts of what they called Alphabet City on the Lower East Side. In April, though, I stumbled on a liquor store robbery not far from the Second Avenue Gym. A colored man who was high on something had a gun, and he was determined to relieve the proprietor of all the cash in the register. It was a place Freddie and I went to sometimes, so I actually knew the owner. Nice old Irish man; name of O'Malley.

I was on top of a building across the street when it happened. I should explain—I had mapped out a rooftop route from the gym as far as I could get going east toward First Avenue. It was impossible, of course, to go west—Second Avenue was a bit wide, ha ha, and I could only go so far north and south before hitting the respective 2nd or 1st Street impasses. Usually I left my bedroom window, climbed to the roof by means of the fire escape, ran east along 2nd Street to a spot I knew where I could shimmy down a telephone pole to the ground. It was in such a dark and unobtrusive spot on the street that no one ever saw me. From there I'd make my way on foot to my destination, wherever it might be.

Anyway, I was at that telephone pole, about to descend to the sidewalk, when I looked down and over at the liquor store. Through the window I saw the robber pull a gun and watched poor old O'Malley raise his hands. I was down that pole in a flash. Before O'Malley had managed to get the cash register drawer open, I was in the store.

Since the crook had a loaded weapon, I drew the stiletto and pointed it. "Drop the gun and nobody gets hurt," I said. Well, my voice must've startled the guy, who was already hopped up on some of those drugs they take, and he turned and *fired* at me! Luckily, he was a very bad aim, but the bullet shattered the glass window on the storefront. I ducked down an aisle for cover—and the guy fired again at the bottles above my head. It was vodka or gin—I can't remember—but I was drenched. It took me days to clean it out of my suit.

"Call the police!" I shouted at O'Malley, but he was too scared to move. He kept his hands raised, fearful that the robber would turn back and shoot him out of spite.

I kept hidden, but I ran down the aisle and up the next one so I'd be behind the crook. The sight of me had shaken him pretty badly, so he wasn't thinking straight. I could hear exactly where he was, too. When I came around the edge of the aisle, his back was to me. He pointed the gun down the vacant aisle, wondering where the heck I was.

"Psst," I whispered.

As soon as he turned around, I punched him in the nose. Before a second had elapsed, I'd grabbed his gun hand and redirected it. Another round discharged, as I expected it would. From there it was easy to disarm him, hit him one more time, and send him to Dreamland.

I turned back to O'Malley and said, "*Now* will you call the police?"

He nodded, his hands still raised.

About two weeks after that, I was in the area they call SoHo, on Wooster Street between Spring and Broome. I was darting along from shadow to shadow, when I heard a woman scream. Pretty amazing that I heard it at all—the sound came from behind closed doors in an apartment above me. But I had an estimation of where it originated, so I stepped out into the street to look up at the building. I caught the movement of two silhouettes on a drawn shade over a window. A man and a woman. The body language told me all I needed to know—the man was threatening the woman with violence.

My lockpicks got me in the front door of the building. I ran up the stairs—three flights—and heard the couple arguing outside their door. She was hysterical, crying, "No, Jim, no!" I heard a slap.

I kicked the lock *once, twice,* and *three times* before the door flung open.

The couple stood there in the middle of the room, scared and shocked as all get-out. She was crying and obviously in a defensive position. The smell of booze was overpowering—the man was apparently a mean drunk.

I didn't ask questions. I simply went up to the guy and delivered two jabs and a cross. He was down before you could count to three.

Turning to the woman, I asked, "Are you all right? Did he hurt you?"

Much to my surprise, the lady went to *him*, knelt by his side, and tried to revive him. She looked at me and shouted, "That's my husband, you idiot. What did you do?"

I was dumbfounded. It was a situation I'll never understand—how could a woman let her man treat her like a punching bag and then defend him? It was the same way with my mother, I saw it with Lucy and Sam, and there it was again.

"He has no right to hurt you," I said.

She stood and pointed a finger at me. "Get out of here!"

I held up my hands. "Look, I'm just trying to hel—"

"I'm calling the police."

She went to the phone on the wall and started dialing.

Fine. Let 'em have their wedded bliss.

I left and was long gone before the cops got there.

By May, the newspapers were having a field day with the Black Stiletto. I read about incidents in which I allegedly took part, but was nowhere near. A couple of mob-related shootings were blamed on me. I had nothing to do with them. Some teenagers up in Harlem got hold of a gun and it accidentally went off. A kid was killed. They blamed it on the Black Stiletto, who had "shown up and tried to take away the weapon." You wouldn't believe the kind of dog poo I had to read about me. It was sickening.

Still, no one had managed to photograph the Stiletto. The police sketch from the Washington Square Park incident had stuck, so that was what every paper ran whenever I "made the news," even if it wasn't really me.

The police commissioner issued a statement saying the Black Stiletto would eventually be caught. I was a "menace, just as bad as the criminals I was pursuing."

Maybe I was, but I hadn't really done anything wrong from my point of view. One thing was for sure—the people didn't agree with the press. They were talking about me in a different light. I heard 'em, too. In the diner, on the subway, in the gym, and on the street the word was that the Black Stiletto was some kind of hero and the police should shut up and let her do her job.

My intention was to do just that.

19
Judy's Diary
1958

JULY 6, 1958

Well, dear diary, we are up to date. I can now begin writing entries as they occur instead of reflecting back on what's happened in the past. It's been a therapeutic—sometimes painful—exercise to write all that stuff down. But now I can move forward.

I suppose you could say I'm in an unusual position for a single twenty-year-old woman in New York City. Most women in the workforce are either secretaries or waitresses, and all the others are housewives. I've learned a lot in my short life about how the world treats women. Basically, we're considered inferior until it comes to childrearing, and that's what men want us to do. Have sex with them and raise their kids. That's it. Here in the big city, there's a prevailing illusion that women have wondrous opportunities to get a higher education or advance in a career. But in the end it's all the same—you work for the man, and by that I mean the *male*. It's even worse back in Texas. I was young when I left Odessa, but I saw it even then. Women were the doormats of life.

Sometimes during the day when I'm not working at the gym or training with Soichiro, I take walks along Madison and Fifth Avenues. I see and hear the working women on their lunch breaks—smoking cigarettes and gabbing about their bosses, complaining about their pitiful pay, wondering if so-and-so will ask them to get married, and I just feel sad. I'd never survive in that kind of environment. I could never be an office girl, answering phones, taking messages, fetching coffee, having an illicit tryst with the boss, even though that's what all the other women my age are doing. I don't like to smoke, either, and it seems that's a requirement to work on Madison Avenue. I tried it a few times and coughed my lungs up. Freddie smokes, so I'm used to the gym and our apartment smelling like cigarettes. That part I don't mind. Heck, everyone I know smokes. Lucy and Sam do. I don't think Soichiro smokes, at least I've never seen him. Maybe I'm wrong.

Those office ladies drink a lot, too, I've noticed. When they're out at lunch, they'll order one or two cocktails—sometimes three or four. If they're with "the men," they usually get completely plastered and go back to work that way because the guys do it. Me, I'll drink when I want, and I've done so since I turned eighteen. Freddie and I often have a drink at night if we're both at home. Lucy and I drink *a lot* when we're out on the town together. But I can't see drinking during the day, at lunchtime, when you're supposed to be working. I guess that's one of the many differences between me and all the other women I see around me.

One friend of Lucy's—a girl named Rebecca—works in one of those Madison Avenue buildings. It's an advertising firm, I think, or maybe a publisher. I can't remember. Anyway, a couple of weeks ago she was in the diner crying her eyes out because her boss, with whom she was having an affair, informed her that he'd decided not to leave his wife. So she's stuck working for him and dealing with a broken heart. She had to apply for a transfer and it might mean less money or a demotion. I felt sorry for her, but I also wanted to shake her and say, "Why the heck would you do that, knowing he was married?" I know I'm not in her shoes and sometimes people can't help what their hearts tell them to do—

look at me, I fell in love with a *gangster*, for Christ's sake—so I suppose I shouldn't be talking. The thing is, let's say Rebecca got married to this guy, he'd probably continue to have affairs with his secretaries and she'd still end up with a broken heart.

I don't want any of that. I'm happy where I am. I love working in the gym—and I'm probably the only woman in the city of New York, maybe the whole country—who can claim that privilege. The patrons at Second Avenue Gym used to give me a lot of "shit"—Freddie's word, not mine—by making fun of me, saying sexually suggestive things, you know. But now they mostly leave me alone. I've become "one of the guys." It's great.

And then there are my nighttime activities as the Black Stiletto, a whole other side of me. A secret identity. Most people would think leading a double life is dangerous, and it is, but it's just so exciting and fulfilling. I feel as if I'm contributing something to our society.

The only thing I don't have is romance, but right now I think that's something I can do without.

July 18, 1958

Something terrible happened last week, on the twelfth. Looking back on it, I probably should have played it differently, but no one has that kind of hindsight. Not even me, with all my heightened senses. All my acute hearing and intuition can't keep me from making stupid mistakes.

The Black Stiletto was out on the prowl. It was about eleven o'clock and I was on First Avenue and 23rd Street. The sky decided to suddenly open up and let loose with a downpour. I mean, it rained *hard*. I had to find shelter, and the first mistake I made was to step into a bar. Full of people. I don't remember the name of the place, but I thought—*why not?* They're just ordinary folks, having a drink, and I was something of a local hero. What could be the harm?

And, at first, it was very pleasant. You should have seen the faces when I walked in. There were maybe fifteen customers. Dean Martin was singing something on the radio, or maybe it was a jukebox, but I doubt that—the East Side Diner was the only place in town I knew that had a jukebox. Anyway, most of the clientele were men. There were two women. Everyone was amazed to see me. Someone asked if I was the real deal, and I told him, "Yes, I am." One guy asked me for an autograph. That was a first. I signed a paper napkin—*To Joey, lots of love, the Black Stiletto*. One woman was very excited to meet me. She told me she reads about all my exploits and cheers me on, and that I'm doing "good work." That made me feel good. More than one person offered to buy me a drink. I had a Scotch and soda the autograph guy paid for. Then a man with camera came up to me, told me his name was Max, and that he worked freelance for the *Daily News*. Could he have a couple of photographs? I thought it would be all right, especially since no photos of the Black Stiletto had ever been published. I knew Max would make a lot of money for the pics, too.

So I posed for photos in that bar. Max took shots of me alone—standing on a table, sitting, holding a drink, displaying my stiletto—and he snapped some of me and the customers together. There was even one of me kissing the bartender on the cheek—I think I'd finished my drink by then and was feeling good.

All the photos appeared in the paper the next day. And the next. Then they got syndicated and picked up by every major newspaper in the country. I hope that photographer made a fortune, because for the last week those pictures have been everywhere. I thought they were pretty good ones, too. Unfortunately, they remind me of the trouble that came afterward that night.

So there we were, having a great time in the bar—a bunch of neighborhood lushes and the Black Stiletto—when in comes a policeman. I swear everyone in the joint froze. The cop did a double take at me and then drew his gun. He said I was under arrest. Everyone in the bar told him to leave me alone, I wasn't hurting anyone. The cop insisted I was wanted by the law and he was going to bring me in.

The second mistake I made that night was to play along, humor him, and then try something sneaky. Maybe it was having the audience clearly on my side that gave me a false sense of security. I laughed, raised my hands, and told the crowd, "It's all right, folks. The nice police officer is just doing his job. I'm going to cooperate." There were cries of protest and even calls for me to run for it. I said, "No, I'm going with the nice policeman."

The guy still had the pistol trained on me. I went to him, my hands still raised, and then I swiftly kicked the gun out of his hands. The weapon flew across the room and discharged, scaring the bejesus out of everybody. No one was hit, though. Anyway, before the cop could react, I performed a *judo* maneuver on him and threw him over my back and onto a table. *Slam!* Then I ran outside.

It was still pouring down rain. I should have started running south; I probably could've avoided everything else had I done so. But I looked up at the building and noticed scaffolding attached to the side, going all the way up the five stories. Everything above the bar was residential—apartments. My idea was to climb the scaffolding, get on the roof, and make my way west to Second Avenue over the tops of buildings. That was the third mistake.

So I took hold of the poles on the scaffolding and started to climb. By then, some of the bar customers had come outside to see where I'd gone. They didn't notice me and I heard one guy said, "She must've got away."

I reached the scaffolding's second floor level, and something happened. My right boot slipped on the plywood that lay across the frame; it was just too wet. I tried to grab the pole, but it was also slippery and the friction between my glove and the metal wasn't good enough. It was like hanging on to a noodle.

I fell. Landed on my right leg and toppled flat on my face, right there in front of the group—just as the policeman joined them. I howled in pain. I sprained my ankle badly; at the time I thought I'd broken it. The policeman told everyone to stand back. There were cries of "She's hurt!" "Leave her alone!" "Call an ambulance!" "Is she okay?" But the cop—*not* a nice policeman, as it turned out—shouted at them to get back inside. They didn't, but the group gave him some room.

He had retrieved his gun and pointed it at me. He told me to slowly unsheathe my stiletto and toss it on the pavement. I had no choice but to do so. Then, with the gun still trained on me, he moved closer and *kicked* me on my injured leg! That caused the crowd to protest even more, and it just made me mad. The policeman then removed handcuffs from his belt. He ordered me to lie face down on the wet sidewalk and put my hands behind me.

The crowd turned ugly. "No!" "She didn't do nothing!" "Let her go!" "Boo!" "Stinking cops!"

With my stiletto on the ground in front of me, I continued to lie on my side, curved into a ball as I nursed my injured leg. The cop must've thought I was too hurt to try anything, so he didn't repeat the order for me to lie on my stomach. He bent over me, ready to snap on the cuffs. I reached into my left boot and drew my back-up weapon, the homemade wrist dagger. Grasping the handle firmly between my right thumb and the side of my index finger, saber-style, I lashed out and sliced the back of the cop's gun hand. That was my fourth and most serious mistake of the night.

The policeman dropped his gun and shouted. I leaped to my feat and *clobbered* him. I mean, I hit him hard on the side of the face and knocked the guy out. He went down, flat on his back. I picked up my stiletto and then I ran. Well, I limped. The crowd in front of the bar wasn't sure how to react. Some of them cheered me on. Others were a little shocked, I think.

I got away and made it home in one piece, which was a minor miracle. It was a painful journey. I even managed to climb the telephone pole on 2nd Street and hobble across the roofs to the gym building and slip inside my bedroom window. Once I was out of my costume, I wrapped my swollen ankle. The next morning, Freddie took a look and rewrapped it. Ordered me to stay off of it for several days. It's better now but it will probably take another week to get back to normal.

What isn't better is my relationship with the NYPD. I'm now wanted for resisting arrest and assaulting a police officer. Serious stuff.

The cops are really out to get me now.

20
Judy's Diary
1958

AUGUST 1, 1958

I saw Tony the Tank today. He came in the gym to see me. I'd spent the last couple of weeks working out and nursing my sprained ankle. It was nearly 99 percent healed. I told Soichiro about the sprain and that I wouldn't be in to see him for a couple of weeks. He tsk-tsk'd me but seemed to understand. I'm very close to obtaining my black belt. Probably in another month I'll have it. I just want to make sure my ankle is in perfect condition before I go on.

Anyway, Tony came in the gym and I was in the middle of spotting Jimmy with some new free weights we'd just purchased. At first I didn't recognize him—he'd lost a lot of weight. When he waved, though, I knew it was him. Suddenly all the memories of Fiorello that I'd swept under the rug came blowing back at me.

"Jimmy, I gotta see someone," I said, and then I went over to the front of the gym where Tony was waiting. We embraced and went through the "how ya doing, long-time-no-see" stuff, and then he asked if I had some time to get a cup of coffee with him. I checked the clock on the wall and figured I could take a break. I yelled at Freddie, who was coaching some young kids in the ring, and told him where I was going. He didn't care, as long as I came back. I think he was always afraid of losing me, not only as assistant manager, but as his substitute daughter.

So Tony and I went to the East Side Diner. Lucy was working and she sat us at a booth near the jukebox. Tony put some money in and played some of the more recent hit songs for me—"Purple People Eater" by Sheb Wooley, "Yakety Yak" by the Coasters, and "All I Have to Do is Dream" by the Everly Brothers. Tony teased me about liking that music. He was more of a Frank Sinatra and Dean Martin kind of guy.

"You're lookin' good, Judy," he said. I told him *he* looked fantastic, seeing as how he'd lost the weight. He was still heavy, but not as bad.

"Yeah, I hadn't been eatin' my usual amount of pasta and meatballs. And I been runnin' all over the place, doin' this, doin' that."

"Well, they say exercise is good for you," I told him.

We had coffee and talked about how he'd been in California doing some work for the family and was finally allowed to come back to New York. All perceived transgressions forgiven. As he spoke, I was thinking there was something he was avoiding, an important topic he wanted to bring up. He was nervous and fidgeted a lot. My intuition read him like a book. So I finally asked him straight out, "Tony, is there anything special on your mind?"

He lit a cigarette and said, "Yeah." He waited a few seconds and then said it. "Judy, the family's reorganized. You know, there's a new don and everything. What with all the organized crime hearin's in Washington goin' on, the family's kinda on the run. Movin' business west to places like Las Vegas and L.A."

"Yeah? Who's the new don?"

"His name is Franco DeLuca, Giorgio's little brother. You remember meeting him?"

"I don't think I ever did."

"Oh. Well, Franco's the new Don DeLuca."

"Okay." I didn't care. I wasn't involved with any of those people any more.

"Judy, I came here to warn you."

"What do you mean?"

"There's a price on your head. Franco's made it his mission in life to whack you."

I felt my stomach suddenly churn. "Me? Why me?"

His voice dropped to a whisper. "Because of who you are at night. You know, the Black Stiletto."

I swear my heart skipped a beat. *How did he know?* Jesus, I was real scared all of a sudden. "What are you talking about?" I asked him, trying to keep my cool.

"Judy, I know it's you. No one else does, though. At least, I don't think so."

I was real quiet for a long time.

"Judy, say somethin'."

"How did you find out?"

"I just put two and two together. I know you train at that gym and take those weird Jap fightin' lessons. Fiorello taught you how to use a knife—yeah, I know that, too, he told me. And I realized—*I'm* the one who told you Don DeLuca gave the order to clip Fiorello and the Ranelli boys did the job. I sure didn't tell anyone else. Just you. I figured it out."

In a way it made me a little angry that someone else besides Freddie knew the truth about me. But I couldn't blame Tony. It was my own dumb fault.

"So what happens now?" I asked.

"Nothin'. You just gotta be careful. I don't think the Black Stiletto should show her face, er, mask, er, you know what I mean. There are standin' orders to kill you on sight."

"Great. The Mafia wants to kill me, the NYPD wants to kill me. I'm quite the popular girl in town, aren't I?"

Tony shrugged with his hands. "Hey, you don't have to keep doin' all that stuff. You could make it go away by makin' *her* go away."

"Look, Tony, you're gonna keep this a secret, right?"

He looked at me like I was nuts. "Of course! Judy, I ain't no rat. I'd never tell 'em. I'd never tell anybody."

"Promise?"

"I swear on my mother's grave, bless her heart."

"Oh, I'm sorry, did she pass on? She lived in Italy, right?"

"She still does. She ain't dead yet. But you know what I mean."

"Tony."

"I swear, Judy. I'll never tell a soul. Your secret's safe with me."

"Okay, Tony. I'm countin' on you," I said.

Still, I was uncomfortable with the fact that two people—Freddie and Tony—knew I was the Black Stiletto. I remembered something my brother John once told me when I was little—once a secret is known by more than one person, it's no longer a secret.

21
Roberto
THE PRESENT

I found out for a fact our *thing* don't exist anymore. Not like it was, anyway.

The only guy from the old crew who was still around and easy to locate was Guido Rossi. He was a little younger than me, maybe by two years. I didn't know him all that well in the old days, but he knew who I was. I remembered him, though, as soon as I saw his beady eyes and long nose. His nickname was "Swordfish" because of the nose. Some of the guys would laugh at him and bring up the old Marx Brothers routine where "swordfish" was a password to get into a speakeasy durin' Prohibition. That's all I remembered about Guido. I never knew what he did for the family.

Guido was in a retirement home, one of those places they call "assisted living." I hope I never have to be in one of them fuckin' places. Not as bad as nursin' homes, but still pretty awful. Might as well be in Sing Sing.

You shoulda seen his face when he saw me. Well, at first he didn't recognize me. I went into the place and asked to see Guido Rossi, and the lady at the desk pointed to a room where some people were playin' cards and board games. My eyes landed right on him, and that's when I remembered who he was. Guido was in the middle of gin rummy with some other old geezer. I walked over to the table and said, "How's it goin', Swordfish?" Man, he nearly dropped his hand. Guido peered up at me and adjusted his glasses.

"It's Roberto Ranelli," I said.

His jaw dropped. I thought he'd lose his false teeth. When he realized I was tellin' the truth, he got up and gave me a big hug. I let him, although he smelled like piss. That's the trouble with those places. Everything smells like piss. Sing Sing smelled like a lot of things, not just piss, so at least there was variety.

We went over to a bench and talked. He treated me with respect, just as he shoulda. I asked him who was still around, that kind of thing. Guido said just about everyone was dead. He didn't know I was still alive. None of the family existed as a unit anymore. He told me he served a little time in the sixties, three years for racketeerin'. Got out on parole and good behavior. Three years is nothin'. I told him to try fifty.

I asked him where I should go if I wanted to work. He didn't have a clue. Told me the Russians and Eastern Europeans butted in and moved all the Italians out of organized crime. I said I could try joinin' their crew. He said, "With respect, Roberto, you're too old. They'd just laugh at ya."

He was probably right.

"You're retired," he said. "Enjoy your freedom."

I planned on it. As long as my money held out. Before I left, I asked him about Tony the Tank. Imagine how good it felt when I heard the guy was still alive—and livin' in Queens.

"Is that so? Tony and I, he was my *compare*," I said, even though I couldn't stand him back in the day.

"Oh, he'll be happy to see you then," Guido said.

He gave me what I'd been after all along: Tony's address and phone number.

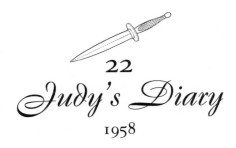

22
Judy's Diary
1958

AUGUST 12, 1958

Had a nightmare last night that really shook me up. It was about Douglas Bates and what happened to me back in Texas. The entire episode replayed in all its perverse glory, only this time I wasn't a little girl of thirteen. I was myself, grown, at age twenty. But I didn't know any of my self-defense moves. I mean, I *knew* them, but I couldn't remember how to do them or I was simply unable to perform. It's like the dream you have sometimes when you're running from someone or something and it feels like you're in quicksand and can't budge your legs. That's what it was like.

It was horrible.

This morning I started thinking again about taking a trip back to Odessa. For a solitary moment I missed my mother and brothers. I never did send that postcard. Mostly, though, the journey would be to visit Douglas. He and I have unfinished business.

AUGUST 14, 1958

I'm about to go out as the Black Stiletto, only without my disguise. It will be a first. *What do I mean?* you ask. Well, I'll tell you. I'm gonna spy on some spies. That's right! I overheard some Communist spies today and I'm gonna see what they're up to. But the only way I can do that is by appearing in public. So Judy Cooper is gonna do a little freelance work for the government this evening.

It started this afternoon at the gym. There was the usual crowd of men, training, exercising, and taking boxing lessons. I was busy repairing one of the sets of wall pulleys 'cause one of the springs had come loose. Freddie had shown me how to maintain all the equipment in the gym, so that was just another part of my job. Anyway, I was standing there with my screwdriver and pliers, when I overheard two men nearby. Actually, they weren't very close at all—maybe fifteen feet away—but my heightened hearing picked up on a few words that I thought were a little suspicious, so I intentionally eavesdropped.

One of the men was Eric Draper, a regular. The other guy was his guest, visiting the gym for the first time. I didn't know Draper except by sight. He was in his forties, balding, a bit of a paunch. He came to the gym twice a week to work feebly with some of the exercise equipment. The other man was maybe a little younger. I speculated he was probably in the military, for he had a crew cut and was in fine shape. He carried himself like an officer. Draper's body language indicated his guest was superior both in social and professional standings.

The words my ears picked up were: "documents," "State Department," "the revolution," "Cuba," "Castro," and "Khrushchev." Okay, they could've been diplomats or something like that, and they were simply discussing current events. We'd all been hearing about Cuba lately, how a revolution was brewing there, and that the Communists were supporting it. Khrushchev was the new guy in Russia. President Eisenhower was concerned, but so far the Cuban government seemed stable enough. I normally didn't pay much attention to world affairs; I most likely never would've paid any attention to the two guys had that stuff not been prominently in the news lately.

Additionally, it wasn't just the words I heard that were

shady—it was their demeanor. They talked in whispers, and I could see that Draper in particular was nervous. His eyes darted around the room and he kept turning his head to make sure no one was listening as they talked. Finally, I heard Draper say, "Let's go in the locker room, it'll be more private. We can talk there."

My God, these guys are Commies! The thought was alternately scary and exciting. Well, my curiosity got the better of me, so I had to listen in on the rest of their conversation. And I knew a way I could do it, too. Of course, I couldn't just go in the men's locker room. There was a limit to me being "one of the boys." But there was an adjoining closet where Freddie and I kept cleaning supplies, like mops. It was accessible from a hallway that shared a wall with the locker room. The employees' washroom—the one I used—and the office were along that same corridor. Gym patrons entered the locker room directly from the gym through a separate door. I was certain that with my acute hearing ability, I'd be able to follow the conversation with ease. So I put down my tools, left the wall pulley hanging there, went through the Employees Only door, and stepped into the hallway. I made sure no one was around, and then entered the closet. I turned an empty mop bucket upside down to use as a seat and then shut the door. Pitch-black. I could've turned on the light but I didn't want Freddie or anyone else to notice it and spoil the fun.

With my ear to the wall, I heard a shower running. After a moment, Draper and his friend entered the room. There were clangs of locker doors and small talk. The shower stopped. Wet footsteps and then greetings from Draper to the fellow who came out of the shower—Louis, one of our regulars. Draper introduced his friend as "Colonel Ward, visiting from D.C." More small talk, and then, "Colonel, why don't you go ahead and shower?" I figured Draper wanted Louis to leave before they finished their conversation. So I waited while Colonel Ward—I was right about him being in the military—showered. Draper and Louis shared more small talk and then Draper hit the showers. Finally, Louis left the locker room. After a couple of minutes, the colonel and Draper returned and sat on benches. Even though they spoke quietly, I could hear every word.

"What time is your flight back to Washington?" Draper asked.

"Nine a.m. tomorrow. I told you that."

"I guess the Pentagon can't function without you for more than forty-eight hours?"

"Hardly."

"Just want to make sure we'll have time for breakfast before you head out."

"No, you just want to make sure you get your cut. Come on, give me the details. When's this Pulgarón fellow arriving?" The colonel sounded testy.

"He should already be in town. He'll meet you tonight at the Plaza Hotel, in the Oak Bar. You know where it is?"

"Yes, yes."

"His flight from Cuba got in an hour ago if it was on time. He wanted you to meet him at nine tonight. I hope that's all right."

"I don't have a choice, do I? Why so late if he's getting in now?"

"I don't know. It's what Rafael requested."

"How will I know him?"

"Pulgarón is about thirty two, I'd say. Dark, tan. Looks like a movie star, I guess. Hell, he's from Cuba. Think Ricky Ricardo, only thinner."

"Fine," Ward said. "What do I do in the meantime? I don't like carrying around this stuff."

"What are you worried about? It's just a briefcase like everyone else has. Go out to dinner someplace nice off Fifth Avenue.

There are a lot of good restaurants in the area. Or you could go to the Plaza for dinner. I'd go with you, but I have to get back to the office. There's a report due tomorrow."

"Sounds like you're the one who's worried, Draper. Afraid of being seen with us, is that it?"

"N-n-no, that's not it at all. I have responsibilities. I'm sure you understand."

"Sure. Pulgarón better have the money, that's all I can say."

"He will. Just don't forget my, um, percentage?"

"We're meeting at six o'clock at my hotel, tomorrow morning, right?"

"Yes."

"Fine. Let's get out of here. This place makes me sweat."

"Colonel, I think that's the idea."

A locker door slammed shut. I heard footsteps and then silence. They'd left the locker room. I quietly stood and opened the closet door. All clear.

Back in the gym, I watched Draper and Colonel Ward go out the front door together. I went over to Freddie, who was working on the broken wall pulley.

"I was gonna finish that," I said.

He shrugged. "I didn't have anything else to do. Where were you?"

"Ladies' business."

Freddie nodded and made a silent "Oh" with his mouth.

"Hey, Freddie, you know that guy Draper that comes in here?"

"Yeah. What about him?"

"What kind of work does he do? Do you know?"

"He works at the United Nations. I'm not sure what he does there."

It's all I needed to know. From what I gathered, Draper was the liaison between Colonel Ward—who worked at the Pentagon—and some Cuban named Rafael Pulgarón. Something was being exchanged for money and it was all a big secret. Couldn't be good.

So in a few minutes I'm off to the Plaza Hotel to find out more.

23
Judy's Diary
1958

AUGUST 16, 1958

Continuing where I left off two days ago—

I dressed in one of the nice cocktail dresses I'd bought during a shopping trip with Lucy, put on stockings and heels, and applied makeup. I placed my stiletto and other items in a handbag and took that with me. Freddie saw me strutting out of the apartment and he whistled. That made me smile.

"You must have a hot date," he said.

"Maybe I do," I replied, winking at him. Then I went downstairs and out the door. Walked up a few blocks and over to Third to catch the bus going uptown, got off at 59th Street, walked west to Fifth, and then stood in front of the magnificent Plaza Hotel. I couldn't imagine staying in a room there; it was so fancy and expensive. I'd never even been inside. The hotel had been in the news a lot lately because of the success of a recent children's book featuring a little girl character named Eloise, who supposedly lived on one of the top floors. I hadn't read it. Not my thing.

I stood in front of the main entrance on 59th Street and watched the uniformed doormen. Like little soldiers, they helped people in and out of taxis and stood at attention. Very exquisite.

This was a new way of doing things for me, so I was a little nervous. A drink would help, so I went on inside. A doorman greeted me warmly and called me "madam."

The interior took my breath away. I felt as if I were in some sort of palace. The center of the lobby was an elegant sitting area surrounded by palm trees. Apparently this was the famous Palm Court I'd heard so much about. Again, a concierge called me "madam" and asked if he could help. I told him I was looking for the Oak Bar, and he pointed the way.

This room, too, was very stylish. It lived up to its name, for the walls were indeed made of oak paneling. Central Park was some sort of decorative theme, for not only did the bar's windows overlook it, but colorful murals depicting the park in different seasons of the year hung all around. A man played soft standards on a grand piano. The atmosphere was somewhat masculine but very pleasant. I took a seat at a vacant table near one of the windows. Before long, a waiter took my order for a gin and tonic.

At exactly nine o'clock, Colonel Ward entered. He was dressed in a suit and tie, and he carried a briefcase. The man scanned the room, frowned, and took a seat, coincidentally, at a table a few feet from mine. Eavesdropping was going to be easy. Although the bar was full of people and there was live music, it was a relatively quiet and relaxing place.

Five minutes later, Rafael Pulgarón came through the archway. Oh my Lord, he was handsome! I've always heard about "Latin lovers" being dreamy, and this man did not disappoint. He was probably my height, had black slick-backed hair, dark eyes, a mustache, and thin, cruel lips. The first thing he did was light a cigarette, as if he needed it for a prop. Then he, too, surveyed the room, and his eyes fell on Colonel Ward. The Pentagon man made a slight gesture with his hand and Pulgarón nodded. The Cuban joined Ward at the table.

"*Señor* Ward?"

"Yes."

"I am Rafael Pulgarón." The men shook hands. "Pleased to meet you. May I?"

"Yes, please."

I listened as the men ordered drinks and engaged in small talk. Nothing interesting, but I did enjoy Pulgarón's accent. I couldn't help stealing glances at him. He was so good looking. I hated the fact that he was a Communist spy. When you have images in your head of such men, they're usually ugly and sinister looking. It just goes to show you that anyone can be a bad guy.

After fifteen minutes or so, Colonel Ward finally asked, "Can we get down to business?"

Pulgarón replied, "Of course. I suggest we go up to my suite. Let me get this."

My heart sank. *His suite?* How was I going to eavesdrop?

I, too, gestured for the waiter to bring me the bill. It was the most expensive drink I'd ever had, but it was worth it simply to sit in such a prestigious place. But now it was time to go to work, with a great deal of improvisation involved.

The men got up and left the room. I followed closely behind, trying my best not to attract too much attention. When they got into the elevator, I slipped in at the last second. Besides Ward and Pulgarón, there were three other passengers. I was simply another guest of the hotel.

"Floor, madam?" the operator asked.

"I beg your pardon?"

"Your floor, madam?"

Oh, no! I thought. I wanted to get off on the same one as my prey. To my relief, the other guests called out their floor numbers, and then Pulgarón said, "Three."

"I'm three as well," I answered.

When we got there, the men expected me to get off first, so I did. I turned toward the corridor lined with rooms and walked ahead, praying that Pulgarón's room wasn't all the way at the end. Thankfully, I heard the Cuban unlock a door behind me. I turned slightly and saw them entering a room not far from the elevator. Good. I slowed my purposeful gait, turned around, and quietly stepped back to Pulgarón's suite. Then I stood there, my back to the wall, and my handbag in front of me to "dig through" in case someone appeared and wondered what I was doing all alone out in the hall.

My ears pricked up, tuning in on the men's voices, which I could hear through the door and wall. Pulgarón asked Ward to sit for a moment while he "retrieved" something from his bedroom. Probably the money.

Finally, the Cuban joined the colonel and their conversation went something like this—

Colonel: "Everything you requested is here. The documents are classified top secret, outlining the Pentagon's plans for Cuba. Eisenhower signed off on them, as you can see. They're copies, of course."

Pulgarón: "Very good, colonel." The Cuban ruffled through the papers. "*Si. Si.* Oh, this is good. And what is this?"

Colonel: "Oh, that's our nuclear capability with regard to Cuba. In other words, it shows you what we have aimed at your country." He laughed uncomfortably.

Pulgarón: "I see. *Señor* Khrushchev will be very interested in this."

Colonel: "You really think Castro and Guevara are going to succeed?"

Pulgarón: "There is no question. Batista and his regime will be on the run within months. But if Castro trades these documents to the Soviets for much-needed arms and equipment, Cuba will be in the hands of the revolutionaries a lot sooner. Maybe by October. This is very good indeed."

Colonel: "Fine. Now, what about my money?"

Pulgarón: "It's all here. You may count it if you wish."

Colonel: "Thanks. I think I will."

Pulgarón: "Take your time. I must make a phone call."

I heard the Cuban go into the bedroom; his voice became much fainter. It didn't matter much, for he spoke Spanish into the phone—I couldn't have understood him had he been right in front of me.

Suddenly, the elevator bell dinged! I froze.

An elderly couple came out and walked past me. I pretended to look through my handbag. "I know that key's in here somewhere." I muttered.

The couple didn't pay any attention to my "predicament." The man simply said, "Good evening," as they walked past. They unlocked and went through a door a little farther down the hall.

Then I heard movement behind Pulgarón's door. The two men were about to leave! I quickly skirted away from the door and went to the elevator. Next to it was a stairwell door, so I slipped through it just as I heard Ward and Pulgarón exit the suite.

Pulgarón was saying, "One more drink, but then I must retire. It's been a long day and I have another one tomorrow, getting back to Havana."

"I'm always up at the crack of dawn. Earlier, in fact," the colonel said. "You get used to it in the army."

The elevator arrived and they got in.

I emerged from the stairwell and pondered what to do next.

24
Martin
THE PRESENT

Had to put down the diary and go to work on Monday morning. Mondays are hell as a matter of course, but I knew this one would be particularly crappy when I walked in the office and found one of the secretaries in tears.

"What's wrong, Nancy?" I asked.

"Martin, Barbara just got laid off," she answered. Barbara was another office assistant, Nancy's best friend there.

"Oh, no. Gee, I'm sorry. Where is she?"

"Probably in the bathroom. I feel so bad for her."

So George had been right. Brad really was axing people. I went into my private office and saw the blinking red light on the phone. Picked it up, checked the voice mail, and learned that our fearless leader wanted to see me as soon as I got in. So I went.

Brad looked harried and more frown-faced than I'd ever seen him. His balding head was moist from perspiration. I guess firing people wasn't so easy for him.

"What's up, Brad?" I asked.

"Sit down, Martin." He indicated the empty chair in front of his desk.

Suddenly, I got a sick feeling in my stomach.

He wouldn't dare.

I sat. Brad opened a folder on his desk and studied some numbers. Kept me in suspense for a whole minute. Bastard.

"Martin, as you know, the firm has lost a lot of business over the past year. Our profits are down and we're not getting new clients at the rate we'd like."

"I'm aware of that. It's the damned recession."

"Yeah. Well, I have no choice but to make some cuts in staff. I hate to do it, but it's necessary."

I nodded. "I perfectly understand. Who are you letting go?"

"Well, you, for one."

I'm pretty sure I blinked a few times and looked like an idiot. "What?"

"We've talked about your performance, Martin. Your last two evaluations weren't up to the standards I ask of my senior auditors. We're giving you a month's notice."

"Brad, I've been with the company for nearly twelve years."

"And you have one of the highest salaries. I'm sorry, Martin, but it's the way it's got to be. Now we'll have Human Resources draw you up a nice severance package, and—"

Everything else he said just faded out. I was stunned. I'd fucking lost my job. Unbelievable. I never saw it coming. Blindsided.

Back in my office, I sat and stared at all my stuff—the computer, the filing cabinets, the knickknacks on the desk, and the two framed photos. One was Gina's beautiful senior picture, and the other was one of me and my mom, taken about twenty years ago. We were in front of our house in Arlington Heights. I was twenty-eight, I think. Mom looked great; her hair hadn't turned too gray yet. I forgot the occasion, but we had our next-door neighbor snap the picture.

I was really pissed off!

I thought, *screw it*, I wasn't about to stay in the office that day and work. I had vacation and personal days left, so I got up and left. Told Nancy I wouldn't be back until tomorrow.

As I drove home on Deerfield Road, I cursed and shouted and

hit my fist on the steering wheel. I wanted to strangle Brad. Son of a bitch. I wasn't a slacker. He expected way too much from his employees, always did.

What was I going to do?

Well, hell, there was always a need for accountants. I'd find another job. A better one. I'd look in the classifieds when I got home. I still had the Sunday paper. I could call a headhunter I knew.

Yet, I was worried.

The BMW passed Woodlands North and I had a sudden compulsion to see my mom. So I parked the car and went in. She was sitting in the common area of the Alzheimer's unit. Some kind of nature program was on the television. The residents sat and stared at it, my mom included. "Hi, mom!" I called cheerfully as I approached. She looked at me, again with that blank look, but I thought there might be a hint of recognition in her eyes.

"Hello," she answered dully.

"How are you today?"

"Okay."

"What you watching?"

She turned back to the TV and nodded. Didn't answer the question.

"You feel like walking around a bit? I'll walk with you and you can hold my arm?"

She seemed to like that idea. I helped her stand and we took a few steps away from the chair. Her legs were like sticks now, but they seemed to be strong enough. As I've indicated before, her body was still fit—she'd just lost a lot of weight in the last few years. Walking back and forth in the unit was one of our pastimes when I came to visit. She seemed to enjoy it, and I also think she liked putting her arm through mine. We always strolled slowly, going down the hall toward her room. From there we turned around and went the other direction. After five or six repetitions, she'd indicate one way or another that she was tired and we'd stop. So much for the day's entertainment. I had to appreciate what little time I had with her, in whatever way it came.

As we walked, I dared to bring up the subject of her past again.

"Do you remember living in New York City, Mom?"

She was quiet for a moment, but then she answered, "Yes."

"I'll bet that was an exciting place to be in the nineteen fifties, huh, Mom? What kind of things did you do? Did you have a job?"

She stopped walking and gave me a funny look. As if she was asking why I wanted to know such a thing.

"Never mind, Mom, let's keep walking."

She put her hand through my arm again and we continued. After a pause I tried again.

"Hey, Mom, did you ever see the Black Stiletto? A lot of people in New York saw her in person in those days. On the street. Did you ever have a sighting?"

Suddenly, Mom pushed away from me. "Who are you?" she hissed.

"Mom!"

"What do you want? Go away!"

Her eyes flared with anger, or fear, or *something*. I'd never seen that expression on her face before.

"Mom, I'm your son! I'm Martin!"

She started breathing in fast, shallow breaths, and I *swear* it looked as if she was about to hit me. Her body actually changed posture for a brief moment, assuming some kind of strange stance with her arms up and legs apart. Some kind of deeply rooted reflex, a mechanism of self-defense.

I put up my hands, palm out. "Mom, calm down. It's just me, your son."

It took several seconds, but she eventually relaxed and put her arms down. Her body language and facial expression transformed back to the sick, confused old woman who lived in a nursing home.

"Shall we continue?" I asked, holding out my arm. She slowly put her hand on it and we continued our walk.

I thought it best not to mention the Black Stiletto to her again.

25
Judy's Diary
1958

I used a lockpick to open Pulgarón's door. Considering the exclusiveness of the hotel, I found it surprisingly easy to do. Once inside, I figured I had at least ten minutes to prepare. The suite was exquisite—it consisted of a sitting area and a view that looked over Fifth Avenue, a large bathroom, and a bedroom with a king-sized bed. I imagine it cost a fortune.

This is going to sound sordid, but I had to admit I found Rafael Pulgarón very attractive. The blood surging through my body felt as if it were on fire. So I took off all my clothes, removed the stiletto from my handbag and hid it, and got into the bed. It seemed so *illicit*, feeling the soft linens against my skin. It was the most daring thing I'd ever done in my life. I was nearly dizzy from the thrill.

It was a half hour before the Cuban returned to the room. I thought I'd die of anticipation. Finally, though, I heard his key in the door and he entered. He lingered in the sitting room for a moment, completely unaware I was in his bedroom. I couldn't stand it anymore, so I lightly cleared my throat to get his attention.

Rafael Pulgarón stepped through the door, and you should have seen the look of surprise on his face! There I was, naked under the sheets of his bed. He said something in Spanish I didn't understand. Realizing his mistake, he said, "Who are you? What are you doing in here?"

"Hi," I said. "I don't speak Spanish. Is that all right?"

"Answer my question, please."

"My name is Eloise." It was the first name to pop into my mind. I'd been thinking about that children's book earlier. I don't think he knew the reference. "And I already know your name, Rafael."

He didn't know whether to run, kill me, or get in bed with me. After all, he was in the country performing a dangerous and illegal task. And I knew his name. I attempted to put his mind at ease by saying, "I overheard you talking to that man earlier, in the bar downstairs. When I saw you, I knew I had to meet you. So here I am."

Pulgarón squinted at me and then smiled. He wagged a finger at me. "I remember seeing you there. You were at the table next to us. You kept glancing in my direction."

"I hope I didn't distract you."

"You did distract me. You would distract any man, I think."

"Oh, is that a compliment?" I asked, fluttering my eyes. I couldn't believe I was playing the role of a *tramp* so well!

"It is."

"Well, I think you're very handsome, Rafael. I couldn't resist meeting you."

He stepped farther into the room. His eyes moved up and down the shape of my body beneath the sheets. "And this is how you meet men? How did you get in?"

"Oh, I've *never* done this before, Rafael! That's the truth, God be my witness. I bribed a bellboy to let me in. It cost me a dollar and a kiss on the cheek. The kiss came first; otherwise I doubt I would have gotten anywhere with my request."

He laughed and wagged his finger at me again. "You are a very naughty girl, Eloise!"

"Why, did I do wrong?" I put on the sweetest Marilyn Monroe voice I could muster. In my mind I conjured up an image of the actress in *The Seven Year Itch* and tried to mimic her. "*Señor*

Pulgarón, I don't think it's wrong to go after what you want, do you? When something is as *irresistible* as you are, a girl can't help herself!"

The flattery was working. He sat on the bed and placed a hand over the sheet on my leg. As he spoke, he gently caressed it. "Eloise, how do I know you're telling the truth? You are not working for someone else, are you?"

My intuition indicated he was indeed suspicious, but that he wouldn't hurt me. Not yet, anyway. So I feigned confusion. "What do you mean? Working for someone else? I don't understand."

Pulgarón shook his head. "Never mind."

I tried to act hurt. "You think I'm lying to you? You don't like me?"

"No, no, it's not that," he said. "I do like you. I like you very much."

I switched over to the Marilyn voice again. "Then what are you sitting there for? Why don't you join me?"

He did exactly as I hoped. Pulgarón stood and began to undress. I watched him with fascination. The spider had lured the fly into the trap, and I felt a surge of pleasure flow through my body. How far was I willing to let this go?

As soon as he was completely vulnerable, I threw back the sheet. His eyes flared as he gazed upon me, and I knew I had him. He got into bed beside me. I let him kiss me, for I have to admit being curious about him. He tasted of the liquor he'd had earlier, but otherwise his musky scent was very appealing. And he was a good kisser. I almost hated to end it.

I reached beneath my pillow and pulled out the stiletto. With a flash so quick that he didn't have time to blink, I held it to his neck and whispered, "All right, you Commie fink, don't make a move. Don't make a sound. You try anything and this blade will pierce your skin faster than you can say, '*Olé!*'"

He froze with a priceless look of shock and dismay on his face. I rotated my body around and straddled him. With my free hand, I reached behind the headboard, where I'd stashed the rope. In three minutes, he was tied spread-eagle to the bed, exposed and helpless.

I then got up and put on my clothes. He watched me with hatred in his eyes. An outpour of Spanish erupted from his mouth, but I ignored him. A quick search produced the documents Colonel Ward had given him, and I laid them on the bed between his legs. I found some stationery on the desk in the living room and scribbled a note—"Compliments of the Black Stiletto." This I placed on top of the classified material. I made sure I had everything I came with, except the rope, of course, and then went to the in-room phone—another luxury the Plaza provided its guests. I dialed the operator. When she answered, I asked her to place a call to the FBI. When I was finally connected to an agent, I explained there was a Cuban spy in the Plaza Hotel who had stolen classified military documents from the Pentagon. That Colonel Ward was the man who had sold the material to Pulgarón, and they would find everything in the Cuban's suite. Before the FBI agent could ask questions, I hung up and left the room. Avoiding the elevator, I took the stairs to the ground floor and quickly exited the hotel.

I wasn't too concerned that Pulgarón had seen my face—and that's not all, ha ha. I didn't think there was any way he'd be able to identify me.

It was the most fun I ever had.

26
Judy's Diary
1958

AUGUST 18, 1958

The next morning—yesterday—there was nothing in the papers about Pulgarón. I wondered what the heck had happened. Had he gotten away? Had I messed up somehow? It wasn't until today that the front page of every New York newspaper displayed headlines about Pulgarón's arrest and the interception of Colonel William Ward at Idlewild airport on his way back to Washington, D.C. COMMUNIST SPIES CAUGHT! proclaimed the *Daily News*. FBI FOIL ESPIONAGE PLOT screamed the *New York Times*.

Apparently not long after I'd left the Plaza, several FBI agents swarmed the building and insisted on entry to Pulgarón's suite. He was found as I'd left him—naked and tied to the bed, along with the incriminating documents. The Cuban was arrested and questioned, and I suspect they quickly figured out where the classified material came from and nabbed the Pentagon man before he boarded his flight.

The *Times* went into more detail about Pulgarón's arrest, saying that an "unidentified female" called the FBI office with the tip. It was the only mention of my involvement. Needless to say, I was annoyed. They could have given me a little credit. I wonder what Pulgarón told them about me. "There was a naked woman in the bed! She got the best of me and tied me up!" Ha ha, I'm sure they enjoyed that confession.

There wasn't any news about Draper, though. I hope I did the right thing last night. Yesterday when there hadn't been any coverage of the arrests, I decided to do something about Draper's role in the scheme. So I looked up his records in our membership files, noted his address, and thought perhaps he could use a visitor. (PS—I still need to figure out how the Black Stiletto can make daylight appearances. It just isn't practical trying to change clothes in a phone booth—I don't understand how Superman does it!)

After dark, the Black Stiletto made her way all the way up to York Avenue and 83rd Street, where Draper lived in a brownstone. It took a long time, flitting from shadow to shadow on foot. I think it was the most distance I'd traveled as the Stiletto. Luckily, Manhattan's East Side was more conducive to stealth, for it was more residential and neighborhood-oriented than the West Side. The most difficult parts are crossing the major cross-streets like 34th Street, 42nd Street, 57th. Usually I don't use the intersections. It works best to dart through the moving traffic in the middle of a block.

It was around ten thirty when I got to Draper's building. I found his name on the downstairs intercom box, noted the apartment number, and then used my lockpicks to get in the front door. It was a walk-up, all the way to the fifth floor—but I was in great shape; it didn't wind me at all.

Listening outside his door, I heard classical music—a record he was playing on a phonograph. I didn't know the title, but it was a famous piece. The one with the cannons going off at the music's climax. Isn't that a patriotic tune? I found that ironic. Anyway, I knocked on his door, stood to the side so he couldn't see me through the peephole, and waited.

"Who is it?" Draper called.

"Eloise," I said. *Why not?* I thought.

"Who?"

"I'm a friend of Rafael Pulgarón."

Dead silence. I could sense the sudden fear emanating from behind the door. What could he be thinking? He didn't know about Pulgarón's arrest—no one did, not last night.

Finally, I heard the sound of a lock turning. The door swung open and I pushed inside.

Draper yelled in terror when he saw me.

I slammed the door shut behind me and said, "Shut up!" I pointed to a chair. "Sit down. Now."

"W-w-wait!" he stammered. "You can't do this. What do you want with me?"

"I said *sit down*!" I found I could be pretty dominating when I wanted. He did as he was told. "You know who I am?" He nodded. "Good. Don't move," I added. Then I walked slowly around the apartment—two rooms and a bath. Small, but comfortable. I stuck my head in the bedroom just to make sure we were alone. There was an open suitcase and a pile of folded clothes on the bed. He'd been in the process of packing.

"Going somewhere, Draper?" I asked.

Sweat poured freely from his bald head. "What?"

"Are you deaf? I asked if you're going somewhere."

"Um, yeah. I'm on vacation. I'm going to Canada."

"Canada? What's in Canada?"

"N-n-nothing. I'm just going there."

"Rafael didn't know you were going on vacation. Neither did Colonel Ward."

At the mention of the second name, his eyes *really* bulged.

"How was your breakfast this morning with the colonel?" I asked him. "Did he give you what you wanted?"

Draper was too frightened to speak. He couldn't believe I

knew his secret. I removed a coil of rope from my knapsack and proceeded to tie him to the chair. "Don't worry, I ain't gonna hurt you," I said. "Just want to make sure you stay put while I have a look around."

"W-what do you want? I'll pay you!"

"Pay me for what? I don't want any of your treason money." I finished securing him with heavy knots, and then I patted his sweaty bald head. "Now you stay quiet and I won't have to gag you."

I went to the bedroom and examined the suitcase. Sure enough, he had stuck several stacks of currency in brown envelopes that lay under clothing on the bottom of the luggage. I started counting, but I gave up when I got to six thousand. That wasn't even half of it.

Returning to the living room, I said, "Draper, do you know what happened last night?" He shook his head. "Rafael was arrested at the Plaza." Another wave of terror passed behind his eyes. "And Colonel Ward was picked up at Idlewild this morning, right after your breakfast. Now, what I want to know is why no one has come to get you. Surely Pulgarón or Ward would rat on you to get a better deal for themselves? What have you got on them? And why the sneaky escape to Canada, or wherever you're going? Talk to me. I'm a good listener."

He was quiet for a long time. I stayed patient, but finally, I simply drew the stiletto from its sheath. I ran my finger along the blade and said, "Well?"

"There's no evidence against me," he said, hoarsely. "All I did was introduce them. I was the liaison, that's all. There's nothing a court of law could charge me with."

"What about all that money in your suitcase?"

He hadn't realized I'd found it. Still, he remained stubborn. "All I did was introduce two men. Whatever business they conducted with each other was no concern of mine."

I could tell he was hiding something. I've always been good at flushing out liars. So I went back in the bedroom. Examining the suitcase more closely, I noticed some odd stitching on the inside perimeter of the lining. It had been resewn. So I slashed it with the stiletto and ripped it open, revealing a large envelope.

Maybe I've led a sheltered life or something, but the photographs I found inside truly shocked me. It was something I've always heard about, but never seen with my own eyes.

They were pictures of Colonel Ward and Draper. In bed. Need I say more?

I brought them back to the living room and dropped them at Draper's feet. The man reacted in horror to my discovery. He actually started crying.

"So, it's the other way around, isn't it? Pulgarón had these pictures of you and the colonel. That's why you both cooperated?" The poor man nodded. "So why doesn't he name you in the conspiracy? He's in jail as a foreign spy. Why haven't they come for you yet?"

"I don't know," he said softly. "He's a very proud man." Draper continued to cry. "He was supposed to phone me when he got to Havana. When I didn't hear from him, I started to pack. I didn't want to take any chances. Billy won't name me."

"Who?"

"The colonel."

"Oh." The newspapers had called him William Ward. I got it.

"I guess it *is* only a matter of time before Rafael tells all," Draper sobbed.

"I would think so. Look. I'll make a deal with you." The poor man raised his head and looked at me hopefully. "I'm gonna make a call to the FBI. You're gonna turn yourself in. You're gonna admit your role in this scheme."

"No!"

"Wait." I held up my hand. "In return, I'll take these photos with me and destroy them. Who has the negatives?"

"Rafael!"

"Well, I doubt he has them on him. They're probably in Cuba, right?"

"I guess so."

"What are the chances of other people knowing who the people in those pictures are?"

"I don't know. Slim, I think."

"That's what I think, too. The negatives are probably hidden in a safe place, and I don't think Pulgarón is gonna be retrieving them anytime soon. By the time someone finds them, no one's gonna know who you are or care. Now, isn't that a fair trade?"

"Not really."

"Okay, then I'll leave the photos on the floor and still call the FBI. Either way you're going to jail."

"No!"

"Well?"

"All right, I'll confess!"

"Yeah?"

"Yes!"

I went to his phone and dialed *O*. Went through the rigmarole of getting connected to the FBI again. The same agent answered the line. I asked him for his name, and he replied that it was Richardson. Once more, I told Agent Richardson about a U.S. traitor, trussed up in his apartment. I held the phone to Draper and nodded at him. He spoke slowly and succinctly, but he confessed it all. How he worked at the U.N., had met Pulgarón on a flight to Cuba, and one thing led to another. When he was done, I spoke to Richardson again. After I revealed Draper's address, I said, "Listen, Agent Richardson, I'm the Black Stiletto. I better get some credit for busting this spy plot, don't you think?"

"That's not up to me, ma'am," Richardson answered. "But I'd

appreciate it if you give me your real name and address. We'd like to talk to you."

I laughed aloud. "Nice try, buster. See you in the comic books." I hung up, grabbed Draper's photographs, and stuck them in the envelope. The traitor cried again. I felt kinda sorry for him, but he was still a Commie spy. I patted his head and said, "Take care of yourself, Draper."

As I made my way home to the gym, I tore the photos into tiny pieces and left them in a trashcan here, a trashcan there, and so on, all the way down to the East Village.

Like I said, I was a little miffed when I saw the papers this morning and the Stiletto wasn't mentioned. And neither was Draper. That concerned me, too.

I went outside to a pay phone, called the FBI, and asked to speak with Agent Richardson. When he finally answered, I told him who I was.

"Yes, ma'am, what can I do for you?"

"My, you're polite. Did you pick up the package I left for you last night?"

"We did. Thank you for the tip."

"You're welcome. I didn't see anything in the papers about him."

"That's right. We're keeping his arrest under wraps for now."

"Oh? Why?"

"He's a bigger fish than the others. United Nations and all. Sorry, I can't reveal more. Oh, and by the way, we found Mr. Pulgarón dead in his cell last night. He'd hung himself."

At first I was stunned. Was Richardson telling the truth? Had the Commie really committed suicide or was he the victim of an "accident?" In all honesty, I didn't care much. After all, the guy *had* seen my real face. Now there was no one who could identify me.

"I see," was all I said about that. Then I asked him, "Any reason why I didn't get any credit for these arrests?"

"Ma'am, you're a fugitive wanted by the NYPD. The FBI can't very well tell the world you're the one who gave us the tips, now could we?"

"I suppose you're right, but it's not really fair, is it?"

"Can't help it, ma'am."

"I hope you're not going to hurt Mister Draper. He's the sensitive type."

"We'll take good care of him, ma'am."

"Thank you. You're a nice man, Agent Richardson. Maybe someday we'll meet."

"I'm sure we will."

We will?

"Nice talking with you. Goodbye."

I hung up and went back to the gym. It sounds silly, I know, but I was hoping I'd get some press for what I did. Was it naïve to think it might help my standing with the cops? I guess it was. But by writing it all down—all the events of the past couple of days—at least that's made me feel better. It was satisfying enough, knowing I helped put away some Reds.

Score one for America.

27
Roberto

THE PRESENT

I found where Tony was livin' in Queens, just where Guido said. The guy was in a dump almost as awful as mine. A ground-floor apartment in Astoria, not too far from the park. Crappy neighborhood. I guess the rent was cheap. Saw Tony leave his building. Tony the Tank had become a fat old man. He walked with a cane. Went down to the corner grocery store, slowly strolled back to his buildin' with a shoppin' bag in one hand and the cane in the other. I didn't feel sorry for him.

This was gonna be easy.

I crossed the street and approached him from behind, just as he unlocked the front door to his buildin'. I reached beyond him and held the door open for him.

"Thanks," he said, barely lookin' at me.

"My pleasure, Tony," I replied.

He turned his head at me again and squinted. Maybe his eyes weren't so good. "Do I know you?" he asked.

"You sure do. It's me, Roberto. Roberto Ranelli."

He dropped his bag of groceries. "Oh, lemme get that for you," I said, so I did.

We stood there in the open doorway for what seemed like a whole minute. He was speechless. Finally, I said, "You gonna ask me in, or what?"

"Uh, sure, Roberto. Come on in. It's good to see you."

I followed him down a dingy hallway to a room at the back, carryin' his groceries. He unlocked the door and we went inside. Just a studio apartment. Smelled like cat litter. Sure enough, there were two of the mangy things, slinkin' around and makin' them noises. I hate cats. I used to hunt stray cats when I was a kid and have some fun with 'em when I caught 'em. Gave me practice for what I'd do to my enemies later on.

"I heard you were gettin' out," Tony said. "It was in the paper, did you know that?"

"No. Why would they put it in the paper?"

"Just a small item. It made more of the fact you'd been in for fifty years or whatever it was. Now you're out and you're, what, seventy-something?"

"Seventy-eight."

"Yeah. How do they think a man can get a job at our age? And when you can't, what do they think you can live on?"

"You sayin' I'm better off in prison, Tony?"

"No, Roberto, I'm not sayin' that. Sit down. You want coffee?"

"Nah. Thanks." I took one of two chairs at a small dinin' table.

"I'm gonna make some for me. You sure?"

"I'm sure."

Tony went over to his gas stove and boiled water. He had one of those cup thingies with a filter that you put on top of a mug. I watched and waited.

"So where you livin'?" he asked.

"Brooklyn. Got a place kinda like yours."

"A dump? You live in a dump, too? Is that what happens to all us old gangsters?" He laughed. I didn't. "Not many of us still around, Roberto."

"I know."

"Actually, I can't think of anyone else. Do you know of anyone?"

"I saw Guido Rossi."

"Oh, yeah. I forgot about Guido. How's Guido doin'? Haven't seen him in a long time."

"He's alive. Still."

"Good for him." Tony finished makin' the coffee and sat down across from me. "So to what do I owe this wonderful visit?" he asked.

"Nothin'. Just came to see you is all."

"Well, thank you, Roberto. I appreciate it."

"Actually I wanted to know somethin'."

"What? If I know the answer, I'll be happy to tell you." He lifted the mug of coffee to his mouth.

"Is Judy Cooper still alive?"

Tony spurted the hot liquid. I guess I touched a nerve. He put the cup down and wiped his mouth, pretendin' it was nothin'. "Judy who?"

"Judy Cooper."

"I don't know a Judy Cooper."

"Sure you do. You did. She was Fiorello Bonacini's girlfriend, remember? The good-lookin' dame from Texas?"

"Oh, yeah! Golly, Roberto, I haven't thought about her in years. In, like, *forever.* Why in the world would you want to know if she's still kickin'?"

"Kickin'. I like that, Tony. Kickin' is the right word for her, ain't it."

"Huh?"

"Why do you think I wanna find her, Tony?"

"I don't know."

"So answer me. Is she still alive?"

The man looked away, sipped his coffee. "How should I know? I haven't seen her since Kennedy was president."

"You know where she lives, Tony?"

"Couldn't say."

"Can't say or won't say?"

"Roberto. Jesus, what's this all about?" He turned to me as he put his mug on the table. His hands were shakin'. He was hidin' somethin'.

I stood and went around the table. I picked up his cane, held it in both hands, and placed it across the front of his neck.

"Roberto! What are you doin'? Hey!"

I pulled the cane, chokin' him a little. He struggled and gasped and made all the right noises. Then I stopped. He coughed and spit and wheezed.

"You know where she is, Tony," I said. "And you'd better tell me."

"Roberto, I don't know nothin', I swear." He was really scared now. Tremblin' like a frightened puppy. He'd placed his hands on the table and nervously fiddled with his fingers. I popped the cane down hard on 'em. He yelled. I'm pretty sure I broke some of the bones in his right hand. I didn't care if he attracted anyone's attention. If someone came, I'd just hurt them, too. Tony musta seen I meant business. He said, "Okay, okay, Roberto. Hold on. Wait." He held his hurt hand under his arm and rocked back and forth. "Why didja do that, Roberto? Fuck, Roberto. It hurts!"

"Of course it hurts. That's the idea," I said. "You gonna tell me what I want to know or you want me to break the other one?"

"No, no, I may have somethin'. Just a minute. Please. Don't hit me again."

"I'm waitin'." I didn't want to let on I was feelin' a bit of pain in my chest from all the excitement. Damn heart murmur.

He stood and went to a nightstand by his crummy bed. Opened a drawer with his good hand, reached in, and pulled out a couple of envelopes. "I might have somethin' here from Judy. It's really, really old." Tony sat on the bed, pulled off a rubber band, and started goin' through 'em. I stood there and watched. I shoulda taken 'em from him, but I didn't. I was stupid.

Eventually he picked out three envelopes. I wasn't sure what the hell he was doin' at first, but he started tearin' a strip off the top of each one. Maybe I thought he was gonna give me the pieces. I was dumb, 'cause as soon as he'd torn corners off all three en-velopes—*he stuck 'em in his mouth and swallowed 'em.*

"You piece of shit!" I shouted. I struck him several times with the cane and he rolled over onto the floor. I quickly grabbed the torn envelopes and realized what he'd done. He'd ripped off the return addresses and postmarks and then ate 'em. I went through the rest of the letters, but they were from people I didn't know. I took a card out of one of the envelopes. It was a birthday card and she'd written, "Hi Tony, I hope this finds you well. Will write more later." Signed it "Judy." The other two were handwritten letters. I read 'em, but there wasn't a single clue about where she lived when she wrote 'em.

I beat Tony to death anyway and left his buildin'.

28
Judy's Diary
1958

NOVEMBER 12, 1958

Something bad has happened, dear diary, and I'll tell you about it
in a minute. First, let me bring you up to date. I've been *very* re-
miss in writing!

The Black Stiletto kept a low profile through the rest of
August, September, October, and the first half of November. I
went out a few times and nothing happened. Didn't see a single
crime being committed. So I concentrated on getting my black
belt in *karate*—which I did—and saving up money by working
in the gym. Soichiro seemed to be more proud of me than I was
of myself. I don't think he ever had a female student like me before. After I was awarded the black belt in front of my class, he
asked me to stay for a few minutes. When the other students had
left, he broke out a bottle of Japanese liquor he called *sake*. He
poured a couple of tiny cups for each of us, saying we should cel-
ebrate my achievement. The *sake* tasted sweet and sour at the
same time, if that's possible. It was good, though.

Another thing I did during the last three months was revise
my disguise. It needed to be something I could change in and out
of when I was away from home. Something portable. I also
wanted something more appropriate for warmer weather. My first

costume was perfect when the temperature was frigid, but it was a sweatbox in July.

The solution was simple—thinner leather. It also had short sleeves, but the matching gloves came up to the midway point of my forearms. Otherwise it looked exactly like my winter equivalent. Instead of tight leather pants, however, I opted for black leotards. I could wear them with a skirt or dress and they looked like colored stockings, which, in fact, they were. I found some shorter boots at Bloomingdale's that worked perfectly. I could wear them with civilian clothes and no one knew any better. When all was said and done, I could keep my mask/hood and utility belt in the knapsack, which I could wear on my back just like a college student. I figured in the winter I could go back to wearing the trench coat over my warmer costume if I wanted to be capable of becoming the Black Stiletto at a moment's notice.

Now on to the business at hand.

Yesterday I went to the East Side Diner for breakfast. I knew Lucy was working the morning shift, so I thought it'd be fun to go see her. Well, I was shocked as all get-out to see she had a black eye. A real shiner, as they call it at the gym.

"Lucy! What happened to you?" I asked her, but she didn't want to talk about it. I let her serve my food, but she looked like she might cry. Someone put a coin in the jukebox and played that new song, "Volare." I never can remember the name of the Italian singer who does it. Anyway, when I was done eating, she took a short break and sat with me in my booth. "Are you gonna tell me what's wrong?" I asked again. But I knew. It was the same old problem, rearing its ugly head.

"It was Sam, wasn't it," I said. She nodded as a tear ran down her cheek. I got mad. I started feeling my blood boil the way it does when I see an injustice.

"It was my fault," she said. "I accused him of being with another woman."

"And was he?"

"I think so. I found lipstick on his collar, and it wasn't mine. And he comes home smellin' of perfume I don't use."

"That bastard!"

"Still, it was my fault. I shoulda kept my mouth shut."

"It is *not* your fault! He has no right to hit you. No matter what. The only reason he could have to hit a woman is if she's coming at him with a gun or a knife."

I hadn't been out with the two of them recently. Sam and I didn't get along anymore. I'd called him on his shenanigans once too often. If he knew I would be anywhere they were going, Sam opted to stay home. He and Lucy were living together now; had been for a few months.

Then, out of the blue, Lucy whispered, "Judy, I have to leave him."

"I'll say."

She shook her head. "You don't understand. I have no place to go. My parents didn't like me moving in with Sam, so they won't let me come home. Besides, I wouldn't want to. I want to stay here in Manhattan."

"So find another apartment. You had one when I first met you."

"I know. I'll have to start looking. I'm not very good at that. I hardly have any time and not a lot of money, either. And if Sam found out, he'd kill me. I mean, *really* kill me. He's very possessive. Won't let me do anything without him knowing about it."

"Sam's a jerk," I said. "Lucy, I've been telling you this all along. Leaving him will be the best thing you can do."

"There's . . . there's something else."

"What?"

"I . . . I met somebody."

I blinked and then smiled. "You mean another man?" She nodded. "Well, talk!"

"His name is Peter. He's—well, he's got money."

"Really! What's he do?"

"He's a lawyer. Works at one of those big firms on Wall Street."

"How'd you meet him?"

"In *here*, if you can believe it. He was just having lunch one day with a colleague. Before he left, he asked me for my phone number. Well, he couldn't very well call me at Sam's place—"

"You mean your place. It's your place, too. You live there."

"Judy, you know what I mean. If another man called me and Sam knew, he'd wring my neck."

"So what did you do?"

"I told him flat out I wasn't available. But he came back the very next day and turned on the charm. Brought me flowers, can you believe that? So, on my break, we went for a walk. He's so nice, Judy. I really like him."

"So leave Sam and move in with him," I suggested with a laugh.

"I can't do that and you know it. Besides, Pete is an up-and-coming lawyer and everything. He wouldn't want to live with a girl and not be married. It wouldn't look good. Not everyone is as free-spirited as you or me, Judy."

She was right. I hardly knew any unmarried couples who lived together. It just wasn't done. I was unusual when I lived with Fiorello, and I guess Lucy is, too, with Sam.

"Well, you gotta do something, Lucy," I said. "You can't go on being miserable and getting beat up."

"I am doin' somethin'," she said. "I *am* gonna leave, as soon as I find a new place to live."

"Heck, Lucy, you can stay with me at the gym until you find a place."

She looked at me with surprise. "Really?"

"Sure. There's plenty of space in my room. We could put a cot or a floor mat or something in there for you to sleep on. As for all your stuff, that building is big enough. We'd find some temporary storage space."

"Wow, Judy, that sounds great." Then she got a worried look on her face. "Unfortunately, there's Sam. As soon as he finds out, he'll go berserk. He'll kill me first, and then he'll come over and kill you for puttin' the idea in my head."

"Let him try!" I scoffed. "I'll go over there right now and kick his butt."

"He's not home. He's on one of his binges."

"Binges?"

"He gets drunk. A lot. You never knew this, I kept it from you. He gets drunk and that's when he roughs me up. Then he leaves our apartment and goes and stays on his father's yacht for a night or two to cool off and sober up. I think that's where he takes his mistresses, too."

"His father's *yacht*?"

"Yeah. His dad has money but won't give any to Sam. I think that's one reason why he's the way he is. Sam's parents live in New Rochelle. His dad is a member of the New York Athletic Club, and he keeps a small yacht anchored there on Travers Island. You ever been there?"

"No."

"It's real pretty. Sam's taken me out on the boat before."

I thought about this and asked, "Where exactly is the boat?" She told me Travers Island straddles the border between New Rochelle and Pelham Manor, overlooking Long Island Sound. Then I instructed her to get as much of her things in a suitcase and bring it to the gym after work.

Well, Lucy never showed up last night. She got off work at five o'clock, and I waited until eleven before calling her at home.

There was no answer. I was a little worried but not overly concerned.

This morning, there it was in the newspaper. The *Daily News* reported that a woman had been beaten behind the East Side Diner last night. She survived, but was in critical condition at Bellevue Hospital. Didn't give her name.

All of my crazy senses, that animal intuition of mine, told me it was Lucy.

And I was right.

LATER

I went to Bellevue to inquire about the "victim," and found out she was indeed Lucy. She was in a coma, having sustained serious injuries. The assailant had beaten and clubbed her on the head. It was too early to know if there would be brain damage.

I was devastated.

The nurse asked if I was a relative. I told her, no, I was a friend. I wasn't allowed to see her. She wouldn't have been responsive anyway. According to the newspaper report, the police were looking for her roommate/boyfriend, Sam Duncan, for questioning; but otherwise they had no suspects for the crime. The police didn't consider Sam a strong one because Lucy was attacked outside the diner, which wasn't consistent with domestic violence.

I knew better.

Imagining Lucy's ordeal reminded me all too much of what happened back in Texas. Douglas Bates. More and more, memories of that night returned to haunt me in my dreams. It came to me that the reason I was saving all my money was so I could take a trip back home to deal with my demons.

But first I had to deal with another one.

I went to Freddie and asked him about the New York Athletic Club. It turned out he had some connections. He'd met Sam before, so I told Freddie I wanted to find out who Sam's father was and where he moored his boat. Freddie asked me why I wanted to know, but I made up some excuse. I told him it had to do with a surprise birthday party for Lucy. I hated lying to Freddie, but it was best he didn't know what I was planning.

Freddie made a call and found out where Duncan Senior kept the yacht, which was named *Carolina*. I went up to my room to prepare. First, I studied a map of New Rochelle that was in a New York atlas I bought a couple of years ago, and traced the route I would take once the train dropped me off in New Rochelle. Then I made sure I had the necessary tools in my knapsack.

Now it's time to go. Wish me luck, dear diary.

29
Judy's Diary
1958

NOVEMBER 13, 1958

Late afternoon yesterday I rode the train from Grand Central to New Rochelle and then took a taxi to the New York Athletic Club. I asked the driver to pick me up in exactly one hour and promised him a big tip if he did. I also winked and blew him a kiss. He assured me he'd come back. By then, the sun had set. I walked into the Main House like I owned the joint. I'd been careful to dress appropriately in casual business wear. I had one outfit that worked—something you'd see the secretaries on Madison Avenue wearing. Anyone looking at me probably thought I worked in the office. It was dinner time, so most of the people there were in the dining room. No one bothered me. I went straight outside toward the Yacht House on Pomeroy's Hill. I'd done my homework and learned that the New York Athletic Club formally created their Yacht Club just a year earlier, and a new marina had been built just in the past few months. That was my destination, but I needed to find a place where I could change clothes. Luckily, no one was outside.

Marina A had slips for about twenty boats. I found Mr. Duncan's *Carolina* docked in one of them, but there was no indication anyone was aboard. At first I feared I'd made a mistake. What if

Sam wasn't inside? I almost turned around and went back, but then I heard a faint strain of music. My sensitive ears again. The melody was coming from a radio in the cabin. No question about it. So I put aside my worries and found a nice, secluded spot up the hill amidst the trees. I took off my jacket, blouse, and skirt, revealing the Stiletto costume I wore underneath. I folded the clothes neatly and put them in the knapsack. The mask and hood came last.

The marina was not well lit, but there was enough illumination along the dock's walkway to expose me. I had to be careful, so I darted from object to object, staying in one place for several seconds before moving again. Standard commando tactics my brother John taught me when we played "Americans vs. Japanese" back in Texas. If the enemy only *thinks* he saw something and you're not visible if he looks again, chances are he'll forget about it.

Now a dim light shone through the *Carolina*'s cabin windows. Sam was on board all right. I don't know much about boats, but I expected something bigger. When someone says the word "yacht," I picture in my mind something huge, as big as a house. The cabin on this one was more like the size of my room at the gym.

A lamp on a ten-foot-high wooden post cast a bright circle of light on the pier in front of the *Carolina*. I didn't like it. Would anyone see me if I stepped into it? I glanced at the Yacht House, up the hill, and the coast was clear. Still, I didn't want to take the chance. How would I turn off the light? It was probably on a switch somewhere, most likely in the club house.

This is where all that practice throwing a knife came in handy. I spent hours—*days*—throwing knives at targets. I got to where I could hit them 99 percent of the time. Perhaps I could strike the bulb with the stiletto. However, if I missed, the knife might easily drop into the water. Even though it was shallow by the pier, I wouldn't want to have to fish for it. Especially in the lamp's spotlight.

Aw, heck, I thought. Go for it. I stepped on the pier and stood in the shadow just beyond the beam's perimeter. It wasn't the ideal angle from which to throw, but it was the best I could do without being bathed in luminescence. I drew the stiletto, raised my arm, held the blade between my thumb and index finger, and aimed.

Relax. Breathe.

Just like Soichiro taught me.

Concentrate.

As Fiorello instructed me.

Picture the outcome in your mind.

I threw the stiletto.

The bulb shattered, plunging the *Carolina*'s slip into darkness. The knife fell neatly but noisily on the wooden planks. I hoped it didn't alert Sam to my presence. I waited a few moments, but nothing happened. Moving forward, I retrieved the knife, sheathed it, and climbed aboard the boat as silently as I could. I tiptoed down the small stepladder to the cabin door and listened.

"Poor Little Fool" by Ricky Nelson was playing inside. Apparently Sam could afford one of those new transistor radios I've seen advertised. Forty dollars was too rich for my blood, but it'd be fun to have one.

I knocked on the door. *Why do I always knock?* Am I too polite? I don't know! It just seemed to be the right thing to do. I'd hate to kick the door down and find the guy undressed or something. That would be too embarrassing.

"What? Who's there?"

It was Sam, all right. He sounded scared. I decided to play with him a little, so I scampered up the ladder and hid around the port side of the cabin. The door opened.

"Someone there?" He stepped up on deck. He was shirtless, wearing boxer shorts and socks. "Dad?" Sam shrugged, turned, and went back inside. The door closed. I moved down the steps again, knocked, and ran around the starboard side of the cabin. The door opened again. "All right, who's out here?" Sam bounded up the steps and wavered unsteadily on his feet. He was drunk. "Damn it. Is someone here?" He looked around the port side— nobody there. I stifled a giggle and then dashed down the steps and into the cabin. A bed had been pulled down from the bulk-head, so I dropped to the floor and slid under it. By then Sam had made a circle on deck, wondering if he was going nuts or not. Eventually he came back in and shut the door. I could see only his feet.

"Oh boy," he groaned as he sat on the bed. As soon as he lay down, I rolled out from under and sprung to my feet.

"Get up, you creep."

Sam screamed like a girl. He jumped and catapulted back against the bulkhead, kicking out with his feet at me as if I was a demon from the netherworld. Perhaps I was.

"The police are looking for you," I said.

"I didn't do anything!"

"No? You didn't beat up your girlfriend behind the East Side Diner?"

"No!"

Once again, my intuition didn't fail me. Sam Duncan was lying like nobody's business. If he was really innocent, I'd be able to tell.

"Why did you do it, Sam? Were you trying to make it look like a random assault? Didn't you think the police would suspect you?"

"I don't know what you're talking about! Go away! Leave me alone!" He started shouting, "Help! Help!"

"*Shut up!*" I couldn't help myself—I drew the stiletto— *swish!*—and drew a thin red line across his pectoral muscles. This caused him to scream again, but at least he wasn't calling for help.

"Be quiet or I'll cut your throat!" I hissed.

That did the trick. He pulled the sheet up over his body, as if that would protect him. He peeked over the edge with wide, terror-filled eyes.

Good, I thought. This was how Lucy felt when she was attacked. Scared to death.

"Now, Sam," I said, "you're gonna admit what you did to the cops. You hear me? If you don't, I promise you I will cut out your heart and feed it to you."

I know that's a pretty rough thing to say. I can be pretty mean if I want to. But I was mad. I really could've killed this guy for what he did to Lucy. It took a heck of a lot of self-control not to hurt him *really* bad.

The stiletto flashed again, this time ripping the sheet. Sam screamed once more. "All right, all right! I did it, I did it! I'm sorry!" Then he started bawling. He climbed off the bed and onto the floor, on his knees, begging me not to hurt him. "Please, I'm so sorry! I didn't mean to hurt her! Please!"

"You didn't *mean* to hurt her? You put her in a *coma*! She could have brain damage! What did you *mean* to do if not hurt her?"

"I'm so sorry! I'll confess! I'll go to the cops!"

It's what I wanted to hear. "Do you have a pen? Some paper?"

"Uh—at the helm."

"Let's go get it." I waved the stiletto and gestured him up. He reluctantly stood and went to the door. "No funny stuff. I'm right behind you."

He opened the door and I marched him up the steps. As I expected, he tried to make a run for the pier—boxer shorts and all. Or less. I leaped forward and tackled him. Sam landed badly and hit his forehead on the edge of the hull. He tried to yell for help again, but I slithered over his prone body, covered his mouth with my gloved left hand, and stuck the stiletto's point against his cheek. There was a cut above his right eyebrow, where he'd hit his head.

"I said no funny stuff. I'm not in a laughing mood."

He was breathing hard and fast, but the fight was knocked out of him.

"You gonna cooperate now?"

He nodded.

"If I take my hand off are you gonna yell for help?"

He shook his head.

"If you do, I will turn you into a pin cushion. Do you understand?"

He nodded again.

"Get up." I released him but kept the knife in play. "Now get the pen and paper."

Sam did as he was told. Meek and subservient, he went to the helm, opened a compartment, and removed a pencil and a small pad of paper. I followed him back into the cabin and shut the door.

"Sit. And write." I pointed to the bed. Funny—at that moment the radio started playing "Tom Dooley" by the Kingston Trio.

It took him ten minutes to write a full confession. Once again, I tied up my prey. I left him on the bed—gagged with a torn piece of sheet—and I placed the notepad on a table for the authorities to find. Then I left.

I changed back into my civilian clothing in the shadows of the pier. No one had noticed the broken lamp. I made my way back up to the Yacht House. It was probably best to avoid people, so I went around the side and climbed over a fence. That wasn't easy in a skirt, but I managed to do it. Walked to the Main House, where dinner was still in progress. I brushed myself off and went inside. No one saw me dart to the ladies' room, where I checked my appearance and made sure I was presentable. When I came out, I ran into a waiter, or butler, or whatever you call someone who works at the clubhouse.

"Is there a telephone I can use?" I asked sweetly.

"Yes, ma'am, right this way."

The gentleman led me to a booth where I could use the phone for free. I checked the time and then dialed *O*. When the operator answered, I asked for the police. I told them where Sam Duncan was and that he had confessed to the assault on Lucy Dempsey.

"May I have your name and address, please?" the officer asked.

"Oh, this is the Black Stiletto, and I have no address," I answered.

Silence on the other end. My cue to hang up.

My taxi was waiting outside the Main House. I was long gone when Sam was arrested and taken away.

That was last night.

This morning I went to Bellevue and learned Lucy had come out of her coma. Her mother and father were there, so I introduced myself to them. They said they'd "heard about me" and appreciated that I was a good friend to their daughter. They were very sweet. Mrs. Dempsey told me the doctor said there didn't appear to be any brain damage. Lucy was expected to make a full recovery after some rehabilitation. That was music to my ears.

They'd also been informed of the other good news—Sam Duncan had been arrested and charged with attempted murder. Stories appeared in all the papers, and this time the Black Stiletto was credited for bringing the assailant to justice. Even NYPD Commissioner Kennedy was quoted as saying, "We would like the Black Stiletto to leave the crime fighting to us, but for locating the perpetrator of this horrible crime and bringing him to our attention, we give her our thanks." If you ask me, I thought they were pretty dumb. Anyone could've figured out Sam was hiding on his daddy's boat if they'd used a brain cell or two.

I went in to see Lucy for a couple of minutes. She was very weak, but she smiled when she saw me. I held her hand and told her the offer for her to move in with me was still good.

"Thanks, Judy," she whispered.

"You get well. By the time I get back, you should be out of the hospital."

"Where you goin'?"

"I have to go out of town for a little while. There's something I need to take care of. But I'll be back. Don't worry."

Yes, dear diary, I've made my decision. I'm going to Texas to find Douglas Bates.

30
Roberto

The Present

Can't believe I passed my driver's test. Had to renew my license since it expired nearly fifty years ago. I got hold of the book they make you study, just in case the traffic laws and signs had changed. Some had and there were some new ones, but it was basically the same. I thought for sure they'd make me take an actual behind-the-wheel test, but they didn't. Just had to pass a written one. Walked out of the NYSDMV with a new license. Un-fuckin'-believable.

Couldn't afford to buy a car, though. Besides, I didn't need one in the city.

After takin' care of a bunch of crap like that to get my life back in order, I resumed my search for Judy Cooper. I remembered she used to work at a gym in the East Village. I couldn't recall what cross street it was on, but I knew it was on Second Avenue. I took the Q line subway into Manhattan and got off at 14th Street. Walked east all the way to Second and then headed south. By the time I got to 8th, things started to look familiar even though it had changed. I mean, all the stores and restaurants were different, but for the most part the streets and buildings looked like they did back in the fifties.

At 4th Street there was a diner. That rang a bell. It was called East Side Diner and it was open. It was important, somehow.

Couldn't quite remember, but the place had something to do with Fiorello and Judy Cooper. I thought maybe it'd come to me in a minute, so I kept walkin'. At 2nd Street there was a gym, some place called Shapes. In my day, there were no gyms for women. This one was for *only* women. Was this the place I was lookin' for? It felt right. This was the old gym. I knew it.

I went inside and there was this delicious dame at the desk. The gym itself looked brand-spankin' new. I guess they'd re-modeled it or somethin'. There were women wearin' skimpy leotards and stuff, doin' all kinds of exercises. I thought I'd died and gone to heaven.

"May I help you, sir?" the dame asked.

"Sure. Did this used to be a gym for men?"

"Gee, I don't know. It's always been Shapes since I worked here."

"I'm lookin' for a gym that mighta been in this spot back in the fifties."

"The *nineteen fifties*?"

"Yeah."

The dame shook her head. "I was born in nineteen eighty-eight. Can't help you."

"Anyone here who might know?"

"I don't think so."

Some other dame was sittin' on a bench puttin' those wooly stocking things on her legs like I seen some women wearin'. She overheard us and said, "What about Lucy? She might know."

The first dame laughed and said, "Oh, yeah. Lucy. She's this old la—um, elderly lady who comes in here sometimes." The dame lowered her voice and giggled softly. "She thinks she comes in to exercise, but she walks for five minutes on a treadmill, stops, and then spends the rest of the hour gabbing. I think she's been around since the fifties."

That name Lucy sparked a memory, but I'm not sure what it was. Was she a friend of Fiorello's? Maybe a friend of Judy Cooper's?

"How can I find this Lucy?"

"Gee, I can't give out members' addresses. But she hangs out at the diner on Fourth Street a lot. Maybe you'll find her in there."

"What's her last name?"

The dame on the bench answered that one. "Gaskin. Lucy Gaskin is her name."

"Thanks," I said. "I think I do know her after all." I coulda stayed and watched those young dames exercise all day, but I had more important things to do. I left and walked back to the diner on 4th Street. I was hungry so I decided to sit down and have a BLT on rye and a Coke. The waitress was in her thirties, I think, not bad lookin', could maybe lose a few pounds down at that Shapes place. Anyway, I asked her about Lucy Gaskin.

"You know Lucy?" she asked.

"Yeah, I'm an old friend of hers. I haven't seen her in ages. I heard she comes in here."

"She used to work here, a long time ago, or so she says. Still comes in a lot. She loves that old jukebox over there." The waitress nodded at the machine in the corner, near the windows. It looked really old.

"Does it work?" I asked.

"Not very well. But it's an antique, so the owner refuses to sell it."

"Where can I find Lucy? Does she live around here?"

"Yeah, she lives in Georgetown Plaza."

"Where's that?"

"Broadway and 8th Street. Big high-rise."

I wondered if she lived alone, but I didn't want to sound too nosy. So I asked, "And how's her husband—?" I snapped my fingers, as if I was tryin' to remember. "—er, what was his name?"

"Oh, I'm sorry, did you know Pete, too? He passed away, I don't know, about five or six years ago. Lucy still lives in their apartment, though. She's a tough old broad." Then the waitress leaned in close to me and whispered, "She's a bit ditzy now. Forgets a lot. I think she'd be better off in assisted living, if you know what I mean."

I grunted. "Yeah, I know what you mean." Fuck assisted living.

I paid the bill and went up to 8th Street, and then walked west to Broadway. Sure enough, there was the high-rise called Georgetown Plaza. Musta been over thirty stories tall. Busy street corner, lotsa shops and young people. Right between Cooper Union, two blocks east, and Washington Square Park, two blocks west.

While I was in the diner, I kept tryin' to remember how I knew Lucy's name. She musta been someone Fiorello knew when he was livin' with Judy Cooper. I bet she was a friend of Judy's. Had to be. That would be my ticket inside.

I went inside the lobby and talked to the doorman. Told him I wanted to see Lucy Gaskin. He picked up a phone and dialed, then asked, "Who should I say is calling?"

"Tell her it's an old friend of Judy Cooper's. My name is Dino."

The doorman nodded, waited, and then spoke into the phone. "Mrs. Gaskin? I have a man named Dino down here who'd like to see you. He says he's an old friend of Judy Cooper's. What? Yes. Okay." He hung up. "She says to come on up." The guy gave me the floor and apartment number, and then buzzed me in.

When I knocked on her door, she took a long time comin' to open it. Finally, though, she did. Lucy was an old broad, all right, maybe in her eighties, but how should I know? She mighta been good lookin' when she was young, but I couldn't tell. She just looked like an old lady now, kinda fat and dumpy.

"Why hello there, it's been so long!" she said as if she'd known me all her life. "Come on in. The place is a mess, please excuse it." I stepped inside and was almost overcome by that old-lady smell. Lots of perfume and soapy scents. Yuck.

"It's good to see you, too, Lucy," I said. "How long has it been?"

"Gee, I don't know. Years and years." She laughed. "What did you say your name was?"

"Dino. I'm Dino. You remember me, don't ya?"

"Oh, yeah. Dino. How've you been? Come on in and sit down. I'll get us a cocktail. What'll you have?"

"Whatever you're havin'."

The place wasn't as much of a mess as she thought it was, but everything was dusty and the furniture and stuff looked really old. She and her husband musta lived in the apartment since the building opened. Actually, it wasn't bad. There was a terrace that overlooked the city.

"Nice place you got here," I said. "Lots of room. Nice view."

She replied from the kitchen, "Yeah, Pete and I bought the place in nineteen sixty-four. It was brand new then. I'm sorry, Pete's not here."

Yeah, I knew that.

I went over to a shelf that had a bunch of framed photos on it. Pictures of Lucy and her husband when they were younger. A wedding photo. Kids. There was also a picture of Lucy and Judy Cooper. It was a shot of them in front of the East Side Diner. Black-and-white. Old, but probably taken around the time in question. Damn. I felt that heart murmur of mine when I saw the photo. In fact, I got a little dizzy. I had to sit down, so I stumbled over to the sofa and collapsed into it.

Lucy came in with two glasses of white wine. Yuck. Didn't she have somethin' stronger? She handed me one and said, "Here you go. I like a little wine in the afternoon, don't you? Cheers!"

She sat in a big chair, not noticin' I wasn't feelin' well. But the cold wine actually tasted good. I felt better after a few sips. Lucy started talkin' and talkin' about nothin', tellin' me about her kids and where they were now, how she loves New York and will never leave the apartment, and other crap I didn't care about. The dame really was ditzy—she didn't realize I was a total stranger to her. Thought I was some long-lost friend she hadn't seen in years.

Finally, I interrupted her and asked, "So what do you hear from Judy Cooper?"

"Oh, Judy." She shook her head. At first I thought she was gonna tell me the bitch was dead, but she said, "I haven't heard from Judy in a long time. We used to write pretty regular, y'know? After she moved to California and all. Then she moved somewhere else—" She was havin' trouble rememberin'.

"Where did she move?" I prodded.

"You know her name isn't Judy Cooper anymore?"

"No, I didn't know. What, she got married?"

"I guess she did. Talbot. She's Judy Talbot now. Uh, just a minute. I think I have her last few letters somewhere." She got up and went to a desk. Rummaged through it, and then came back with a stack of envelopes.

Bingo.

She looked at one and said, "Oh yeah, she moved to Chicago in the sixties. Never came back. Here's the last letter I have. What's the date, can you read it? I don't have my glasses."

I took the stack and looked at the postmark. Nineteen eighty-seven. Maybe a long time ago, but not too bad in the grand scheme of things. J. Talbot. That explained why I couldn't find her as Judy Cooper. A return address of Arlington Heights, Illinois. I didn't know where the fuck that was.

Before Lucy sat down, I downed my glass of wine and handed it to her. "I couldn't trouble you for a little more, could I?"

"Why, of course. My pleasure. I'll have more, too."

As soon as she was out of sight, I stuck the envelope in my pocket. It may or may not be Judy Cooper's last known address, but there was a good chance it was.

I guess I was relieved I didn't have to kill Lucy Gaskin for it.

31
Judy's Diary

1958

December 11, 1958

Today I took my first airplane ride. Actually it was two airplanes.
First I flew from Idlewild to Dallas, where I had to wait five hours
before I could board another plane to Midland Air Terminal. It
was so much fun! A little scary, I have to admit, but it was kinda
like going on a ride at an amusement park. It reminded me of
when I was little and my mother took us three kids to a carnival
in Odessa when the rodeo was in town. I think we went twice,
two years in a row, but after that it got to be we couldn't afford to
go. Anyway, getting on the airplane and feeling it take off was
something I can't describe. I looked out the window and everything on the ground looked so tiny. The stewardesses were nice,
too. They gave us food and drinks. The only thing I didn't like
was the passengers smoking cigarettes. There was a section set
aside for the smokers, but the smoke still filled the entire cabin. I
still haven't gotten used to tobacco, I don't know why. Everyone
I know smokes. I must be some kind of freak, ha ha.

I'd almost forgotten how flat and desolate West Texas is. It
was nearly sundown when we landed, and the horizon was as
straight as all get-out. Just a line, dividing the sky and the earth.
The sunset was mighty pretty, though. I do remember that about
Texas. The colors in the sky could be breathtaking. The rest of

the place—all the sand and mesquite and tumbleweed—you can keep, thank you very much.

It was a good thing I saved up a bunch of money to take with me. Since I didn't know how to drive a car—I never learned!—I was going to have to take taxis everywhere. No public transportation like buses and subways in Odessa. Well, there were buses, but not like what I needed. I also couldn't remember too many things about the town's geography, so I bought a map at the airport before going outside and finding a cab. Even the taxis were hard to come by—I had to get someone to call one to take me to town. The airport was situated in the middle of nowhere, between Odessa and Midland.

A nice Mexican man named Luis picked me up. I gave him my false name—Eloise—and told him I'd like to hire him for a couple of days to be my personal driver. He'd never heard of an arrangement like that. His English wasn't great, but we understood each other all right. He said he'd have to check with his boss at the taxi company he worked for to find out what it would cost.

In the meantime, I paid him for a ride to the west side of Odessa, which is where I used to live with my mom and brothers. Whitaker and 5th Street. Once we got into the city, it all came back to me, even in the dark. I'd forgotten, though, how close we were to the railroad tracks that separated white Odessa from "colored town." When I was growing up, there was a creepy mystique about the south side of Odessa, an area of nothing but shanties where all the Negroes lived. Whenever my brothers and I were upset about how poor we were, John or Frankie would say at least we weren't as bad off as them. After living in New York and working in a gym where Negroes and whites trained in the same room together, I realized how prejudiced the rest of the country is. Odessa was no different. I guess I grew up with the concept of prejudice instilled in me, too, but now I see it's all so wrong. Not much I can do about it, though.

I had Luis drive by the old house. Imagine my shock when I saw it wasn't there anymore. Several homes on the street had been torn down and new ones were being built. It's not surprising. My old house wasn't much better than the shanties across the tracks. Well, obviously, my mom didn't live there. I guess I had some detective work to do to find her.

Luis dropped me at a motel on 2nd Street and waited while I checked in, again using a false name. I asked him to call for me tomorrow morning at nine, regardless of what his boss told him about me hiring him for a couple of days. Luis said not to worry, he'd be there.

Now I'm settled in, about to go to bed. It's nearly midnight and I have very mixed emotions about being back in Odessa. Seeing that street disturbed me. I know I haven't thought much about my mother and brothers since I ran away from home. I guess I'm feeling guilty about it, and I had a good cry a few minutes ago. I considered going down the street to a bar and get a drink, but I'm afraid people would think I'm just some floozy. So instead I'm staying in.

Perhaps tomorrow will bring some answers.

December 12, 1958

Dear diary, I've had a very emotional day. Luis picked me up this morning, as promised, and told me he could be my driver for ten dollars on a daily basis. I thought that was all right, so I hired him. Did I mention he was a chain-smoker? He lit one after another the entire time I was with him. I had to keep my windows down a bit to air out the car. I didn't mind too much. Like I said before, everyone in New York smoked, too. I was getting used to the smell.

First I had him take me to Odessa Junior High School. He waited in the parking lot while I went inside. It hadn't changed much. The halls were still full of kids from lower-class families.

They didn't look any happier than I'd been. I tried to imagine myself back there, walking with my books in hand, going to gymnastics, and reading books in the library. For some reason, the image wouldn't form properly in my head. It figures, I guess. I've moved on. I'm just not the person who once roamed those corridors and classrooms. Even though it was only seven years ago, it was really a lifetime.

In the office, I asked about Mr. and Mrs. Douglas Bates. I didn't tell them I was the prodigal daughter. They looked at me like I was crazy. Why would they have any information on a couple if their child didn't currently go to the school? I realized they were right, so I left the building. That was dumb on my part.

So I went to our old church. It was the First Christian Church, on Lee. We didn't go very often. Mom dragged us kids there for Easter every year and occasionally on some Sundays. We hated it. I never took to Sunday school and I especially fidgeted during actual services. But we were members, so I thought maybe they'd have some records.

A nice lady in the church office remembered my mother, but hadn't seen her in a long time. She didn't ask who I was; I just said I was a relative and wanted to find out where Mr. and Mrs. Douglas Bates might be. She couldn't find a listing in their directory, so she went into another room to ask someone. When she came back, the lady had a look of concern on her face. I immediately felt a surge of extreme sadness. My intuition foretold what she was about to say.

"I just heard from our church secretary that Mrs. Bates—her name was Betty, right?"

"Yes, ma'am."

"Well, Mrs. Bates passed away three years ago. Caught the cancer, she did. Died in nineteen fifty-six."

The news took my breath away, even though I half expected it. Before I could no longer stop myself from crying, I had the presence of mind to ask about her husband and sons. She didn't know anything about Douglas or where he might be. However, she told me Frank Cooper lived in town and was, surprisingly, still a member of the church. At first, the lady hadn't connected Frank with the name Betty Bates. She said he worked at a hardware store on 8th Street. I thanked her and went outside to Luis and the cab.

In the car, I broke down and cried my eyes out. My mama was dead. And I'd run away from her, probably when she needed me the most.

I found Frank at the hardware store on 8th Street, not far from Dixie Drug, a pharmacy and deli where my brothers bought comic books when they were little. You shoulda seen his face when he realized who I was. At first he didn't. I recognized him as soon as I walked in. He wasn't as tall as me—he never was, ha ha—but he'd filled out and was all grown up. Still had a baby face, but there was also something wrong with his right eye. When I was up close I could see the problem—it was made of glass. He'd somehow lost his eye since I'd last seen him.

Anyway, I spotted him behind the counter. He was helping a customer with some tools or something. I waited patiently for my turn, and then he looked at me and asked, "May I help you, miss?"

"You sure can. I wonder if you might have time to play a little "Americans vs. Japanese" when you get off work."

"I beg your—" And then his jaw dropped. I couldn't help but laugh.

"Judy?"

"It's me, Frankie."

"Oh my God, Judy!" He was too shocked to move.

"You gonna give me a hug?" I held out my arms, he practically leaped from behind the counter, and we embraced. It felt great.

"Where—oh my God, Judy—where have you *been*? Where did you go? We were so worried about you!"

"I know. And I'm sorry. Listen, when can you get a break? I'd love to sit and talk."

His head went up and down, taking in my entire body. "Judy. Holy cow. You're a woman now. You're *gorgeous*! Oh my God, my sister is a beautiful young woman!"

"And I'm smart, too," I said. "When can you take a break?"

"Right now. Just a sec, lemme find someone to watch the counter." He ran to the back of the shop, stuck his head through a door, said something, and came hustling back. After a moment, another man—older, probably senior in position—followed him out.

"Ray, this is my sister Judy," Frank said.

"Pleased to meet you, ma'am," the older man said. He, too, seemed to be taken by my appearance. I guess I did turn some heads, but I never thought about it much.

"Come on," Frank said, gesturing me toward the front door. "There's a coffee shop a couple doors down. You feel like walkin'?"

"Sure."

I stopped at the taxi to tell Luis what I was doing. He was happy to wait. I think acting as my driver made him feel important somehow. He thought I was some high-class businesswoman from New York.

Frank and I sat and ordered coffee at this cute little place full of blue-collar folks on their breaks, smoking their cigarettes and having coffee. A waitress with a thick Texas accent took our order. I'd forgotten how much of a drawl people had, and I imagine mine came back full force once I landed in the state.

"I can't get over how good you look," Frank said.

"You look good, too, Frankie, but, my Lord, what happened to your eye?"

He winced and replied, "Oh, that's a long story. But first, Jesus,

Judy, tell me what happened to you. You can't imagine, well, Mom was real upset when you ran off. We thought you were dead. We had the sheriff and the police and everyone lookin' for you. We were goin' crazy."

Hearing this made me want to cry again. "I'm sorry, Frankie. I really am. It's just—I had to get away. Because of—you know. Him. Douglas."

At the mention of the man's name, Frank stiffened. He looked away and then nodded. "Did he hurt you? Do something to you?"

"Yeah. He did. It was bad, too."

"What happened?"

So I told him enough that he'd get the picture without going into the gory details. "I was so young, Frankie. I was afraid to tell anyone. He threatened me. Said he'd make it sound like it was all my fault."

"That's bullshit."

"I know that now. When I was thirteen I didn't."

"I'm sorry that happened to you, Judy." He looked away. "Douglas is the reason I have a glass eye."

"What?"

"It wasn't long after you left. Maybe three or four months. Mom was in bad shape, drinking all the time, really unhappy. Douglas went on binges and beat her when he could, and if she was already passed out then he'd beat me. One day we were in the kitchen. He had an ice pick, chippin' away at a block of ice for the fan 'cause it was startin' to get hot outside. Anyway, he just got through yellin' at Mom for somethin' and I hollered right back at him. I told him to get out of our house. He meant to slap me, but the ice pick accidentally flew out of his hand. Judy, that thing hit the ceiling and then fell, just as I was lookin' up at it. Landed right in my eye. It was a freak accident, but I still blame him. Went to the hospital, and now I've got this crappy glass eye. I hate it. I look like a freak."

"No, you don't, Frankie. I hardly notice it." It was a white lie, but I had to say it.

"Thanks for sayin' that, Judy, but I know you're fibbin'. The only good thing about it was it got me out of military service."

"Oh, that reminds me, what about John? Where is he?"

"He's still in the army. I guess he likes it, 'cause he never left once he joined. He's makin' a career out of it. He's an officer, stationed at Fort Sam Houston in San Antonio."

"Well, I'll be. Are you in touch with him?"

"A little. Not much. He came back for Mom's—oh my God, Judy! Do you know?"

"About Mom? Yeah, Frankie. I know."

"How did you find out?"

"A lady at our church told me today." I felt tears welling up in my eyes; I couldn't help it. "I'm sorry, Frankie. I shoulda been here. I feel so bad."

He reached out and touched my hand on the table. "I think she woulda liked to see you again."

That did it. I started bawling all over again. Frank was a dear and got me some tissues. He was crying a little bit, too. This entire trip had turned into nothing but a series of waterworks. But I settled down after a while and he told me a little about her final days. In 1954 they had moved to an apartment on the far northwest side of Odessa, out closer to the oil fields. She'd gotten a job as a secretary at one of the parts companies and wanted to be near work. When Frank graduated high school, he moved out and immediately started making his own living. He had no desire to go to college, and besides, neither he nor Mom could afford it. Her illness came on suddenly and advanced quickly. Apparently during the last three months of her life, Douglas just upped and left. Abandoned her when she needed him the most.

Finally, after Frank told me where Mom was buried, I asked

the question. The reason I'd come to Odessa. "So, where is Douglas now?"

Frank made a face. "I don't know and I don't care. I hate him."

"Is he still in Odessa?"

"Hell, I don't know. Far as I know. After Mom died, he sold the house and left. We never heard anything more about him. He just disappeared from our lives. Good riddance. What a son of a bitch. Pardon my language, Sis."

"That's okay. I've cursed him myself. I really want to find him, Frank."

"What for?"

"I just do. He and I have some unfinished business."

"Judy, don't be stupid."

"I know what I'm doin', Frankie. Can you find out where he is?"

"Well, actually the last I heard he was still workin' as a rough-neck out in the oil fields. Near Goldsmith. You know where that is?"

"Vaguely. It's a little-bitty place outside of town?"

"About fifteen or twenty miles away; you go out Kermit Highway, and then turn north on a ranch road to Goldsmith. Smack dab in oil field country. It ain't much to speak of."

"You think he's still there?"

"Hell if I know. Like I said, I could care less. I hope he falls in an oil well and drowns in it. What a mean, spiteful, horrible person."

"I couldn't agree with you more."

We talked a little longer, but then it started feeling strange. I don't know why, but I suddenly got real uncomfortable. Like I didn't belong. I was a stranger in my own hometown. I decided to end our visit, so I looked at my watch and told Frank I had an appointment.

"Will I see you again?" he asked.

"I don't know. Why don't you give me your address and phone number?" He did, but I didn't return the favor. I suppose he must have sensed I was a very private person now. We said goodbye back at the hardware shop. I told him I'd call before I went home, but I knew I probably wouldn't. I hadn't told him anything about my life in New York, and he never asked. In fact, I don't think I ever said I lived there. Frank doesn't know where to find me.

It's probably best that way.

It was getting dark, so I had Luis drive me to the cemetery where Frank said Mom was buried. It was the Ector County one, just south of the tracks on Dixie, so it wasn't very far from the hardware store. It was probably the oldest cemetery in Odessa, but I'm not sure about that. The place was closing in less than a half hour, so I had to hurry.

I left Luis in the car and found my way through the gravestones until I located the place where my mother now rested. The stone read: ELIZABETH WALDEN COOPER, BELOVED MOTHER. I was glad to see my father's last name on it. Had that been Frank or John's decision? Perhaps my mother requested it before she passed on. I have no way of knowing, but it felt right. Dad's body was never recovered from the Pacific Ocean, so he had no burial site. It's a shame.

Standing there, looking at the headstone, I cried for the third time that day. I was overcome with guilt for running away from home and not sending word back to my mother that I was all right. I'd caused her unnecessary worry. At the time, I supposed I despised her for putting up with Douglas and being blind to what he was doing to her, to me, and to my brothers. I hated her alcoholism. To me, she was a weak and pathetic person—drowning her sorrows—*our* sorrows—with a bottle and then spending days in bed. Now, though, I see it was the only defense mechanism she had. Those were tough times, especially after my dad was killed. Mom sacrificed a lot, demeaning herself to be a cleaning lady for women who were better off than she. She was dealing with so much—and then I had to run away. Yes, it was something I had to do to get away from the monster that lived in our house. But I guess I could have done it a little differently.

"I'm sorry, Mama," I said out loud. Tears ran down my cheeks as I spoke. "I hope you didn't worry too much. I shoulda told you I was safe. I guess I was afraid you'd have the authorities come and bring me back here if you knew where I was. And I'm sorry you died of cancer, Mama. You know it was Douglas who was the cause of it all—my leaving, your cancer—yes, I'm sure Douglas brought that disease on you. He is malignancy itself, a devil who has no right to walk this earth while you lay buried in it. I'm gonna make him pay, Mama. I promise you that."

I felt a presence watching me; I turned and saw the cemetery keeper standing by the gate. Closing time. I had to go.

Looking back at the grave, I had nothing more to say, except, "Goodbye, Mama. I love you. I really do."

Then I wiped the tears off my face and walked back to the taxi.

"Where to, Miss Eloise?" the driver asked.

"Luis, how would you like to make a few extra bucks and keep working tonight?"

He smiled broadly and nodded eagerly. "*Sí, sí!*"

"Good. Take me back to my motel, and then we've got some things to do."

The Black Stiletto was going to visit Goldsmith, Texas.

32
Martin

It's been a lousy couple of days. I went in to work yesterday and today, and tried to act like I cared. Brad avoided me at all costs. Nancy had heard the real reason why I didn't stay at the office on Monday, so she was suitably sympathetic. It's weird when a company gives you two or three weeks' notice—in my case, a whole month—because you don't really feel much like working for a firm that's just fired you. You'd think they'd know that. Nevertheless, I thought I'd give it my best shot until I found another job. Maybe I could leave before the month was over. I hadn't done much to look for a new job, though.

I'd spent Monday and Tuesday evenings drinking too much and trying to read the rest of Mom's diary. I still have a ways to go. I'm still angry at her for keeping all this stuff a secret. Then there were those other things I found in the strong box—the roll of film, for example. I should get off my butt and find an 8-mm projector so I can see what's on it. Those things aren't so easy to come by these days. I want to view the film in private, so I'll either have to find a place where I can rent a machine or buy one on e-Bay.

It was mid-afternoon and I didn't feel like working anymore. So I pulled out the diary and started to read—I didn't give a damn if Brad walked in. But my cell phone rang—and I saw it was Carol. The ex.

"Hi," I answered.

"How are you, Martin?"

"Okay."

"I heard about your job. I'm sorry."

"Yeah. I'm not too worried, though. I'll get another one."

"I know you will."

I could sense she wanted to tell me something. My mind reeled. What, she was getting married to that Ross guy?

"Martin, Gina got some news yesterday and I thought maybe I'd warn you before you hear it from her."

"News about college?"

"Yeah."

"*Warn* me?"

"She's afraid you're not gonna like it."

"Well, let's hear it."

"She got accepted into Juilliard and she wants to go."

I had to think a second. Juilliard was in New York. And it was *an arts school*. Performing arts.

My blood started to boil. "Since when did she apply to go to *Juilliard?*"

"She was afraid to tell you. It's what her heart's been set on all along. She got accepted in the School of Drama."

"Drama!"

"Martin, she wants to study theatre and dance."

I felt a headache coming on. "She's out of her mind! She'll be a pauper for the rest of her life."

"So? Martin, it's what she wants to do. You can't expect her to be what *you* want her to be."

"Where is she? I want to talk to her."

"She's at school."

"Oh, right." I drummed the table. "What do you think about it?"

"I think it's great, Martin. She's realizing a dream."

"Oh, give me a break. You tell her to call me when she comes home."

"You can call her yourself. Besides, I think she's going over to visit your mother after school."

"She is?"

"Yeah. She wants to tell Judy about her going to New York."

"My mom doesn't remember much about New York."

"Well, maybe so, but Gina really likes her grandma."

We didn't talk much longer. I hung up and decided I'd go to Woodlands after work and head off Gina. I had visions of a knockdown, drag-out in the nursing home parking lot.

Damn. I was upset. Mad at my mom, mad at my daughter, mad at my boss, and mad at my ex-wife. Angry that I had to go job hunting.

But wait.

I was sitting on a gold mine.

My mother was the Black Stiletto.

That was news. BIG news.

What would a major news organization pay for a story like that? Thousands? *Millions?* My God, it was possible I wouldn't have to work again for the rest of my life!

I immediately started thinking about whom I should call. The *Chicago Tribune?* Nah, I needed to go national. CNN? *The Today Show?* How does one even *call The Today Show?* I opened up my web browser and Googled. Found their website. On the Contact Us page, there were links to the show and other NBC news programs. Would have to send an e-mail. No calling.

On an impulse, I clicked the link and a Compose Mail window popped up with *The Today Show*'s address in the TO: box. I typed in the Subject line, "Identity of the Black Stiletto Revealed!" Tabbing down to the body of the e-mail, I typed, "To Whom It May Concern," and then I stopped.

What the hell was I doing?

I couldn't do it.

Not yet, anyway.

It was too soon.

I had to think about it more. Maybe even hire an attorney. Uncle Thomas wouldn't be right. I'd have to get some big shot who'd know what to do with this information and how I could control it.

Slow down, Martin. Take a deep breath.

I closed the e-mail and browser and looked at the clock. A couple more hours of work to go. So I picked up the diary.

33
Judy's Diary
1958

December 13, 1958

It's morning and I'm nursing a sore jaw and a few bruises here and there. Had an interesting evening last night, to say the least. I'm about to go out with Luis to pick up a paper and see if there's a story about me. I was sleeping when the morning news was on television. I'd be surprised if there wasn't something. I made a little noise, so to speak.

When Luis brought me to the motel after the cemetery visit, I tried to decide if I was hungry or not. I wasn't. All the crying had upset my stomach. I had too much tension and frustration to release, so I quickly dressed in my Stiletto disguise. West Texas was nippy in December, so I used the cold-weather one. Didn't bother with outer clothing. Put the mask/hood in my handbag, grabbed the knapsack, and went back outside to Luis's cab. The poor man had just lit his billionth cigarette of the day. He blinked and did a double take when he saw the outfit. My uniform did indeed accentuate my curves, no doubt about it. The stiletto on my thigh also provoked a bug-eye or two.

I got in the backseat and said, "Luis, how would you like to make not only the money I promised you for each day and evening, but another hundred dollars as a tip? You don't have to give any to your boss. It would have nothing to do with being a driver."

He didn't really understand what I was saying, but the words "a hundred dollars" appealed to him. It was probably more money he saw in two or three weeks, so he nodded eagerly. "Okay, Luis," I said, "what I'm paying you to do is to keep a secret. You know what that is?"

"Secret, *sí*." He made a gesture of zipping his mouth closed.

"Good, *sí*, you must never tell anybody about what we're about to do. All right?"

"No tell. No, *señorita*, Luis keep secret."

"It would be very bad if you told anybody about me." I dug into my handbag, found my money, and handed him fifty dollars in cash. Luis couldn't believe his eyes. "That's half. I'll give you the rest when I leave town, on the way to the airport. Okay?"

"*Sí! Sí!*"

"Okay, let's go to Goldsmith. Do you know Goldsmith?"

"*Sí.*"

And we were off. As the cab drove out of Odessa's city limits, I was once again struck by the eerie flatness. The sky was pitch-black; the stars and half moon were so bright that the landscape around us seemed to glow with a soft, pale luminescence. No trees to speak of, just short mesquite bushes, stretches of desert-like prairie, and, of course, the oil wells. Mysterious, tall sentinels standing watch over the gold mine that West Texas had become. The rocking pumpjacks became exotic, other-worldly animals that dipped and grazed on the barren ground. Gave me the shivers.

It took twenty minutes to reach Goldsmith. It was a little whistle-stop community with few buildings and a population made up mostly of oil worker families and ranchers with spreads outside the town limits. I think I saw two or three cafés, two gas stations, two liquor stores, three or four bars, a grocery store, maybe four small apartment complexes, a motel, and three churches—all within a square mile.

I had Luis pull up in front of the bar that had the most cars in front of it.

"Keep the car running," I said. "I'll be back in a few minutes. Now, remember, you can't talk about anything you might see tonight."

"*Sí.*"

I put on my mask and hood.

Luis's cigarette dropped right out of his mouth. He'd never seen anything like me in all his days. I had to laugh. I knew the Black Stiletto was known in New York and maybe in some of the bigger cities in the country, but had anyone in West Texas heard of her? I was about to learn the answer.

I got out of the car, walked up to the door, and opened it.

Seventeen men in the place—believe me, I counted—not including the bartender. All white. Twenties through forties, maybe one guy in his fifties. Roughnecks and cowboys. Good old boys who, with a little liquor in their bellies, were probably not so good. The place itself was a dreary dive containing a pool table, a dart board, a couple of tables, but mostly one long bar and stools. That latest country and western hit, "It's Only Make Believe" by Conway Twitty, was playing on the radio.

I strutted in and stepped up to the bar. Unsurprisingly, everyone in the place stopped what they were doing and stared at me.

"I'm looking for someone," I said to the bartender. He was speechless. No "Yes, ma'am?" or "What can I do for you?" or "Would you like a drink?" Someone in the joint whispered, "Son of a bitch, will you look at that?"

I turned away from the bartender and addressed everyone. "I'm looking for someone. Maybe one of you gentlemen can help me find him."

A whisper: "That's the Black Stiletto!"

Another: "No, it ain't."

"Sure, she is."

"She's an imposter, you damn fool. The Black Stiletto lives in New York."

My ears tuned toward the last comment. It had come from a dumb redneck sitting at the bar with a long-neck beer bottle in his hand. He was grinning like the village idiot and eyeing me lasciviously.

"I'm no imposter," I said. "I'm the real deal." To prove a point, I quickly drew my stiletto and flung it at the dartboard on the wall.

Bull's-eye.

I paused for effect. Probably a corny thing to do, but it worked. The men had turned to stone, with frozen facial expressions of awe, lust, disbelief, and shock. I winked at Village Idiot and then strode across the room to the dartboard, retrieved my knife, and sheathed it.

"As I was saying, I'm looking for someone. Any of you know a roughneck by the name of Douglas Bates?"

A few of the men looked at each other and mouthed something. They knew him. I gestured to them. "You. Do you know him?"

One of them, a tall skinny guy with black teeth, said, "I know him. He used to work out here."

"Where can I find him?"

"Don't know. He don't work here no more."

"That's right," his buddy said. "Moved back to Odessa."

I focused on the two men to see if I could detect untruths, but as far as I could tell, no one was lying.

"Anybody else?" I asked the room. "Got any idea where I can find Douglas Bates?"

"Come on, baby, take off your mask," Village Idiot said. "You don't fool us. You got lucky with the knife. What's your name, sweetheart?"

Ignoring him, I moved back to the bar. "If anybody knows where I can find him, I'd appreciate it."

Village Idiot stood and took a step toward me. "Would you like a drink, honey? How about havin' a seat and you and me get to know each other better?"

"Some other time," I replied, the irritation in my voice probably a little too obvious.

"Oh, come on, you and me's gonna have a little fun." Then he reached out and tried to touch my mask. I slapped his hand away; not hard, but there couldn't have been any doubt I meant business. The man recoiled and then laughed. He was probably the type of guy who, when he was young, used a magnifying glass on ants and enjoyed watching them burn in the sun. At any rate, I felt an immediate rise in tension in the place and it was very uncomfortable.

"Aw, come on guys, she's an *imposter*." Village Idiot announced too loudly. He took another step closer. "Who the hell d'ya think y'are? Comin' in here like this and askin' questions? If you was a man, we'd beat the shit outta you and throw you outta here on your ass." He turned back to a couple of buddies, one a big fellow who looked as if he ate steel for breakfast, and another guy with greasy hands and three days' prickly growth on his face. "Ain't that right, boys? That's what we'd do, ain't it!"

The boys nodded. "Yeah." "Sure would." "Damn straight."

"Oh, but because I'm a *woman* you're not going to do that?" I asked sweetly.

"Hell, no," Village Idiot answered. "For you I think we got somethin' better. Better for us, that is." He guffawed and his buddies joined him. Some of the other men in the place laughed, too. I didn't.

He got real close to me—too close—and I could smell the

whiskey on his breath and the sweat and scent of petroleum on his clothes. It was disgusting. And it reminded me all too much of Douglas.

This time he spoke with genuine menace. "Now why don't you take off that mask of yours and let us see how pretty you are under there?"

He made the mistake of reaching for my mask again. Reflexively, I knocked his arm away, a little harder this time. He didn't like that.

"Now, look, honey—" He grabbed my upper left arm and I punched him in the face with my right. The creep let go and retreated a few steps. He was more surprised than hurt, although I'm sure his pride was damaged more than anything.

"Don't touch me," I said. "Back off. If you know what's good for you."

"She hit me!" Idiot proclaimed as if it was news. "Bitch hit me!" He looked to his entourage for support. "We can't let her come in here and do that!"

Unfortunately, his buddies agreed with him. The three of them—Village Idiot, Steel Eater, and Needs-a-Shave came at me. I immediately assumed the *hachiji-dachi* stance—feet at shoulder width, toes open at forty-five degrees. Darn it, I didn't mean to go looking for trouble, but it found me.

Village Idiot made a move; I let loose with a *mae geri*, a front kick that struck him in the chest. By then Needs-a-Shave had invaded my space and wasn't playing around. He swung hard enough to knock down a man, but I dodged it, pivoted my body around and delivered an *ushiro geri*, a back kick that struck the guy on his right knee. He hollered in pain and fell to the floor. I don't think I meant to break it, but I might've. Then Village Idiot surprised me by grabbing me from behind in a bear hug, pinning both my arms to the sides. He was very strong and I couldn't wiggle out of it. Steel Eater, the big guy, stepped in front of me and walloped me one on the side of the face. The guy hit me so hard that I thought he might have broken my jaw, which is why it's still sore now.

Someone in the room yelled, "Hey, don't! She's a woman, for Christ's sake."

But another person rooted for their team, shouting, "Grab her legs so she can't kick ya!"

Steel Eater went for them but it was too late—for him, that is. I raised my knees with the speed of a snake and thrust the heels of my boots full force into the big man's belly. He doubled over, stumbled to the side, and eventually fell, moaning in pain. I wouldn't be surprised if I'd dislodged some internal organs.

I had only Village Idiot on my back—literally—when two more dumbasses decided to join the fray. They got up from their stools, rubbed their hands with glee, and ran at me. I had to dispose of the Idiot before I could deal with them. *Judo* training depends on breaking an attacker's leverage, and this was how I broke the bear hug. I quickly squatted in what Soichiro called "sumo position"—Idiot's arms were still tightly around mine with his hands locked against my chest—and then I bent my elbows, brought up my forearms, and placed my gloved hands over his. This posture allowed me to step *around and behind* him so that the front of my left thigh was against the back of his right thigh. At this point, he was slightly off balance, enabling me to grab his legs from behind his knees and pull them *up*, thereby toppling him backward over my leg! Once he'd hit the floor, I stomped him in the chest with the sole of my boot.

Seeing this, the two newcomers hesitated.

"Come on," I taunted. "You want some, too?"

One guy chickened out and retreated, but the other fool advanced. He put up his dukes, boxing-style, and proceeded to dance around me as if we were in a ring. I thought, okay, if that's the way he wanted to play—so I did the same. He tried a jab and a cross that I blocked with ease, and then I let him maneuver around me some more. Another jab, an attempt at an uppercut, and a cross and then I pummeled him with three fast, short straight-punches right to his chin, as if he was a punching bag hanging from the ceiling. A right hook knocked him on top of a table, splitting it in two and sending bottles of beer crashing to the floor.

"STOP!" the bartender shouted. "DON'T MOVE!" He had a shotgun trained at me.

Four men were on the floor, rolling and writhing in pain. One table was busted, and a handful of glasses and bottles had shattered. Not too much damage, all things considered.

"I'm leaving," I said to the bartender. "You gotta admit, all I did was defend myself."

"Just get out of here," the man said. "I'm gonna call the cops and they'll be here in a *minute*. Leave now and you'll have a sixty-second head start."

I nodded to him, held up my hands in capitulation, and walked away toward the door. Behind me, one fellow offered, "Try Schlumberger. I think Bates works for them now." He pronounced it *Shlum-ber-jay*.

Turning back to the speaker, I said, "Thanks," and then I opened the door and stepped outside.

Just before I closed it, someone else declared, "I guess it really *was* her!"

34
Judy's Diary
1958

The Black Stiletto is ready to confront Douglas Bates. Earlier today I came back to the motel for a quick rest and some preparation. Luis is due to pick me up in a half hour.

After I wrote the previous entry, I ate at the motel's adjoining eatery, the Texan Café, which was a far cry from the East Side Diner in New York. The eggs were good, but nothing else compared. Seeing the waitress made me miss Lucy, even though they were nothing alike. I saw the day's *Odessa-American* newspaper. Sure enough, there was a piece about me buried in the middle. The headline was: BAR BRAWL WITH BLACK STILETTO? The paper took a dubious slant, reporting that a woman had "impersonated" the Black Stiletto and caused a fight in a bar in Goldsmith. Two patrons were sent to the hospital—one with a broken knee and another with unspecified injuries. Not much else to it. Big deal.

This afternoon, Luis took me—in civilian clothes, ha ha—to the Schlumberger headquarters, which was located on Andrews Highway, outside of town. West Texas was sporadically dotted with towns much like Goldsmith, often with long stretches of flat road between them. It struck me as peculiar that nearly all the highways heading out of Odessa are named after the towns to which they led.

Schlumberger was larger than most oil field supply distributors, but it wasn't the only one. These kinds of businesses were what kept towns like Odessa thriving. They all smelled of machinery and metal and oil and gas and men. At least the ones I've been in have, and that isn't many. As I walked into this one, I suddenly had a vivid memory of going with my father to such a place. I must have been three or four. And, afterward, I now recall, we visited one of the oil derricks where he worked. I was terrified of it! Loud, noisy, dirty, greasy, and full of men yelling instructions to each other over the cacophony.

I found it strange to unexpectedly experience this recollection, and for some inexplicable reason it provided me with even more resolve and courage to continue my mission.

To my surprise, a woman was at the reception desk. She was middle-aged, dowdy, and had a beehive hairdo. A pushover.

"Yes, ma'am, can I help you?" she asked sweetly.

"Yes, please, I'm looking for an employee of yours, Douglas Bates."

"And what is this in reference to?"

"He's my *uncle* and I need to deliver his father's hunting rifle to him. I lost his address."

The woman was confused. "I'm sorry, you have his hunting rifle?"

"Yeah, his father—he lives in Andrews, oh, and so do I—borrowed it and asked me to return it to him 'cause I was headed this way. My great uncle wrote down his address and gave me a key—he has a key to his son's house—but I lost the piece of paper with the address on it. Uncle Douglas is gonna want it. I have the key, could you just give me—?"

"Of course, honey!" the woman gushed, happy to help. "Let me look in our files. What did you say his name was?"

"Douglas Bates." I sure hoped that guy in Goldsmith was telling the truth and Douglas *did* work at Schlumberger!

The woman opened a filing cabinet drawer and thumbed through the tops of the folders. To my relief, she pulled one out. "Here it is, Douglas Bates." She read off the address and I wrote it down on a piece of Schlumberger's note pad there on the desk. Ripped off the sheet and stuck it in my pocket.

"Thanks a whole lot."

"You're welcome, dear. Anything else I can do for you?"

"That's all, thank you."

I practically ran out the door, triumphant. Got in the car and had Luis take me back into town so I could do a little reconnaissance in Douglas's neighborhood. He lived in a trailer park near the new Ector County Coliseum, a gigantic building that was built since I went away. It was also on Andrews Highway, not at all far from Schlumberger. Not much housing development around there. Seemed like trailer parks were the big new thing, especially for lower-income people.

Suited me just fine.

Now it's nine o'clock and I'm ready to go. If for some reason I don't make it back to finish this, dear diary, I leave everything I own to my friend and mentor Freddie Barnes. See you later.

35
Roberto

The Present

The airplane trip to Chicago made me feel lousy. The goddamned heart murmur or whatever the fuckin' thing is started actin' up as soon as I sat in my seat. I was in a plane once before, in 1956. Flew to Las Vegas with the don. I didn't like it. Made me feel like I wasn't in control. I don't like not bein' in control. Same thing happened today. I hated the security checks at the airport. The waitin' drove me nuts. Then there was a delay and we sat in the plane for another thirty minutes before it took off. Fuck air travel.

I was a little worried about takin' my Colt Detective Special. The rules said you're supposed to declare and check it, but I thought for sure they'd stop me 'cause I'm an ex-con. In fact, even possessin' the damned gun was a violation of my parole. So I used that FedEx service and shipped it ahead of me to the Hyatt Hotel that's at the Chicago airport. Booked a room there and had 'em hold the package for me. Anyway, I was glad I didn't have a problem with *that*. It was the only good thing about the trip.

But I made it. Rented a car at the airport, checked into the hotel, and picked up my gun. Took me a while to get used to all the modern crap they got in cars now. Automatic this and automatic that. The wheel was so easy to turn I almost crashed into a wall. Got a car with one of them new GPS contraptions, so I wouldn't have to depend on a paper map. It worked pretty good, but drivin' on the fuckin' Chicago expressways was a nightmare. Made my heart pound like it was gonna burst. Had to give the Italian salute to a couple of other drivers who pissed me off. Think I'm gonna use side streets from now on.

I got to Arlington Heights in the early afternoon. Found Judy Talbot's house, and nearly smashed the car window with my fist when I saw the place was for sale. Vacant. Nobody home. Fuck, where was she? Did she die?

Still, I thought maybe I should take a look around. Got out of the car and went up to the front porch. Front door was locked. I gazed up and down the street to make sure no one was looking—and then I kicked it. Opened with one try.

The place was empty except for a chair or two. Smelled old and musty. I went in the kitchen, found a few tools the real estate people probably kept handy. Nothin' in the fridge. Checked out the bedrooms—they were empty, too. I was beginnin' to think the trip to Chicago was a bust. On my way out, I noticed the door and stairs to the basement. Not much to see, but there was a punchin' bag hangin' from the ceilin'. That made sense. I could see footprints in the dust at the bottom of the stairs, too. Someone had been there recently.

I went back upstairs and outside to look at the FOR SALE sign. The realtor's name was Kathy Reynolds. Noted the phone number and used my new cell to call her. When she answered, I told her I was interested in the house and would like a viewin'. She seemed real excited about that and said she'd meet me in a half hour. I didn't tell her I was already at the house and had broken in.

Maybe she knew where Judy Talbot was.

The realtor was fifteen minutes late, which didn't improve my mood. She parked in front—my rental was in the driveway—and ran up to me apologizin' for bein' "tardy." She was heavy, maybe in her mid-forties, and wore too much makeup. Dressed in a women's business suit. Her voice was high pitched and annoyin'. I already wanted to strangle her.

"Well, Mister Johnson, this house is a real *bargain*!" she said as we walked to the front porch together. I'd given her a phony name over the phone. "The owner has priced it to sell. As you can see, it needs a little sprucing up, and the owner understands that."

"Let's see the inside," I said. Then I did a good job of fakin' surprise when we got to the broken door. "Hey, look at that. Someone's broken in."

"Oh, my Lord! I should call the police."

"Later. Show me the house first."

"But somebody could be in there."

"I doubt it. Come on." I went inside and Kathy Reynolds hesitantly followed me. I closed the door as best I could behind her. "Roomy," I said.

"Yes. Well, if someone did break in, there was nothing whatsoever to steal. I hope they didn't vandalize anything."

She went into the kitchen and I trailed right behind her. "Who's the owner?" I asked. "I like to know who I'm buyin' from."

"Oh, I'm not allowed to give out that kind of information unless there's a sale. Hmm, the kitchen looks all right. My tools are still here. This is a real mystery!"

"I'll say. This house is old, right?"

"Built in the nineteen thirties. That's pretty typical for this area."

"So the owner was some old person, right? A lady, right? Is she—or he—still alive?"

This time the realtor nodded. "Yes, but it's a sad case. The poor old woman is in a nursing home. Stricken with Alzheimer's. Terrible thing."

"A nursin' home? Which one?"

"Oh, I'm sorry, I'm not allowed to say. Would you like to see the bedrooms?"

"So who's handlin' the sale? She have relatives?"

"Her son. Follow me, let me show you the wonderful master bedroom."

Son, huh. That explained the Talbot name. Judy Cooper musta got married at some point. Interestin'.

I followed the ugly dame into the bedroom. I noticed she was carryin' a notebook-style briefcase. Probably had all the information about the house's owner. If it didn't have the nursin' home address, it would surely tell me how to find her *son*.

My hand slipped into my jacket pocket and felt the cold, hard handle of the snubby. When the lady stepped into the bedroom, I pulled the gun out of my pocket. Held it by the barrel. Raised my arm.

"You get a lot of light in the morning," she said, indicating the windows. "I like sunshine in the mornings, don't you, Mister John—?"

She didn't know what hit her.

I used her jacket to wipe her blood off the butt. She was dead. I probably broke her skull. Oh well. She got on my nerves somethin' awful.

I took her notebook, went back to the kitchen, and opened it on the counter. Sure enough, there was all the info I wanted. The son's name was Martin Talbot. Lived in some place called Buffalo Grove. But I didn't need him after all. There's a note from him to the realtor written on Woodlands North stationery. The address and phone number printed right on it. Looked like a nursin' home to me.

I called the place and asked to make sure. Asked to speak to a Judy Talbot and they said they'd transfer me to her unit. I hung up before it rang. So she was indeed a resident. Looked at my watch and saw it was a little after five o'clock. Perfect. I got in my car and headed that way.

36
Judy's Diary
1958

DECEMBER 19, 1958

Yes, dear diary, it's over a week since my last entry. I'm back in New York now. I'll try to write down what happened in Texas, although a lot of the past week is a blur.

It was about nine thirty on the night of the 13th when Luis dropped me off at the entrance to Douglas's trailer park. I told him to drive by again in an hour—if I was ready, I'd signal him somehow. If not, he was to come around again every half hour after that.

Trailer parks are kind of spooky at night and this one was no different. There was a light that illuminated the entrance and a few here and there on the property—but mostly the place was dark. That was actually beneficial for me.

I darted through the shadows, moving from trailer to trailer, until I stopped to linger in the cold blackness behind a mobile home directly across the path from Douglas's unit. He wasn't there. No vehicle was parked beside it and the lights weren't on. If he was out of town on a job or something, I was going to be mighty disappointed. Nevertheless, I skirted across one last beam of light and made it to his front door. It was locked, of course, but my lockpicks opened it easily enough.

Trailer homes are narrow and claustrophobic. Not much room to move around in. I dared to turn on a light; I wanted to see how Douglas lived. The thing was divided into three distinct sections. A tiny kitchen was at one end. Had a fridge, sink, stove, a small round café table with one chair, and a phone on the wall. A carpeted living room area was in the middle, furnished with a television and rabbit ears antennae, a comfy chair, a tiny coffee table, a magazine rack, and a love seat that needed reupholstering. Barely three or four feet between furniture to walk through. On the other end was the bedroom and bathroom.

The place reeked of cigarette smoke and booze. As I took it all in, my intuition went haywire—my nerves started tingling the way they do when there's danger. Looking back, I think it was because of Douglas's mere presence in the home. Just the fact that he lived and slept there set off my "alarms." I sensed him, all around me. It was an unnerving sensation.

The second thing that struck me was there were no family photographs. No pictures of my mom—his *deceased wife*—or any of us kids with whom he lived for several years. Of course, he left Mom on her deathbed, but still you'd think the guy would have a memento or two.

In the bedroom I found a few empty booze bottles, ashtrays overflowing with cigarette butts and ashes, and a few magazines that had pictures of naked women in them. That was shocking. I'd seen Fiorello's copies of *Playboy*, of course, but that was a classy publication. These were simply filthy, not something you'd buy at the drugstore or newsstand. It figured that Douglas would look at trash like that.

Once I was done snooping, I turned off the lights and sat in the comfy chair in the living room.

And I waited.

He got home around ten fifteen. I saw his car's headlights through the trailer windows as it pulled into the small drive on the side of his home. I went into the bedroom and stood in the doorway.

Heard the car door open and slam shut. Footsteps on the gravel outside, then on the two wooden steps at the front door. Key in the lock. I held my breath.

Douglas Bates came in and turned on the light. He'd aged considerably in the last six years. He had a beer gut drooping over his belt and his hair had turned gray. He was still a big man, though. I was a tall girl at age thirteen and he seemed huge then. I hadn't realized until now how large he really was.

He threw his keys on the little coffee table, went into the kitchen, opened the fridge, and removed a long-neck bottle of beer. I ducked into the bedroom so he wouldn't see me when he turned around. I heard him switch on the TV, and then he plopped into the comfy chair. The set warmed up and came on after a few seconds—it was tuned to the news.

As soon as I knew he was settled, I made my appearance.

"Hello, Douglas."

He jumped and dropped the beer bottle. Said a curse word. Started to get up, but I drew the stiletto and pointed it at him. "Don't get up!" His eyes darted around the room as if he was looking for a weapon or an escape route. I moved between him and the front door.

"Who are you?" he asked.

"I'm the Black Stiletto."

"What's that?"

"You haven't heard of me?"

"No."

"You don't read the papers, much? Follow the national news?"

"No."

"You're watchin' the news on TV."

"I was waitin' for the sports."

At first I thought of turning off the set, but then I decided to leave it on. In fact, I went over and turned up the volume.

Wouldn't want his neighbors to hear him scream. I sheathed my knife.

"What do you want?" he asked. "Why are you here? How did you get in?"

"You ask a lotta questions."

"If it's money you want, I don't have much. I'll give you my damn wallet. I think there's six dollars in there."

"I don't want your money," I said. "Say, how come there ain't a picture of Betty Cooper in here? You know, your *wife*? Didn't you love her? Oh, I forgot, you left her to die in the hospital."

That raised his ire. "*Who are you? What do you want?*"

"Let's see—what do I want? I'll tell you, Douglas. I want to hear you apologize for killin' Betty Cooper and rapin' her daughter, Judy."

His eyes flared. "What?"

"You heard me."

"I didn't kill Betty! She died of cancer!"

"But you left her on her own to deal with it, didn't you?"

"I—well, I—no—what business is it of yours?"

"That's irrelevant. Is that too big a word for you? It means it doesn't matter why I'm interested in all this. What's important is how much you're willin' to atone for your many sins."

"Fuck you, lady. Get out of my house. Right now. I'll call the cops."

"You will?" I nodded at the phone in the kitchen. "Go for it. Go ahead. See how far you get."

Suddenly my protective instincts went crazy. I sensed terrible peril from this man, but I couldn't understand why. I had him under control, I knew I could best him physically, and he was sitting in a chair. I was missing something, but I didn't know what it was.

I watched him carefully as he slowly started to stand, as if he was actually going to accept my challenge. Then he looked at the dropped beer bottle and the spreading stain on his carpet. "Now see what you made me do," he said, "and I just had the carpet cleaned last week." He reached for the bottle—and again I felt the tingling of jeopardy.

"Leave it!" I snapped, but it was too late. Instead of grabbing the beer bottle, he reached under the comfy chair and pulled out a handgun. It was there the entire time and in a place where he could quick draw it. And he was fast. The only thing I could do was leap sideways toward the kitchen just as he pulled the trigger. The discharge was terribly loud and I felt a horrendous, burning *thump* in my left shoulder as I sailed in midair. The pain messed up my trajectory and I crashed into the café table. I fell hard on the kitchen floor and cried out in anguish.

I'd been shot.

In hindsight, I should've remembered Douglas and his guns. The constant target practice out in the field. His obsession with cowboys and gunslingers. I was dumb and I paid for it.

Before I had a chance to take stock of the damage, Douglas was standing over me, the gun barrel pointed at me.

"Take off that mask," he ordered.

It was difficult to catch my breath. All I wanted to do was nurse my shoulder, which was bleeding profusely. My left arm was useless.

"Ain't your neighbors gonna call the cops, hearin' a gunshot like that?" I asked.

He laughed. "My neighbors don't give a shit about what other people do. Folks fire guns all the time around here. There's a practice range out back of the trailer park. Now take off that mask. I want to see who was stupid enough to try and fuck with me."

"I don't think so."

He aimed the gun lower. "The next shot goes in the leg. I'll do it, too. Who the hell are you?"

Then I noticed how Douglas was standing. Legs apart. Directly over me. An image of Soichiro flashed in my mind and I heard his voice say, *"You do know where the most vulnerable spot on a man is located?"*

My leg catapulted toward his groin, *but Douglas deflected the kick* by swatting the gun against my leg so that I missed the vital area and ineffectually struck his left thigh. The pistol went off again, but the bullet missed me and penetrated the floor mere inches from my right hip.

Acting quickly, I used my other leg to kick him. I managed to strike him hard on the inside of his right knee, which caused him to buckle. Ignoring the excruciating pain in my shoulder, I performed a "kip-up," in which you go from a supine position to a standing one by thrusting the legs upward and outward while pushing off the floor with the shoulders. With adequate back arching, you land on your feet. It requires a powerful hip extension, contracting the glutes and the back in one swift motion.

Once I was standing, I immediately disarmed Douglas by grabbing his gun arm, twisting around so my back was to him, and then chopping the forearm sharply with a *shuto-uchi*—knife-edge strike. He yelped and dropped the weapon. It bounced on the carpet and landed somewhere out of sight. I then elbowed him in the stomach, completing the succession of attacks that finally toppled him. Goliath fell hard, shaking the trailer home as if an earthquake had struck.

I spun around to continue the onslaught, but the man was devilishly fast. He rolled onto his side and managed to pick up the small coffee table by one leg, and then he flung it at me with great strength. The best I could do was to use my bad left arm as a shield against the impact, and it hurt like the dickens. I remember screaming in torment. The table dropped to the floor between us. By then, the monster was on his feet, ready for more. He lunged at me over the table, attempting a tackle at the waist. As soon as his heavy arms were around me, I focused on a *karate* vital point and used a knife-edge strike on the back of his neck right at the base of his skull. He jerked from the shock to his nerves and plummeted to the floor, but he still had some fight left. Douglas succeeded in grabbing my legs and felling me yet again! The interior space was just too constricting for me to maneuver properly; otherwise I could've easily avoided him. I crashed into the floor hard, effectively stunning me. Then the creep managed to take advantage of my condition and slug me in the stomach! He started to get to his feet so he could kick me, but I used his own weapon against him. I took hold of the coffee table and swung it at his legs with such force that the furniture shattered into three pieces. He dropped to his knees and actually landed on top of me before I could get up. His weight on my bad shoulder was agonizing. Then he got his hands around my throat and started to squeeze. His fingers were powerful and strong; they dug into my neck as if it was made of cotton. I couldn't breathe! He was choking the life out of me!

I tried to break his hold, but my left arm was no good and my right wasn't enough to do it alone.

Dear diary, I might've died right there on Douglas Bates's floor. I felt my spirit ebbing away. A darkness enveloped my vision and my senses waned. And then, I swear I don't know how it happened, but I had a vision—a vivid memory recall—of the night my stepfather raped me. I was thirteen years old. In my room. Douglas Bates, on top of me, ripping my insides, making me bleed, causing me intense pain...

This man had to pay for what he did!

So I did the only thing I could think of, essentially a last resort. To execute a deadly *nihon nukite*—a two-finger attack, I formed my hand like an imaginary gun, with the index and middle fingers straight and together like two sharp spears. Then I jabbed Douglas at the base of the throat in the fleshy vital point below his Adam's apple as hard as I could.

It crushed his windpipe.

Now helpless, gasping for oxygen, he released me and rolled off. I inhaled precious air and moved away from him across the carpet until I was sitting with my back against the television. The man pleaded with his eyes for me to do something.

"No, Douglas, I'm not gonna help you," I said. "You beat your wife and your stepkids. You poked out Frank's eye. You caused your wife such intense unhappiness that manifested itself into a cancer that killed her. And you had the audacity to leave her as she was dyin'. But most of all, I'm not helpin' you for what you did to *me*."

I reached up and pulled off my mask and hood.

As he lay there, choking and gurgling, the horror of recognition spread over his face.

"That's right, Douglas," I said. "I'm Judy. And you're dead."

It took nearly three minutes. When he was finally still and lifeless, I weakly got to my feet. Blood covered my jacket and pants. I didn't know how much I'd lost, but I needed medical attention or I would end up like the sorry son of a bitch on the floor. I had the presence of mind to take a look around to make sure I didn't leave anything behind. All I saw was Douglas's handgun on the bloody carpet. I ignored it.

I left the trailer and limped to the park entrance. I had no idea how long it would be before Luis picked me up. It seemed to be an eternity, but it was probably only a few minutes. The taxicab rolled by and stopped. I got in the backseat and said, "Luis, I've been shot."

Then I passed out.

Sunlight from a window woke me up the next morning. My head was in a cloud and I felt terribly sleepy. At first I was frightened, for I didn't know where I was. It was a child's bedroom. The wallpaper had flowers and gingerbread men all over it. There were dolls and toys on the floor, pushed out of the way. The door was closed, but not all the way. I felt a dull ache in my shoulder and saw that my arm was in a sling and my gunshot wound was bandaged. I think I moaned loudly to see if anyone could hear me.

A Mexican woman came into the room. She approached me cautiously and spoke to me in Spanish. I couldn't understand her. She had a glass of water for me, which I gulped greedily. Then Luis entered. He explained in broken English that I was at his house in south Odessa, and the woman was Juanita, his wife.

"What happened?" I asked him.

He said he took me to a doctor who was a friend of his. Not a hospital. It was someone who helped illegal immigrants from Mexico if they needed medical attention. Apparently the doctor removed the bullet and patched me up. I'd lost a lot of blood. I needed to rest and recover. I figured they must've drugged me in order to perform the operation. I didn't remember a thing.

I was too groggy and confused to care, so I went back to sleep.

My stay with Luis and his family—three daughters along with his wife—lasted four days. He had taken care of checking me out of the motel and paying my bill, for which I repaid him. He also showed me the newspapers. Douglas Bates had been found dead in his trailer home, the victim of an unknown assailant. Police had no clues, except that witnesses of a bar fight in Goldsmith had claimed a "woman impersonating the Black Stiletto" may have been responsible. Then he showed me a copy of *Time* magazine, the existence of which I was unaware. One of those photos taken of the Black Stiletto in that bar in New York was on the cover. Luis pointed at it and then to me and asked a question in Spanish. I understood him.

"Yeah, that's me."

Luis swore to me that he and his wife would never speak of it. Again, the gesture of zipping his lips. We both laughed.

I flew back to New York a little over a week from the time I arrived in Texas. I gave Luis not only the promised fifty dollars, but another fifty for his trouble. I think that one hundred fifty dollars was more money than he and his family had ever seen at one time. As for keeping silent, I trusted him. Luis and his wife were good people.

My arm's still in a sling. Freddie fussed like a mother hen over it. Naturally, he pressed me for the story, but I wouldn't tell him. All I said was I'd taken care of some important family business and the wound was simply part of the sacrifice. He asked if I'd settled the matter, and I replied, "Yes, I have." Bless his heart, Freddie didn't say anything more about it.

I wonder how long it's going to be before the events in Odessa no longer occupy my dreams, for they are constant companions during the night. One thing is for sure—the image of Douglas choking to death on the floor of his trailer has now superseded the recurring nightmare of him raping me.

I honestly can't say if that's an improvement.

37
Martin

The Present

Almost done with the diary, but I had to leave the office and get to Woodlands to talk to my daughter. On the way over in the car, I got to thinking, and I gotta say something. My entire life has friggin' changed. It's as if everything I thought was true is not, and vice versa. My mother is not Judy Talbot, the single mom who stayed at home in the Chicago suburbs and looked after her son. No, she was really Judy Cooper, a vigilante, a living lethal weapon, a *killer*.

It's not every son in the world who can say his mother is a murderer. Granted, she had compelling reasons to do what she did. The "law" aside, if Douglas Bates was really the monster my mom said he was, then personally I think he deserved what he got. I'm not sure what I think about the other deaths she was directly or indirectly responsible for—Vittorio Ranelli and Don Giorgio DeLuca. The jury's still out on those.

I'm just going to have to read more of Mom's diaries to learn more. There's also the mystery of the other items I found. What's with the JFK campaign button? The heart-shaped locket? The roll of film? The gold key? And what about that Smith & Wesson handgun that was in the secret closet?

And that brings up a whole different topic. It's something I've wondered about for years. How did Mom support us? She didn't work the entire time I lived with her. She never had a "job-job."

I remember a few times, as I was growing up, when I'd ask her, "Mom, how come you don't go to work?" And she'd say something like, "My job is to take care of you." Then, when I was older, I asked practical questions like, "Mom, what do we live on? Where is the money coming from?" And she'd answer that my father left us an inheritance.

My father. Right. Who the hell was he? Will I ever find out? Did Richard Talbot really exist, or is he a fantasy created by my mother to placate me? Should I grill Uncle Thomas and find out more about her money? I can only hope the other diaries will reveal that answer.

Anyway, I now look at my mother in a totally different light. Can't help it. I've been angry at her for the past few days, but I guess you can say I really have a renewed respect for her. Her bravery. The monumental achievement of escaping a horrible situation at home and creating a new identity. The way she trained herself and learned all those fighting techniques just so she could be the Black Stiletto. It's beyond what any normal woman would do, especially in the fifties!

After reading through the first diary, though, I think I'm beginning to understand a little of why she did it. Every so often, a few individuals appear in this world that transcend us mere mortals and become something unique and important. The Olympic champions and famous athletes, or gifted actors or musicians—the kind that make money!—or charismatic government leaders. That's Judy Cooper. She was one of those. Damn, it's as if I'm meeting my mother—the *real* Judy Cooper—for the first time.

It's made me want to visit her more often. I won't bring up the past anymore. It upsets her, and I don't think *she* even knows why. But there are indeed memories locked up in her brain somewhere, and every now and then a word or name or place triggers a response. Her doctor once explained the disease as a wall around a person's memories, and the brain simply can't get to them. The mind knows the memories are *there*, but they can't be seen, read, felt, touched, or heard. So when Mom feels an emotional response to something that's a memory, she reacts with anger and frustration because she can't get through or over that wall.

It was nearly dinner time at the nursing home when I arrived. Once again, I found Mom in the common room with other residents, blankly watching television. Gina was there with her.

"Hi, Dad."

"I'll talk to you in a minute," I growled. "Hi, Mom."

She said hello to me and then immediately went back to the show. A musical was on—*My Fair Lady*, I think. I couldn't tell if Mom was enjoying it or not. She just stared at the picture without smiling, laughing, or even crying. I had to assume it gave her something to do.

"What's wrong, Dad?" Gina asked.

"Now I know why you wanted to know about Grandma living in New York."

My daughter's mouth opened. "Did Mom tell you?"

"Yes, she did."

"I can't believe it!" She stood. "Look, I was gonna tell you."

"Oh? When? I didn't even know you'd applied to Juilliard."

The nursing staff raised their heads. Our voices were obviously loud.

"Let's talk about this later," I said. "Stick around."

The movie ended and one of the staff switched the television to the local news.

"Mom, you want to go into the dining room and eat?" I asked. The dining room was in the same direction as her room.

She nodded and said, "Okay." I held out my arm for her to take it. She stood and we started to walk away—when I heard the announcer on the TV say, "We bring you this special bulletin—" I wasn't paying much attention to it until I heard the words, "—

the murder of a real estate agent at a home in Arlington Heights. Katherine Reynolds was found dead when a coworker went to the property—"

It was the realtor's name that rang a bell. I knew her. In fact, she was the agent handling the sale of the old place on Chestnut. My head turned toward the TV *and there was a shot of the exterior of our house!*

"Hold on a second, Mom," I said. We stopped walking and I focused on the news bulletin.

There was no question. It was the house, with yellow police tape and cop cars in front of it. Apparently it had happened recently. Like, in the past hour or two.

"Hey, that's Grandma's house," Gina astutely observed.

Then the strangest thing occurred. My whole body started tingling. It was similar to the feeling you get when you have déjà vu. Or maybe it was more like an intense anxiety, a buzz that prompts you to *act quickly*.

Something was very wrong.

"Mom, I think we should get your sweater or jacket. Let's go for a ride in the car. What do you say?"

"That'd be nice."

"You haven't been for a car ride in a while."

"I haven't?"

"Dad, what's wrong?" Gina asked. I waved at her to shush up.

"Let's go to your room and get something to put over you, Mom. It's actually pretty nice outside, but you might get chilly."

I didn't know what was going on; I just knew I had to get my mom out of the nursing home. She was in great danger.

As we walked to her room, she kept her consistently slow pace no matter how much I tried to rush her. I had a feeling she could move faster if she really wanted. Her legs may have been thin, but there was still plenty of muscle there. Gina followed behind us.

"Dad, what's going on? Is something the matter?"

We got to her room. I opened the closet and found a sweater.

"Here, let me help you put this on."

As I did so, my mother said, "You are a nice man."

"Thank you, Mom. I'm your son, you know. You brought me up to be nice."

That brought a smile to her face.

"Okay, let's go. The car's outside. Maybe we can go to McDonald's for dinner. Would you like that?"

She nodded like a schoolgirl. I didn't know if she remembered what McDonald's was, but it must have sounded good.

Then Gina suddenly dropped into a chair, her eyes closed and her hand on her forehead.

"What's wrong?" I asked her.

"I don't know. I feel weird," she said.

"Are you sick?"

"No. It's like—I don't know how to describe it. It's like how I feel before a test or something. Kinda scared."

I think I understood. I was feeling the same thing.

"Can you walk with us?"

"Yeah."

She got up and we slowly moved into the hallway and headed back toward the common room. Mom held my arm as we walked, just like she always did. It was almost as if she was an elegant lady of royalty and I was her escort.

The Alzheimer unit's common room lay between us and the doors leading to the rest of the facility. There was still another long hallway to the main entrance. Several residents, along with a couple of nurses and staff people, were still in the common room, slowly making their way to the dining room behind us.

Then I saw him.

An elderly man had come in the double doors and approached

the desk. He looked a little shabby, wearing clothes that were slightly too big for him. The most striking thing about him was his demeanor: cold, calculating, and to the point.

"I'm lookin' for Judy Talbot," he said.

The nurse smiled and pointed our way. "Why, that's her, right there!"

The man jerked his head toward us and narrowed his eyes.

Oh my God, it was Roberto Ranelli! It had to be!

I froze. I didn't know what the hell I should do. Pick Mom up and run with her in my arms? Confront the guy and send him on his way?

He walked toward us and stopped just a few feet away. Ranelli looked at my mother, up and down, and snarled, "Yeah, it's you, all right. I recognize you, you fuckin' bitch!"

That got everyone's attention. Every head in the room turned toward us. The newcomer emanated such *menace* that it was impossible to ignore him.

"Dad, who's that?" Gina asked.

Mom stared at him unemotionally. I have no idea if she recognized him. And yet, I felt her grip on my arm tighten.

"Do you know who I am, bitch?" he growled. "I'm Roberto Ranelli! You killed my brother Vittorio! And now I'm gonna kill *you*!"

"Dad, he's got a gun!" Gina shouted.

I don't know how she knew that, for it was after she'd announced it that his hand went into his jacket pocket *and he pulled out a revolver*!

"No!" I shouted.

But then my mother did something I'll never forget as long as I live. The woman who was Judy Cooper, seventy-two years old and suffering from Alzheimer's, released my arm, rearranged her entire body in a *different* posture, and then *swiftly kicked the son of a bitch right between the legs!*

Ranelli yelled in pain and anguish, dropped to his knees, and then fell on his side. He curled into a fetal position and gasped. Gina kicked the revolver away out of his reach.

My mother remained in this defensive stance, still as a statue, until she sensed the danger was passed.

And then she relaxed, assumed the deportment of her normal, fragile self, and took hold of my arm as if nothing had happened.

By then, the nurses and staff were going nuts. They called for backup. Someone knelt beside Ranelli and examined him.

"Who is this man?" someone demanded.

"Call the police," was all I said. "He tried to shoot my mother."

A nurse hollered, "He's going into cardiac arrest! Call a code blue!"

I turned my mother around. "Let's go back to your room, Mom. We'll go to McDonald's another time."

As all hell broke loose in the common room, we slowly strolled back to her unit. Gina followed us, slightly in shock. I helped remove the sweater and assisted Mom onto the bed, and then I took off her shoes. I don't believe she was aware of what had just occurred.

She was asleep within seconds.

Needless to say, what I'd just witnessed had shaken me to the core. In those few moments in which Mom defended herself without thinking about it, I felt a change come over me. An enlightenment, if you will. I don't know how to explain it. All I know is that suddenly I wasn't angry anymore. Maybe a little peeved at myself for being a jerk the past few days, but the resentment with Mom and frustration with Gina disappeared. And I knew I needed to keep Mom's secret safe for now. There was no telling how many more Roberto Ranellis there might be out there.

The police asked me and Gina a lot of questions. Of course,

Gina knew nothing. There was a lot I didn't know, but some things I kept to myself. I insisted I had no idea who Roberto Ranelli was or why he'd come to Woodlands North to try and kill my mother. Apparently he was indeed the suspect in the brutal slaying of Kathy Reynolds, and he was a recently paroled convict who had served time for murder.

A detective named Harrigan wanted to talk to my mother. He was convinced she knew Ranelli. Why else would the old man go looking for her at our old house in Arlington Heights? And why would she have reacted the way she did? We woke her up, but, alas, there was nothing my mother could tell him. She didn't even understand the questions. Harrigan quickly realized she was incapable of answering.

Outside her room, the detective asked me if my mother had ever lived in New York. I told him she did, back in the fifties. He shrugged and said, "Maybe it was just an old grudge. But I guess it's a moot point now."

"Why?"

He told me Ranelli suffered a stroke or a heart attack; he wasn't real sure, but it was something pertaining to the heart. At any rate, Ranelli was DOA at the hospital. I guess my mom's assault on his nuts was too much for him.

Harrigan gave me his card and asked me to call if I remembered or found out anything that connected my mother to the killer. I dutifully said I would.

He started to walk away, but then he stopped and asked, "How did she know how to kick him like that?"

I shrugged and replied, "I don't know. Don't most women know how to kick a guy in the balls? Maybe it was just a natural response."

"Yeah, maybe." Harrigan grudgingly accepted that theory and went on his way.

I think perhaps it was true. The maneuver Soichiro taught her long ago had stuck with her like an instinct. They say that with Alzheimer's, certain mental functions—playing and appreciating music, for example—are the last to go. I imagine my mother's self-defense training was the same type of thing. It's something you don't forget.

"Dad, what's going on?" Gina asked me.

I couldn't tell her anything. Not yet. Someday, maybe.

"I don't know, honey."

Gina looked at me and said, "You're lying, Dad. I can tell."

I walked Gina out to her car and we had a composed, civilized talk. I didn't tell her what I knew, but I did say she was more like her grandmother than she could imagine.

"Your grandma was a real individual," I said. "Totally independent. Always went her own way, no matter what."

"I think that's great," my daughter said.

"Yeah. It is. I think she'd want you to be the same way."

I held out my arms to Gina. "Congratulations on Juilliard, sweetheart."

"You mean I can go?"

"If it's what you really want."

"Oh, Dad!" And she hugged me.

Before leaving Woodlands, I went back to my mom's room to say goodbye. She had fallen asleep again, so I quietly entered and stood next to her bed. I tucked the blanket around her, leaned over, kissed her cheek, and whispered that I loved her.

More than ever.

38
Judy's Diary
1958

DECEMBER 31, 1958

It's New Year's Eve again. Yep, that date is definitely significant to me in one way or another.

In ten minutes it'll be midnight and we'll usher in the year 1959. At the moment I'm in my room above the gym, having taken a break from the annual party downstairs. Freddie is there, of course. Lucy is in attendance, thank goodness. She's recovering nicely from her ordeal and still spends some time in rehabilitation, but she seems to be doing great. Lucy lived with me for a month after she got out of the hospital, and she just got her own apartment three days ago. She's even gone back to work at the diner, *and* she's dating her rich lawyer beau, Peter Gaskin. So, good for her! (PS—Lucy says he might ask her to marry him! Wouldn't that be something? The Black Stiletto could be the bridesmaid, ha ha!) Some of the gym regulars are there—Jimmy and Louis and Wayne and Paul and Corky and—well, you probably don't know some of those names, do you, dear diary? Even Tony the Tank decided he'd come to *our* party before going over to Don Franco DeLuca's celebration—which is still a tradition, although they don't have it at the Algonquin anymore.

Anyway, before I go back downstairs, I thought I'd catch you up before I close the book, so to speak, on this incredible year.

A lot has happened, that's for sure. As my personal life has gone through changes, I've also started to pay more attention to what's going on in the world around me more than ever before. Earlier in the year some teenager named Bobby Fischer won an international chess championship and was declared a genius. The government launched a satellite called "Explorer" into space, which means all those scary science-fiction movies are coming true! The Cuban Revolution still dominates the news, and as of yesterday it looks like Che Guevara and his men will take over Havana any day. Fat lot of good my intervention did! Khrushchev is our latest foreign enemy, and everyone is still scared of nuclear war and what the Communists might do. And Alaska is about to become our 49th state.

For me personally I saw a few movies and read a number of books, including the dirtiest one I ever laid my hands on—*Lolita*, by some Russian author whose name I never can remember. Freddie and I have some favorite TV shows and watch them together when we can. We don't like to miss *Peter Gunn* since it started in September. We also enjoy *Jack Benny*, *Ed Sullivan*, *Milton Berle*, and I really, really love *Alfred Hitchcock Presents*! I'm still crazy about Elvis and rock and roll music, although Dean Martin's not too bad. I achieved a black belt in *karate*. And I grew closer than ever with the friends I call my family—Freddie, Lucy, and Soichiro.

But most significantly, Judy Cooper became the Black Stiletto.

Apparently she is wanted for questioning in Odessa, Texas. My little escapade in Goldsmith cost me. Too many of those witnesses in the bar talked to the police and insisted the Stiletto had come looking for Douglas Bates that night. Well, when Douglas turned up dead two days later, naturally they suspected "the masked woman in black." Of course, they don't know for sure if she was the *real* Black Stiletto. I doubt they have any evidence against me from the crime scene. Some blood stains, perhaps, but they can't do anything with those except maybe figure out my blood type, for what that's worth. And I happen to be O+, which I've read is the most common blood type in the world. I mean, blood's not like fingerprints, and I was wearing gloves the whole time. But to play it safe, I guess I won't be going back to Odessa any time soon.

The dreams and nightmares linger in the shadows of my subconscious. They're not a nightly occurrence anymore, thank God. I'm not sure if I'll ever totally be rid of them, but I have no regrets whatsoever. I truly believe my mother is resting in peace now, and I certainly feel vindicated for what happened to *me*. I also don't have any remorse for Don DeLuca or Vittorio Ranelli. Oh, that reminds me. It was just in the papers—Roberto Ranelli's trial ended with a guilty verdict. He was sentenced to life in prison. I guess I don't have to worry about him ever again.

My biggest problem now is the NYPD. And the FBI, to some extent. I'm still curious about that agent, Mr. Richardson, who said we would meet someday. And while I was in Texas, there was an editorial in the *Times* from the police commissioner. He talked a lot about how crime was on the rise in the city and what we as citizens can do about it. He said "the Black Stiletto is not the answer," and he vowed that she will be brought to justice. Doesn't he realize I'm doing everyone a favor? Again, public opinion is on my side. There's actually an advertisement in the back of the *Daily News* to join a Black Stiletto Fan Club! Freddie cut it out and suggested we both join as a joke. Supposedly as a member you get a poster of that old police sketch of me that's still floating around, as well as copies of the now-famous photographs that Max took at that bar on First Avenue. They've been syndicated all over the world. Anyone who doesn't know who the Black Stiletto is by now has been living on the moon.

Well, the Stiletto is not going to disappear. It's become a habit. They call it a "compulsion." So what? It's who I am now. I *must* be the Black Stiletto. I truly believe that what I do is right. What's wrong with fighting crime and protecting the innocent? As long as I steer clear of the cops, I should be okay.

Oh, Lord, the music in the gym downstairs just changed to that silly Chipmunks Christmas song. I laugh every time I hear it. It's getting close to midnight, so I better run, dear diary. I have to go get my glass of champagne and stand close to Freddie when he makes his perennial toast to me.

"To Judy," he always says, "the daughter I never had."

And I'll cry a little bit, hug him, and sing "Auld Lang Syne" along with the rest of the crowd.

Happy New Year!

ABOUT THE AUTHOR

Between 1996 and 2002, Raymond Benson was commissioned by the James Bond literary copyright holders to take over writing the 007 novels. In total he penned and published worldwide six original 007 novels, three film novelizations, and three short stories. An anthology of his 007 work, *The Union Trilogy*, was published in the fall of 2008, and a second anthology, *Choice of Weapons*, appeared summer 2010. His book *The James Bond Bedside Companion*, an encyclopedic work on the 007 phenomenon, was first published in 1984 and was nominated for an Edgar Allan Poe Award by Mystery Writers of America for Best Biographical/Critical Work. Using the pseudonym David Michaels, Raymond is also the author of the *New York Times* best-selling books *Tom Clancy's Splinter Cell* and its sequel *Tom Clancy's Splinter Cell: Operation Barracuda*. Raymond's original suspense novels include *Evil Hours, Face Blind*, and *Sweetie's Diamonds* (the latter won the Readers' Choice Award for Best Thriller of 2006 at the Love is Murder Conference for Authors, Readers, and Publishers). *A Hard Day's Death*, the first in a series of rock 'n' roll thrillers, was published in 2008, and its sequel, Shamus Award nominated *Dark Side of the Morgue*, was published in 2009. Other recent works include the 2008 and 2009 novelizations of the popular videogame, *Metal Gear Solid* and its sequel, *Metal Gear Solid 2: Sons of Liberty*, and *Homefront: The Voice of Freedom*, cowritten with John Milius.

Raymond has taught courses in film genres and history at New York's New School for Social Research, Harper College in

Palatine, Illinois, College of DuPage in Glen Ellyn, Illinois, and currently presents Film Studies lectures with *Daily Herald* movie critic Dann Gire. Raymond has been honored in Naoshima, Japan, with the erection of a permanent museum dedicated to one of his novels, and he is also an Ambassador for Japan's Kagawa Prefecture. Raymond is an active member of International Thriller Writers Inc., Mystery Writers of America, the International Association of Media Tie-In Writers, a full member of ASCAP, and serves on the board of directors of The Ian Fleming Foundation. He is based in the Chicago area.

www.raymondbenson.com